Published in 2018 by Lethe Press, Inc.
6 University Drive, Suite 206 / PMB #223 • Amherst, MA 01002 usa
www.lethepressbooks.com • lethepress@aol.com

isbn: 978-1-59021-671-2 / 1-59021-671-7

Set in Electra and Futura
Cover design: Inkspiral Design
Interior design: Frankie Dineen

YELED TOV

Daniel M. Jaffe

LETHE PRESS

For Andrew

Yeled Tov

As Mr. Katz chanted from the Torah scroll up in front of the synagogue congregation, Jake hunched over his *makhzor*, his High Holiday prayer book, following along. He read the Torah's prohibitions against seeing one's father's nakedness, one's mother's, one's sister's, and the nakedness of one's other kinswomen. Well, of course you shouldn't see those things, he thought. Duh, how obvious. It's 1974, for gosh sakes, the world's civilized.

He continued reading when suddenly what Jake would forever think of as "the Leviticus passage" gleamed before his eyes, nearly leaping off the page: "Thou shalt not lie with mankind as with womankind; it is abomination." Jake blinked, clamped his eyes shut.

He knew he must have stumbled onto the Leviticus passage before now because, even if this were one of those Torah sections the teachers skipped in Hebrew school to be read "one day when you're older," Jake had been reading it in the *makhzor* on Yom Kippur every year. He always paid close attention when reading the *makhzor* because this, the Day of Atonement, was the holiest day on the Jewish calendar, the end of the ten-day New Year period during which Jews the world over repented for sin in the hope that God would forgive them, would seal them in the Book of Life.

Maybe the Leviticus passage jumped out at Jake for the first time because he understood Hebrew better now at nearly age sixteen than he had before? Or, more likely, it bore greater significance now because Jake's feelings and fantasies had grown much clearer over this past year.

/ /

Knitting his thin eyebrows, Jake read further still: anyone who committed such abomination "shall be cut off from among their people." Jake shivered from a chill. What did it mean to "be cut off"? Would he be expelled from the congregation if anyone found out? Would Dad kick him out of the house?

No. Not possible. Dad wouldn't do that, he'd protect Jake no matter what.

Maybe Jake was being too hard on himself. Maybe the Leviticus passage wasn't actually talking about what Jake wanted to do. Sure. That's right. Jake knew what it was for a man "to lie with a woman." His fantasies were just about hugging guys and maybe kissing them. That's all. Even the ancient Greeks wrestled naked together, and that was just innocent athletics that led to the Olympics, for gosh sakes. Innocent athletics couldn't be labeled "abomination," right? And kissing wasn't that big a deal, was it?

No. Jake was upsetting himself over nothing. He hadn't violated anything. He was still a *yeled tov*, a good Jewish boy, not some sinner who went around breaking all the Torah's rules. He didn't swear using God's name. He didn't do homework on *Shabbes*. He tried hard to treat his parents with respect. He didn't steal or murder or do anything else bad. He ate only kosher food, put on *tefillin* and *davened* every morning, saying every word of his prayers. No, the Leviticus passage couldn't possibly have been meant for him. Not at all. Tugging distractedly on his ears that stuck out just a tad, Jake glanced quickly up to see if Dad had somehow noticed Jake's sudden interest in the Leviticus passage. After all, Dad noticed everything, like the time last week when Dad caught Jake masturbating. That had been the most embarrassing moment of Jake's life: he'd been lying in bed late Thursday afternoon, on top of the blue-and-yellow striped sheets, his red t-shirt lifted to expose his belly, his briefs and shorts down to his ankles, and a facial tissue laid carefully over his pubic hair. Concentrating as he was with his eyes closed, picturing himself kissing one of his teachers, muscular-chested Mr. Saltzberg, he didn't hear Dad enter his room and approach the side of his bed until Dad said, in a matter-of-fact voice sounding directly above, "It's time for supper." Jake rolled quickly away, onto his side facing the wall.

"Be right down," Jake mumbled, not looking up at what he knew must be a narrow face gaunt with disappointment and shock. Could Dad tell the fantasy that had precipitated—?

"Your door wasn't clicked closed," Dad mumbled on his way out of the room. Jake knew the household rule of privacy: any room could be entered without prior knocking as long as the room's door had not been clicked closed. Dad now clicked Jake's bedroom door firmly closed behind him.

How stupid Jake had been not to shut his bedroom door completely, not to click it closed. Mom was forever saying that, according to Freud, there were no unintentionally disclosed secrets, that the subconscious mind always wanted naughtiness to reach the exposure of daylight. "That's why you dropped string beans on the floor while playing with them at dinner," she explained. "Your subconscious wanted me to know you weren't eating them." Or, "That's why you tracked mud into the front hall; your subconscious wanted me to know you'd been poking around in the muddy dirt hills up the block before coming home directly from school as you should have. Your subconscious always tells me." Jake had left his door unclicked closed; his subconscious had obviously caused him to do so on purpose; he must have wanted Dad to walk in on him, to find him. As Jake's face burned with shame against his pillow, he wondered why he would invite such discovery.

"Jake!" Dad called from downstairs. "I told you, supper!"

Silently promising the fantasy Mr. Saltzberg that he'd meet him later at bedtime, Jake pulled up his shorts, washed his hands in the bathroom, took a deep breath, slipped blue yarmulke from pocket to head, and slunk slowly down the stairs to the kitchen, every step a march through the mud pits of ancient Egypt. How would Dad flay him?

As usual, Dad and Mom were sitting opposite one another at the round, olive Formica-topped table; little Artie sat in his own spot across from Jake's. They all held torn slices of rye bread in hand. Dad was chewing a bite, so Jake knew he'd already said the *motzi*, the blessing over the bread, signaling that the meal had officially begun. Without Jake.

Mom turned toward Jake her freshly made-up face—she always put on lipstick and rouge before Dad's come-home time. "Your father said you were in the middle of something so we should start without you."

"Uh, yeah. Thanks, Dad."

"You're welcome." So, he hadn't told Mom. Was Jake going to get off easy?

"What were ya doin', Jake?" asked Artie.

"None of your beeswax."

Artie stuck out his tongue.

"You're ten going on five," Jake said.

Artie stuck out his tongue a second time.

"Did you wash your hands?" asked Dad.

Jake turned crimson and nodded.

"Wash them again," Dad said. "And this time say the *brachah* when you do."

Jake dutifully went to the kitchen sink, washed, recited the blessing about God having commanded to wash hands.

Back at the table, Jake said his own *motzi* and began to eat. As he swallowed the first bite, Dad began, "Jake—"

"Good brisket, Mom," Jake said.

"Thank you, dear. Same as always." She brought a hand to the back of her black curls and fluffed them.

"Jake," Dad said again, "Your mother and—"

"Something about the way you do the onions," Jake said to Mom as though not having heard Dad at all.

"How nice of you to notice. I—"

"Hey!" said Dad. "I'm talking!"

"No, Sol, *I'm* talking," said Mom. "Jake asked about my brisket." From the corner of his eye, Jake saw the annoyed expression on Dad's face. Mom knew something was up and was trying to protect him. Dad knew that Mom knew. Jake knew that he knew that she knew…. She continued, "I diced the onions very fine. Lots and lots of onions, that's the secret to a good brisket. And garlic powder. But mostly it's the onions."

"Onions," Jake said. "Who'd of thunk it, eh, Mom? So tell me, how do you peel—"

"Stop with the onions!" Dad exclaimed. "We have something serious to discuss."

"Uh-oh, Jake's in trouble," said Artie with a little giggle.

"It can wait until after dinner," Mom said and then, whispering to Dad across the table as though Jake weren't sitting there, "Maybe you should talk about this with him privately."

Jake stopped chewing mid-mouthful, felt he was going to be sick.

"Baloney," said Dad. "United front, Millie. United front." He turned his attention to Jake. "Jake, your mother and I have been talking, and she knows that you've matured."

Mom and Jake both dropped their heads to stare at their plates as though in silent prayer.

"Jake, you're a healthy teen boy. So, when you have…have… *those* dreams at night or during a nap, you don't have to wipe up with a tissue. Mom'll just change the sheets in the morning, okay?"

"Jake pees his bed!" said Artie.

"Shut up!" Jake lashed.

"Boys," Mom said in her firm, don't-make-me-count-to-three voice.

"Mom'll just change the sheets," Dad repeated. "Do you understand what I'm saying?"

Jake nodded at his overcooked, grayish-green string beans, wished the kitchen floor were the Red Sea ready to part and swallow him up. Where was a hungry whale when you needed one?

Obviously, Dad had been waiting for the right moment to inform Jake that, when waking him for school every morning, he'd been noticing the moist, crumpled tissues beside Jake's pillow. Why, Jake asked himself, had he left the tissues beside his pillow instead of hiding them beneath it with the packet of fresh Kleenex?

Obviously, according to their family understanding of Freud, Jake had wanted Dad to find them. But why? Jake knew about biblical Onan, how he'd been slain for having spilled his seed. That was the whole reason Jake was praying every morning to gain strength to stop this sinful ritual.

And why had Jake not clicked his bedroom door closed this afternoon?

"So, Millie," said Dad, "all these years and I never knew the secret to your brisket was the onions."

That awful conversation had taken place just last week. In *shul* now on Yom Kippur, Jake shook his head to erase the memory.

"What's wrong?" asked Dad from beside him. "Why are you shaking your head?"

"Uh, nothing. It's just some of these prohibitions, that's all. Who'd ever do such things, anyway? Hard to believe the perverted things people think up."

"Some people. Not good boys like you."

Jake nodded and flipped the page, skimmed the Book of Jonah, thought of the day's unseasonal September heat, wished he could take off the *tallit* from around his shoulders, or his navy blue suit jacket or maroon tie, felt wetness beneath his arms and at the back of his neck, felt so hungry and thirsty after nearly twenty hours of fasting—required on Yom Kippur from sunset to sunset—that he could imagine himself having walked all forty years in the desert.

His empty stomach rumbled. Dad looked down at him, patted Jake's knee at his appropriate Yom Kippur suffering. He pointed to broad-shouldered Mr. Goldschmidt, a former college football player, who was standing up on the *bimah*, the dais, and beginning to lift the opened Torah scroll for everyone to see. The congregation stood, chanted in Hebrew, "This is the Torah that Moses set before the children of Israel, at the command of God, by the hand of Moses." How strong Mr. Goldschmidt was, Jake thought, to be able to hold the heavy Torah open so high, nearly over his head. Then Mr. Goldschmidt closed the scroll, propped it on Mr. Heine's lap while Mr. Kagan wrapped the Torah in its velvet cover and silver ornaments. What an honor for those men to be allowed to care for the Torah, and on Yom Kippur no less. Jake envied them, but at the same time, felt he'd be unworthy. Mr. Klezmer stood at the podium now with an ordinary, printed copy of the Bible, and began to recite the Book of Jonah.

Jake thought of Mom's hot and tender brisket, the onions doused with garlic powder—he thought about them in part because he was ravenous, but also because they were not abominable sex. Jake sniffed as if to smell the imagined food and clear his confused head. But what he smelled was not the expected: he smelled the scent of dozens of unwashed men hanging in the sanctuary's warm, humid air.

As part of the fasting ritual, the more observant congregants wouldn't have showered on Yom Kippur: no washing of face or other body parts, no brushing of teeth—not a drop of water was to enter the mouth; only fingers and eyes could be washed clean.

Atonement for sin was serious business. In their Conservative congregation, women and men sat together, but Jake's senses filtered the women completely out.

Gradually, the scent of unwashed men—the actual scent or one that he imagined—enveloped him. He sniffed deeply, wondered whom he was smelling—the wavy-haired man in front of him with the thick, wrestler's neck? The thin man beside him whose bushy beard looked so cute? Strong Mr. Goldschmidt who'd taken his seat somewhere behind them in the crowded sanctuary?

The *makhzor* on Jake's lap began to move seemingly all by itself, but he knew otherwise. Abstinence from sex was as important a part of fasting on Yom Kippur as abstinence from food and drink; knowing that, Jake had purposely skipped his bedtime ritual the night before and his waking ritual this morning, but now—now he couldn't help himself. He just couldn't.\He looked up furtively to his right at Dad, who was engaged in whispered conversation with Artie and Mom on his other side. Jake looked briefly at the two decorative tablets rising high above the Torah's ark on the *bimah* up front, tablets representing the Ten Commandments. He looked away, back to the men seated in front of him. He slipped his left hand to his lap. Under cover of the *makhzor*, he squeezed and rubbed, squeezed and rubbed, smelled, pictured former football player Mr. Goldschmidt, stared now at the perspiration dripping down the thick wrestler's neck in front of him, now at the side of the bushy beard beside him, imagined licking that bushy beard, that thick, perspiring neck until—

"What's wrong?" asked Dad.

"What's wrong?" Jake squeaked.

"I thought I heard you grunt something. You okay?"

"Just my stomach rumbling."

"The fast is working. You'll be inscribed in the Book of Life for sure." Dad patted Jake's knee again; the *makhzor* almost fell from his lap to the floor.

Jake pulled out his left hand from beneath the *makhzor*, gnawed his knuckles until they showed blood.

"What do you think you're doing?" asked Dad.

"Evil hand," Jake said. "It almost dropped the *makhzor*, with *Hashem*'s name in it. Evil evil hand."

"Maybe you've fasted long enough."

"But—"

"Go to the hallway and take a long drink from the water fountain."

"No, Dad. I can hold out."

Dad put his arm around Jake's shoulders and hugged him close.

Sitting there under Dad's embrace, feeling a cold trickle along his left thigh, Jake reminded himself that at least he had not actually done what the Leviticus passage prohibited, that he'd only wanted to do it, had merely fantasized about doing it. But he could not escape awareness of what those fantasies had just led him to—the Onan-like spilling of his seed—and of what those fantasies might lead him to in the future—wasn't that the sort of depravity for which Sodom and Gomorrah had been destroyed? He looked up to the *bimah* at the front of the sanctuary, at the Torah's ark, worried that the tablets of the Ten Commandments might fall from their place, that *Hashem*—God—might hurl them to the floor in front of the entire congregation and shatter them the way Moses hurled and shattered his two tablets after having descended from Mount Sinai and viewed the rabble's blasphemous golden calf idol.

Jake felt horror at what he'd just done. Beside Dad. Beside Dad in *shul*. Beside Dad in *shul* while a scroll of the Torah, God's Law, was out of the ark in front of him on the holiest day of the year. Beside Dad in *shul* while a scroll of the Torah, God's Law, was out of the ark in front of him on the holiest day of the year, the very day Jake was requesting God to grant him another year of life.

How could Jake have been so stupid? How could he have been so defiant? How could he be so wicked? Jake thought of having left crumpled moist tissues beside his pillow every morning, of having left the bedroom door unclicked closed that day last week while masturbating. He thought of what his subconscious motives must have been then, what they most be in *shul* now. Why had he committed such evil in a way that risked discovery? The only possible conclusion was that he wanted to be found out.

Yes, he realized: he wanted to be found out.

Exactly.

Suddenly he breathed easier, relaxed his jaw, which he had not even realized to be clenched, leaned into the underside of Dad's arm of pride. So, Jake was not wicked beyond the pale of repentance-induced redemption: he wanted to be found out. His subconscious wanted him to be found out. At least his subconscious was devoted to God's Law. Sitting there, enveloped in the scent of unwashed men, Jake took comfort in the knowledge that he wanted to be found out, that he wanted to be found out because he wanted, before going too far, to be stopped.

PART 1

The weekend after Yom Kippur, Jake's best friend, Dave, and his parents drove down to South Jersey from Westchester, a New York City suburb, to celebrate Jake's birthday. Dave's parents and Jake's had all grown up together in Manhattan.

A year older than Jake, taller and stockier, Dave had thick brownish-red hair, freckles, a loud laugh and a fun sense of humor. The boys giggled over stupid things like the time when Jake was ten and nearly choked during their potato chip eating contest. (Dave won.) When Jake was eleven, Dave taught him to wrap a brown towel on his head sort of turban-like and drape it down his back as if it were long hair. Then they cuddled like silly girls. So goofy.

Dave's family arrived on Sunday afternoon and planned to stay for two days, the fathers taking time off work for the annual visit, and the boys being granted the unusual privilege of skipping one Monday of school. Sunday evening, they all ate at Katz's Deli, the only kosher restaurant in town and, therefore, the only restaurant where Jake's Dad ever allow the family to eat. Because it was Jake's birthday, they ordered a huge appetizer platter of Jake's favorites—*knishes, kishka, kasha, kreplach,* and potato *kugel*—what Jake called "My favorite 'k' foods."

"'K' is for 'kosher,'" shouted Artie.

As Jake rolled his eyes, Dave whispered into Jake's ear, "'K' is for 'cock.'"

Jake punched him in the arm, Dave punched him back, Jake tickled Dave, Dave tickled him back, and Dad said, "*Genug!* Enough!" He shook his head with a grin, "Teenagers—yet you're still roughhousing like little boys."

"Once they start roughhousing with girls, they'll leave each other alone," said Uncle Irv, Dave's father. Uncle Irv was tall with a square jaw and, Jake always thought, was the handsomest of all Dad's friends. He wasn't really Jake's uncle, but the two families were so close that the boys addressed one another's parents as aunt and uncle. "You fooling around with girls yet, Jake?"

"Irv," scolded pudgy Aunt Flora in her high-pitched canary-like voice. "Stop it, they're just children."

"In a year or two they'll be men," replied Uncle Irv. "Our Dave's already got some fuzz on his upper lip. Soon no girl will be safe around him."

Jake enjoyed the way Uncle Irv was relaxed about things that made Dad uptight.

Dad looked at both boys. "You're turning sixteen today, Jake. And Dave—you're already seventeen. It's time I gave you the same advice my father gave me when I was about your age. You follow this advice and you'll be good Jewish men." Dad shook his finger first in Jake's face and then in Dave's face, stating solemnly, "Whatever you do, never hurt the girl."

"Sol," said Mom, "this is a birthday party. Let the boys eat their *knishes*. Save the advice for some other time."

"You want our boys should grow up to become brutes?"

"Of course not, Sol, but now's not the time."

"It's always the time for moral lessons."

With pleading eyes, Mom looked at Aunt Flora, who shook her head, causing her double chin to wobble. She blotted a paper napkin against the back of her neck, saying, "Even with the AC, it's warm in here. So humid tonight. Indian summer."

Uncle Irv said to Mom, "If we don't let Sol get this advice business out of his system, we'll never enjoy the rest of dinner. Okay, Sol, spew forth."

"Don't mock," Dad replied, then turned his attention to Dave and Jake. "Remember, never hurt the girl. Take that in every conceivable way. A *yeled tov* never hurts the girl."

"But what if Miriam Klotz hits me first?" asked Artie, bits of potato kugel sticking to his upper lip. "She always sneaks up behind me during recess and gives me a *potch* on the *tuchas*."

Everyone chuckled at the image of some girl spanking Artie's butt.

"It's not funny!" exclaimed Artie. "She did it every day in school last spring, and I complained to Mrs. Mermelstein, but she said I did something to deserve it, but I didn't. If Miriam does it again when school starts, I'm gonna hit her back to make her stop."

"No, no," said Dad. "Mustn't hit girls even if they hit first. Maybe she *potches* you because you keep showing her your *tuchas*?"

"Sol, that's rude," said Mom, following Aunt Flora's example and dabbing a napkin against the perspiration on her neck.

"I'm just saying that if the boy doesn't turn his back on her, maybe she won't be tempted to hit. Maybe what she really wants is attention, did you ever think of that, Artie? Maybe if you look at her and talk nicely to her, she won't hit you."

"But she's a girl. Why would I want to talk to a girl?"

"Because it's the only way to get her to kiss you," said Uncle Irv.

"Eeeeewwww," said Artie, wiping the back of his hand across his lips. "Gross."

Everyone laughed and continued eating.

/ /

Back at home, Dad turned on the air-conditioning because the evening didn't seem to be cooling down. Everyone stood around the olive-Formica-topped island in the kitchen and dug into a *parve* birthday apple pie that Jake's Mom had baked from scratch—no milk or butter because *kashrut*, the kosher rules, prohibited eating any dairy products within six hours of eating meat.

("Why do we follow the rules of *kashrut?*" Dad liked to drill Jake.

"Because *Hashem* ordered us to," replied Jake. "Obedience is its own reward."

"And?"

"And because adherence to the rules of *kashrut* teaches us self-discipline, the hallmark of civilized man."

"Good boy.")

Then they all moved into the dark wood-paneled den where the grown-ups and Artie crowded onto the brown-and-white plaid sofa while Dave and Jake lay on the burnt-orange area rug, everyone staring at Dad's pride and joy—the television set into a huge, stubby-legged, maple cabinet with built-in, thin cloth-covered speakers, and bookshelves stacked high with old *TV Guides*, *Reader's Digests*, and Mom's *Good Housekeeping* and *Life* magazines. *Fiddler on the Roof* just happened to be showing on TV that very night. "A good omen," Dad said. "Almost makes your birthday a national holiday."

Jake caught Dave's eye and the two teens snickered. How many times, wondered Jake, had he seen *Fiddler*, that musical about Jewish life in an old Russian village?

When everyone else sang along to the song "Matchmaker," Dave whispered, "How lame."

"You're not kidding," Jake whispered back.

Dad toe-nudged Jake's thigh, said, "Respect your elders," then continued singing. When the father in the movie, Tevye, started his solo, "If I Were a Rich Man," Dad stood, raised his arms the way Tevye was doing, and sang along in his fairly decent bass. Jake and Dave rolled their eyes, the other adults applauded and Dad bowed. "I love the way Tevye talks to *Hashem*," he said.

"You do?" Jake asked.

"Of course. Talking to *Hashem* shows respect. And faith."

Wow, thought Jake, that's really good to know.

"Like God has time to listen to billions of individuals," said Uncle Irv.

Uh-oh, thought Jake. Uncle Irv's going to upset Dad big time.

"Don't start," said Dad, "with your atheism."

"What atheism? I'm not denying God's existence, I'm just saying He can't possibly listen to every single person's private prayers."

"Irv," Aunt Flora said, grasping her husband's forearm, "stop. What are you upsetting the man for in his own home?"

"Who's upsetting anybody? Two old friends can't disagree?"

"We can disagree," said Dad, "but you're wrong."

Mom intervened, "Sol, they're our guests."

Uncle Irv stated, "It's not humanly possible for God to listen to every human prayer simultaneously."

"Why do you impose human limitations onto *Hashem*? He can do anything."

"Next thing you know, you'll say you believe in all the Bible's miracles."

"Of course I believe in all the Torah's miracles. Every single one! You don't?"

The two men stared at one another as if seeing each other for the first time.

"You never were very religious as a boy," mumbled Dad.

"You always took our yeshiva training too literally," mumbled Uncle Irv.

"As soon as you met Flora in high school, you stopped attending *shul* on Shabbes," accused Dad.

"Saturday mornings were the only time we could sneak off and be alone—while our parents were in *shul*." To Dave and Jake, Uncle Irv added, "Flora and I each told our parents we were *davening* in a different synagogue in another neighborhood, but really we were smooching on her parents' living room sofa."

"Shush!" said Dad, standing. His face was reddening. "This is what you teach our children? To disrespect parents? To kiss instead of pray?"

Mom grabbed his hand, "Sol, calm down. Your blood pressure."

Uncle Irv heaved a sigh. "Okay, Sol. Your home—your standards." He stood and offered a hand, "I apologize."

Not shaking the hand, Dad said, "Don't apologize to me, apologize to *Hashem*."

"Sol!" said Mom.

"It's all right, Millie," said Uncle Irv. He turned to Dad and said, "I'll apologize to God in my private prayers. According to you, He'll hear me just fine."

"You want to make a mockery?" Dad said softly through clenched teeth, "You do that. But not in my home."

"We'll leave first thing in the morning."

Aunt Flora's voice was squeakier than high-pitched canary. "Irv!"

"This is ridiculous, Sol," Mom said. "What's going on here, such arguing out of nowhere?"

"It's not out of nowhere," said Uncle Irv. "We've been disagreeing about religion for decades. We just try not to show it in front of you. We try never to talk about it at all."

"Sol, is this true?" asked Mom.

"I don't want to talk about it." Dad stomped out of the den and upstairs.

Uncle Irv went down to the basement guest room, and Aunt Flora followed after mouthing a silent "I'm sorry" to Mom.

"Happy Birthday," Mom said to Jake sadly, kissing his cheek. "I'll put Artie to bed and then set up Dave's cot in your room."

"You need help, Aunt Millie?" asked Dave, his tone more solicitous than usual.

"No, dear, I can do it. I'll leave folded sheets at the bottoms of your beds—even with the air-conditioner, it's so warm tonight. But if you get cold, blankets are in the hall linen closet. Come up whenever you're ready, but please don't make noise that will disturb your father, Jake."

After Mom led Artie out of the den and Jake heard the beige-carpeted stairs creak a little, he breathed deeply. "That was crummy."

"Very heavy," said Dave. "I've never seen your father angry like that."

"Me neither."

"Religion's the only subject my pop gets angry about," said Dave. "He hated being raised religious. He says too much religion prevents people from thinking for themselves."

"My father says religion makes him feel secure, knowing that God's taking care of everyone. He says it's like a contract—we obey God's rules and He takes care of us."

Dave shrugged.

Jake shrugged back.

"I guess we'll be leaving earlier than we planned," said Dave.

"Too bad. There's a zombie movie on TV. Wanna watch?"

After the movie, the boys went upstairs. Dave changed into his pajamas in Jake's room while Jake changed in the bathroom, washed up, and took his nightly antihistamine tablet.

Shutting his bedroom door behind him, being careful to click it closed softly, Jake looked at Dave's hairless chest and asked, "You didn't bring a pajama top?"

"I did, but it's too warm. You should take your top off, too."

Being shy, Jake hesitated.

"Come on," said Dave. "You hiding tits or something?"

"Dufus," said Jake, unbuttoning his pajama top and tossing it on the dresser.

"Wow," said Dave. "You're getting chest hair already. I wish I was."

Jake felt a burst of manly pride.

Dave stood beside the wall opposite the bed and cot, examined the posters of Sonny and Cher, and of Elton John in huge, rhinestone-rimmed glasses. "Your Dad let you put up these posters?"

"He shook his head when I showed him, but he said, 'It's your room.'"

"Cool. He'd probably like it better if you put up a *Fiddler* poster instead."

The boys shared another snicker.

"Oh, Papa," said Dave, stroking his thick brownish-red hair in impersonation of one of Tevye's movie daughters, "please please make me a match."

"Me, first, Papa," said Jake in a mocking falsetto.

"Lame-o," said Dave, plopping down beside Jake on the cot. "*Fiddler* would be more fun if Tevye's daughters stripped."

Jake laughed at the shocking image. Dave tickled Jake's bare belly, making him laugh even harder. "Quit it," gasped Jake between breaths as he rolled off the cot onto his bed right beside it.

"I discovered my pop's stash of *Playboys*," said Dave, lying on his side.

"You did?" asked Jake, turning onto his side.

"Yeah. In a carton in the garage under a pile of dirty overalls."

"Did he find out?"

"Nah. I only sneak out two magazines at a time and hide them under my mattress. Hot chicks in those photos. Lots of big tits."

"Wow. I wish I could see pictures of tits," said Jake. "Have you ever seen any for real?"

"Sure," said Dave. "Lots. You mean, you haven't?"

"Oh…well…sure I have. I just didn't know if you had, that's all. I mean, you're talking like magazine pictures are a big deal."

"Pictures are great because you can look at them any time. It's not like I can look at real tits any time. But I've seen lots. And I've touched lots, too," said Dave.

"No, you haven't, you liar."

"Sure I have. Big juicy ones."

"You never told me that."

"Since the last time I saw you. I squeeze tits a lot now. I've even sucked on a couple."

"No, you haven't."

"Sure I have," said Dave. "Sheila Silverberg loves having her tits squeezed and sucked. She'll let anybody. Next time you visit, I'll call her and we'll go into her basement and have some fun. She really gets turned on if you play with her tits while she's sitting on the dryer. All that vibrating, you know." Dave winked.

"Wow, thanks," said Jake, wondering why sitting on a vibrating dryer would be any fun. Wouldn't it make her a little nauseous? Or make her lose her balance?

"She might even let you finger her. You'd like that, wouldn't you?" asked Dave.

"Of course I'd like it," mumbled Jake, rolling away from Dave to face his wall. "I'm normal."

"Dufus," said Dave, tickling Jake's bare sides from behind.

Jake squirmed. "Cut it out, jackass!" He giggled and turned, tried shoving Dave's hands away, but Dave just kept tickling. And then Dave, a good three inches taller than Jake and huskier, slid over onto Jake's bed, climbed on top of him, wrestled and pinned Jake's wrists back onto the pillow. Dave hawked up a gob of spit and, staring down into Jake's eyes, let the gob fall down toward Jake's face.

"Gross!" exclaimed Jake, turning his face to the side just as the spit splatted on his right cheek. He bucked his hips to knock Dave off balance, then wiped his face. Now it was Jake's turn to roll on top of Dave and pin him. Easily.

Too easily. They'd wrestled some over the years, and Jake could never pin Dave. Yet now…why was Dave grinning, and pressing his pelvis up against Jake's?

Jake could feel Dave's hardness rub against Jake's lower belly. And his own hardness rub down against Dave's.

"Boys!" came Mom's voice from outside the bedroom door.

Jake rolled off Dave onto the cot.

"Boys, please stop making so much noise. We can hear you wrestling and grunting."

They were grunting?

"Save the roughhouse for the morning. Talk late as you want, but don't keep the rest of us from sleeping."

"Sorry, Mom," called Jake, adjusting his blue pajama bottoms.

"Good night, Aunt Millie," called Dave.

"Good night."

Jake listened to Mom's footsteps depart down the hall. "See what you did?" he accused Dave.

"Me? That was you, dufus, can't handle being tickled." He reached out his arms and made spider fingers as if to tickle Jake again.

"Quit it!"

"Now you got me all sweaty," said Dave, still on Jake's bed.

Dave's sweat smelled different from Jake's own, somehow. Musky. Jake liked it.

"You've got lousy air-conditioning," said Dave. "I'm so damn hot." He tugged off his brown pajama bottoms and kicked them to the end of the bed, revealing himself swollen and huge. "You're all sweaty, too. Take off your pajamas."

Jake lay there, frozen.

"Come on. Take off your pajamas and come here."

"No."

"Come on. We're best buds, aren't we? We used to pee together when we were little."

True — years back, they'd stand side by side over the toilet and criss-cross their streams.

"I'm showing you mine, so you gotta show me yours," continued Dave. "I wanna see if it's the kind Sheila'll like."

Shutting his eyes, Jake slipped off his pajama bottoms and just lay there.

"Nice dick," said Dave. "Longer than mine. Sheila'll love it." He reached over and gave Jake a squeeze.

Jake gasped at the touch, at this first ever amazing sensation.

"Yeah," said Dave, "just the sort of dick she likes." Dave began to stroke Jake lightly. "Sheila'll suck this one for sure."

Jake could barely breathe. He knew he should swat Dave's hand away, but the feeling was amazing, way better than when Jake stroked himself, better than anything Jake had ever felt.

"I'm just showing what Sheila's gonna do," said Dave. "So you're prepared, that's all. Not queer or anything, just one friend helping out another, some guy-practice so you're ready and don't make a fool of yourself with a girl. I could use more practice. Do me."

Jake hesitated. He'd done this in his fantasies, but never in real life. Never.

"Come on," said Dave, "fair is fair."

Jake reached out and grasped his friend. So full and thick. How good it felt. Amazingly good.

"Now jerk it the way Sheila will," said Dave, "nice and slow the way I'm jerking you."

Jake hesitated, but followed instructions.

"Yeah, that's it. I'm pretending your hand is hers and I'm fingering her wet pussy and sucking on her big juicy tits. Oh that's so hot, so hot, so—! Ugh! Ugh!"

Jake moaned, too, spasming just as Dave did.

"What a sticky mess," said Dave, reaching for his pajamas at the bottom of the bed, wiping his hand and himself. Jake did likewise. They tossed the soiled clothes to the royal-blue-carpeted floor.

"So that's what you'll get from Sheila next time you come visit. And way more. Won't that be fun?"

"For sure," said Jake, wondering what he was supposed to do now.

"Okay," said Dave. "You take your bed and I'll take the cot. And if you get to thinking about Sheila during the night and pop a boner, wake me and I'll give you more practice."

Each boy pulled a blue-and-yellow striped sheet up over his lower body. Jake lay there until he heard the regular breathing that meant Dave was asleep. Then he brought his hand, the hand that had touched Dave, to his nose, and inhaled deeply, that familiar yet distinct Cloroxy aroma. He licked his palm. Then he reached beneath his own sheet.

/ /

The next morning, Dave slipped on shorts and t-shirt and acted like nothing out of the ordinary had taken place, but Jake, wearing a fresh pair of pajama tops and bottoms at the breakfast table, barely spoke to him over pancakes. The adults made small talk—at least Dad and Uncle Irv were talking—about watering ivy, mowing lawns, planting geraniums.

"So," Mom said to Aunt Flora, "what shall we all do today? You and I could shop at the mall while our men see a movie."

"Thanks, Millie," said Uncle Irv, "but we're heading home this morning instead of tonight."

"Irv, please. You're not going to let last night's little tiff ruin our weekend, are you? We could drive to Atlantic City for the day. It's only an hour away, and warm enough for the beach. I'll make egg-salad sandwiches. Sol, talk to him."

"If the man needs to get home," said Dad, "he needs to get home."

"You men," said Aunt Flora, "are more childlike than your boys."

A quiet rest of breakfast. Quick packing upstairs. Stiff goodbyes all around. "Next time, you come stay at our house," Dave said to Jake in his usual cheery voice, "I'll introduce you to some school friends, like Sheila." Dave winked, turned and followed his parents out to their car.

"Is that a special friend of Dave's?" asked Mom. "That Sheila?"

"Uh, yeah, Mom. A special friend."

"How nice."

From the front door, they waved good-bye as Dave's family drove off in their big-grilled maroon Buick Wildcat.

"*Daven* yet?" asked Dad.

"Not yet," said Jake. "I'm going to pray right now."

"Good boy," said Dad, patting him on the head. "I'll be in my room doing the same."

Upstairs in his room, Jake clicked the door closed, put on yarmulke, *tallit*, and *tefillin*, those leather straps he had to wrap in a ritualized way around arm and head to make sure that Torah quotes sealed in small leather boxes remained affixed to forehead and upper arm—keeping God's words against mind and heart. Jake prayed as usual.

But afterward, before unwrapping the *tefillin*, Jake looked up at the ceiling the way Tevye, in *Fiddler on the Roof*, had looked up at the sky when engaging God in private conversation.

"God, are you there?" Jake asked out loud.

For you, Jake, always, Dave heard echo in his head.

'I'm trying really hard to be a good Jewish boy, God,' Dave thought silently. 'Without even knowing it, I've been great at obeying Dad's rule about never hurting girls.'

Never hurting girls is one thing. Never touching them is another.

'I know, but maybe I've just been extra careful, that's all.'

Are you saying you want to touch girls, but restrain yourself?

'Not exactly.'

I'm God. Tell Me the truth.

Jake looked down at the pattern the *tefillin* strap made on his hand—it spelled out the Hebrew word *shadai*, meaning "Almighty." He looked back up to the ceiling, said out loud, "Please make me normal, God."

Now this is a request worthy of a good Jewish boy.

'I mean it, God. I want to be normal. I want to follow Your rules and be normal and good.'

Obedience is difficult, I know. Try harder. Don't do things you know I'd disapprove of.

'Yes, Sir. Thank you, Sir. 'Bye for now.'

Bad boys didn't want to be good, but Jake did. He wanted to be a *yeled tov*, a good boy, a good Jewish boy.

And he would. He didn't have to see Dave again, even if he was Jake's best friend.

Jake always had his annual physical right after his birthday. In the back seat of Mom's gray Oldsmobile sedan, Jake teased Artie about the doctor's name: "You know why they call him 'Dr. Peril'? Because he straps little boys down onto a gurney and sticks them with needles until they bleed to death."

"Mom!" yelled Artie. "Jake's creeping me out!"

"Behave, Jake, you're a senior in high school, for goodness sake."

"Yeah, but I skipped third grade, so I'm immature."

"Jake," she replied sternly.

"Sorry, Mom." Then to Artie: "You just wait till your next birthday and your physical—Dr. Peril likes to take scalpels and cut some boys' peepees off to feed them to snakes he keeps at home."

"Mom!"

Jake was trying to get his mind off his nervousness. After making Jake strip, would Dr. Peril be able to tell that Jake had had sex with Dave? The man was a doctor, after all, and was trained to notice changes in people's bodies, not that Jake had noticed any change these past couple days. But maybe Dr. Peril would scan Jake's naked body and realize what Jake had done, would recoil in horror now that Jake was...was...one of *those* boys. Dr. Peril would tell Mom, who'd burst into tears, then faint and hit her head and suffer a concussion. She'd call Dad at work at his medical library in Philly, and his blood pressure would skyrocket, he'd turn beet red and fall off a ladder high in the stacks and he'd get a concussion, too. All because of Jake.

"Howdy howdy howdy," Dr. Peril said as usual, waddling into the examination room in his squeaky black orthopedic shoes. Dr. Peril was a jovial sort whose girth gave new meaning to "obese." A chain smoker, he had a big red clown sort of nose, and eyes forever goggling in every which direction behind black-framed glasses. "How ya feeling?"

"Just fine, thank you." Seated on the examining table's white paper, Jake was still in t-shirt and briefs.

"All righty, then. Now take off your shirt and let's have a listen."

Here we go, thought Jake. Clenching his teeth, he did as ordered.

He watched Dr. Peril as he pressed the cold stethoscope against Jake's chest. "Big breath. Cough."

No discernible strange staring. Maybe he hadn't noticed yet?

Stethoscope against back.

"Big breath."

Probe in ears, nose, throat.

"Lie back down for me." Belly thump here, press there.

Still no register of horror in his eyes.

"Sit up, and let's check your reflexes."

Dr. Peril knocked a rubber hammer just below Jake's knee; Jake's foot kicked out.

"Fine and dandy," said Dr. Peril. "Now stand, drop your drawers, turn your head to the side and cough." As Dr. Peril felt under Jake's testicles for hernia, Jake's breathing quickened: did his genitals look (or feel) different now in a way that only a doctor would notice? Surely, Dr. Peril was despairing: a good boy from a good family, but look at those genitals — clearly the boy's engaged in perverse homosexual sex.

"All righty. Now close your eyes, hold your arms out to the sides."

Jake was so nervous, he could feel his shut eyelids twitching.

"Keeping your eyes closed, touch your index fingers to your nose one at a time." With trembling hands, Jake moved his right hand, then his left.

"Okeedokee. Get dressed and come into my office."

Jake opened his eyes, still detected no horror in Dr. Peril's. Well…Dr. Peril never gave results in the examination room itself. He always made Jake come into his office with Mom while Artie sat reading *Highlights Magazine* in the waiting room. Bad enough Dr. Peril was going to tell Mom about the sordid implications of Jake's homo-revealing chest or genitals, but did he have to shame Jake right in front of his own face?

In the smoke-filled office cluttered with shelves of files, magazines, and medical books, Dr. Peril sat behind his big wooden desk, tapping ash off his cigarette with one hand while making Bic pen notes in Jake's folder with the other. Mom was already seated in one of the two leather chairs opposite, and smiled as Jake came in, so he knew the doctor hadn't told her yet.

Jake sat in the chair beside her.

"Millie," said Dr. Peril, "Jake's fine, just fine, except for one thing — "

Here it comes. Jake felt like throwing up.

"Our boy's very tense. Too tense. Eyes twitching and hands trembling. Is something going on at home?"

Mom looked at Jake. "Really? Jake, darling, are you tense?"

"Uh, I'm under a lot of stress this year, being a senior and all. SAT studying, college applications," he blurted.

"Maybe the boy's working too hard, Millie. Too much stress."

"True, his father does make him memorize vocabulary lists for the SATs. And review algebra and geometry in addition to regular schoolwork. Jake skipped third grade, you know. We want to be sure he's ready for college next year."

"Our boy here already gets good grades. Jake, which extracurricular activities are you doing?"

"Nothing so far," said Jake.

"Millie, extracurricular activities would be fun for the boy. They'd help him relax. Besides, they'd look impressive on a college application."

Was this it? Jake wondered. This is the big revelation? That Jake was tense? He wanted to jump up and down with glee.

PART 2

"**B**ut rehearsals have already begun," Jake replied to Deb, his closest friend at school. She'd been cast as the lead in the fall play: with her narrow Jewish face and long black hair, with her overall bubbly personality and acting experience, she was perfect to play Anne Frank.

"One of the actors dropped out," Deb continued. "You'd be perfect for the part. Mrs. Horowitz is looking for someone."

"Dad wouldn't like it because it'd take away from study time."

"The play honors Jewish history. Your father'll love that."

/ /

Jake initiated the conversation with Dad by asking, "Why doesn't Grandpa Morry ever talk about the Holocaust?"

"You know that Grandpa and Grandma, may she rest in peace, left Poland a good ten years before the war began: a cousin in New York had a small tailor shop serving wealthy clients and was doing well. He invited your grandpa, a master tailor, to join him, so they came."

"I know all that. But why doesn't Grandpa ever talk about the Holocaust?"

Dad set a hand on Jake's shoulder. "It's called 'survivor's guilt.' When others suffer tragedy, but you're lucky enough to survive, you feel guilty even though you did nothing wrong. Grandpa and Grandma left their parents and siblings in Poland. By the time the Nazis invaded in 1939, it was too late to get them out."

"They all died in the camps, I know."

"So your grandfather feels weighed down by guilt. He can't talk about it without breaking into sobs."

This was the opening Jake had hoped for. "I've been thinking, Dad. Maybe there's a way I could honor the memory of Grandpa's family."

"Really?"

"You know Dr. Peril advised me to do an extracurricular activity, right? And you know they do plays at school? Well, this fall they're doing *The Diary of Anne Frank*. Deb has the lead. There's an opening for a small part, and Deb thinks I'd be good in it. Grandpa could come see me, and he'd know I'm honoring our family."

"Wow," Dad said, cupping Jake's cheek. "You're more mature than I realized."

Jake didn't like how it felt to manipulate Dad. Sure, if he got the part, he actually would be honoring the six million murdered Jews, but that wasn't the real reason he wanted to audition. He just wanted to have some fun, that was all. Jake was using his grandfather's pain, the suffering of millions, for his own purposes. He felt lousy.

"But I don't know," said Dad, clearing his throat. "A play's a major time commitment, not just some club meeting once a week. What about your grades and studying? French class, English, chemistry, history—can you handle it all? I don't want you getting stressed."

"Rehearsals will be fun, not stressful. They'll be a stress relief. And they'll give me something good for my college apps." All true. Every single word. But still…

"It's a beautiful project, Jake. If you think you can keep your grades up."

"I will, Dad."

"And you've got to keep studying for the SATs, memorizing new vocabulary lists every week."

"For sure."

"And get those college application essays done well and early—I don't want to take the chance of you getting the flu or something last minute and not being able to get the applications in by deadline. Your entire future's at stake."

"I know, Dad."

"And you'll still have to go to *shul* with me on Shabbes."

"It's a deal."

/ /

"It's the part of Mr. Dussel," Mrs. Horowitz explained at Jake's audition. She and Deb were sitting in folding chairs onstage while Jake stood with a script in his hand. "Basically, he's an intruder. Neither Anne Frank's family nor the others want him sharing their hiding space, but they all know that welcoming him is the right thing to do. He shares Anne's bedroom, and is eminently annoying."

"That's Jake!" said Deb.

"Thanks," Jake said.

Mrs. Horowitz continued, "Mr. Dussel's older. In order to play an old man, you need to lower your center of gravity. Imagine that a weight on a string is tied to your chin and weighing you down. Then stiffen your joints a little."

This past year, Jake had spent hours in front of the bathroom mirror monitoring the way he walked to make sure he didn't mince or hold his arms out effeminately. He practiced examining dirty fingernails by curling fingers into a fist rather than by splaying them and examining the nails from the back, which everybody knew was a girlish thing. And he rehearsed crouching down to pull up socks rather than bending knee and foot behind, another girly trait. He could handle self-conscious body movement.

In response to Mrs. Horowitz's direction, he hunched gently forward, walked stiffly across stage in his best old man shuffle. "Like this?"

"Exactly. Very good," said Mrs. Horowitz. "Now try reading Mr. Dussel's lines with a bit of a Yiddish accent. Can you do a Yiddish accent?"

Jake heard Grandpa Morry's accent in his head and said, "You vant maybe I should talk like dis?" Jake asked.

"Kinda like dat I vant," replied Mrs. Horowitz with a laugh. "But don't overdo it."

/ /

At Jake's first rehearsal with the entire cast, everyone sat around a long cafeteria table on stage. "As we know," explained Mrs. Horowitz, "the Franks and others are hiding in their Secret Annex. They're living in a hidden part of an office building where ordinary people work during the day. Close your eyes for a minute."

Jake, Deb, and the others did so.

"Think about what it would mean to get caught—to be deported who-knows-where. To be locked up in a Polish ghetto, maybe. Or sent to a labor camp. Are the rumors of death camps true? If caught, will you be executed? Think about this. Think about what it means for *you*, for your family."

Beside him, Deb sniffled.

"Yes," said Mrs. Horowitz. "That's it. Get into your characters. Feel what it's like to live in cramped quarters for heaven knows how long. Never stepping out into sunlight. Not knowing when you'll get to leave this tiny closet of an apartment and live a normal life again. Imagine what it feels like knowing that if you make a wrong move, creak a floorboard or knock something over, a stranger downstairs will hear and get suspicious and call the police. Think about that for a minute. Think about what it means to live in hiding."

Jake felt a chill run up his spine.

"Imagine the constant terror of being caught."

Jake's breathing sped up.

"Your face, Jake," Mrs. Horowitz said softly. "Your face has been contorting in response to my words. It's clear you're getting into your character, beginning to understand what it means to fear discovery."

He didn't know what to say.

"Don't reply," Mrs. Horowitz said. "Just continue to feel."

He swallowed hard.

"Remember this feeling," Mrs. Horowitz went on. "Remember how the fear inhabits your bodies, remember the tension in your shoulders, maybe the burning of tears you're trying not to shed, maybe the churning of your stomachs…. At the same time, take a modicum of solace in the fact that at least you don't have to hide alone. "

Jake finished rehearsal emotionally exhausted, but with a new connection to his character, to the play, to all his people who suffered during the Holocaust. To Grandpa.

Three weeks after Jake joined the cast, Mrs. Horowitz wanted everyone to walk through Act I. She asked them all to hang out together beforehand, without her, in the courtyard behind the auditorium, "to get the feeling of a collective—camaraderie in real life will translate onto the stage." Steve, the fellow senior who was playing Anne's love interest, Peter, plunked down beside

Jake on a bench and asked routine getting-to-know-you questions about courses and family. They'd seen each other around, but hadn't ever chatted before. Mid-conversation, Steve casually stood, stepped behind the bench, and started massaging Jake's shoulders and upper back. Just like that.

Nobody had ever touched Jake that way before. Jake loved the sensation, but darted his eyes around to see if others were staring. Nobody was. Come to think of it, Steve was kind of a touchy-feely sort of person. Onstage, he was affectionate with the other actors. During rehearsals, Jake had seen him stroke this one's forearm in a conversation or squeeze that one's shoulder. No big deal. Was that Steve or the character he was portraying? Jake leaned back and enjoyed. When Mrs. Horowitz came out and summoned them all to rehearsal, he felt bitter disappointment that the massage ended.

That afternoon, Jake watched Steve intently, felt drawn to Steve's performance of a young man falling in love, playing those tentative romantic scenes with Deb, acting sweet and innocent. For the first time, Jake noticed Steve's full lips resting in a natural pucker that stretched wide in warm grin to reveal large super-white front teeth. Light brown hair drooped over the tops of his ears in curls that Steve would twist when acting a nervous moment, or press against the side of his head. Even from the wings, Jake could see that Steve needed to shave more often than Jake did.

After that day, Jake showed up at every single rehearsal whether his scenes were being rehearsed or not—"so I can learn more about acting by watching everybody else." He stared up at Steve onstage, sponging in his every stride, the lilts of his voice, his frowns and grins. The more deeply Steve inhabited his character, the more sweet and sensitive he appeared, the more handsome, the more masculine. So many emotions played across Steve's actor face as his character grew enamored of Anne Frank.

Jake grew to feel envious that Steve's words and smiles of affection up there weren't meant for him. If Steve were to gaze at Jake that way, Jake would reach out, hug him close, kiss his eyelids and promise to be his friend forever.

The first Saturday in November, Jake and Deb went to take the SATs together. Dad was less than thrilled that Jake would be taking them on *Shabbes*—Jake would have to write them, of course, and writing was prohibited on *Shabbes*—but there wasn't a choice, and Dad emphasized that "Education comes first and foremost. *Hashem* will understand." Will He? Jake hoped Dad was right about that, about God understanding certain violations of His rules. But which ones would God understand and which wouldn't He? When was it okay to break a rule and when wasn't it?

After Jake and Deb took their seats in the cafeteria and set out their No. 2 pencils, Jake spotted Steve across the room and waved. Steve waved back and tossed one of those big-toothed grins of his.

"I think I've got a crush on him," admitted Deb. Jake felt a pang of jealousy. "You've got to stop confusing your character in the play with real life."

"I know. But he's so dreamy. It's stupid because Steve's been with his girlfriend for two years already."

"He's got a girlfriend?" Jake went cold.

"She's a freshman at NYU. He's so mature, of course he's got an *older* girlfriend. He usually takes the bus up to New York to stay with her on weekends. That's why he wants to get into NYU."

Jake felt like he'd just skidded on a frozen pond and fallen through ice he hadn't realized to be cracked.

"Nervous?" asked Deb.

"Nervous?" he replied. "What the hell should I be nervous about?"

"Hey, calm down. You've been studying for the SATs harder than anyone. No need to be nervous. Our whole future depends on this exam, that's all. Hah hah."

"You sound like my Dad."

"I'll take that as a compliment."

NYU. Jake wasn't even planning to apply to NYU. Should he? If he applied there and got in, but also got into his dream school, Princeton, what would he do?

"You may begin."

Jake looked up. The head proctor had just started timing the exam. Jake blinked a couple times, bit his lower lip to force focus. He turned the first page of the test booklet, and began.

Throughout the exam, Jake repeatedly had to block out thoughts of Steve: "If x=375 and y=643.2, then…" Steve had a girlfriend. "Of the three sentences below, select the one that correctly uses the word 'discombobulated.'" Steve wasn't interested in Jake at all. "Mark the closest analogy from the listed choices." Had Steve intentionally led Jake on by massaging him that afternoon? Did he want Jake to think there were possibilities when there weren't?

"Time. Pencils down," called the proctor.

As they left the cafeteria, Deb said, "I wish I'd studied more. Do you think you did well enough to get into Princeton?"

He shrugged.

"I hope I did well enough for Penn's architecture program."

"If you don't get into college, you could always audition for Broadway—you're really talented."

Deb gave Jake a hug just at the very moment Jake's mother pulled up to drive them both home.

The play ran the weekend after Thanksgiving. Dad would have been happier had the opening not been on a Friday night, *Shabbes,* but he said, "Well, it's for a good Jewish cause, remembrance of our people. *Hashem* will understand." Once again Jake wondered which exceptions to the rules God understood.

The opening was a smash. "Four curtain calls!" Jake exclaimed afterward in the den at home. "We know," said Mom. "We were applauding in the front row."

"You make a terrific old man," said Dad. "I'd like to see you in sixty years."

"I loved it," said Jake. "Did you see how the audience laughed when I acted like I got the earplug stuck in my ear?"

"And your character seemed so nervous and frightened!" added Mom. "You performed that perfectly. You're a natural."

"In the dressing room after the show," said Jake, "Steve said he thought I was the funniest actor in school."

"Steve?" asked Mom. "Who's Steve?"

"He's the guy who played the role of Peter."

"Ah, the male lead," said Mom. "A handsome young man."

"Is he?" asked Jake. "I never noticed."

/ /

Saturday night's performance went just as well.

On Sunday morning, the telephone rang. It was Grandpa Morry. He was supposed to be driving down that afternoon from New York to see Jake perform in the evening. "I'm sorry your vonderful play to be missing," said Grandpa. "But I voke up feeling not tiptop. You should never know how it really feels to be an old man—dis hurts, dat hurts. Ech, your grandmodder, may she rest in peace, had da right idea—*genug* already." Enough already.

"I hope you feel better soon, Grandpa."

"Your fadder told me vhy dis play you're doing—to honor da memory of my parents and—" Grandpa's voice caught. He cleared his throat. "You're such a good boy, Jake. Your grandmodder vould have been proud. You're a real *yeled tov*."

Jake felt awful. Grandpa was all emotional because he believed Jake was doing the play for a reason that wasn't totally true. Jake was a fraud. In more than one way.

"Just be sure," said Grandpa, sounding more cheerful, "to mail me your autograph on a program. A stamp you can spare?"

"For you, Grandpa—two stamps," said Jake, teasing the way Grandpa liked.

"Dat's my boy," said Grandpa.

/ /

After Sunday's performance, Steve hosted the cast party. Jake told himself he was attending because everyone else was, not because he really wanted to be in Steve's home.

Steve's house was twice as large as Jake's or Deb's, and on a huge wooded lot. Steve's parents arranged the party in their living room. They set out on their glass coffee table a big crystal bowl of red Hawaiian Punch with floating lumps of melting orange sherbet. Beside it stretched a white-frosted sheet cake with pink rosettes saying, "Congratulations Cast and Crew." The phonograph played popular music from the 1940s, various swing and jazz songs that Jake and everyone else had heard their parents play before. Steve's parents sat on a blue and yellow floral sofa with Deb and made polite conversation. Deb looked stiff and uncomfortable.

Seated in a corner armchair upholstered in blue silk, Jake imagined himself standing, crossing the room, walking over to Steve's mother with her poofy brown hair, pearl necklace and red-painted nails. "Mrs. Kabakoff, could you show me the Lladró figurines in the corner china cabinet?" She rises, takes him by the hand, leads him to the cabinet and proceeds to spend half an hour showing him each porcelain piece—the romantic couples, the lovebirds, the swans facing each other and forming the shape of a heart with their long necks and heads. Jake diligently "oohs" and "aaahs" as if he really cares.

In gratitude for Jake's interest, Mrs. Kabakoff invites him for next Friday night *Shabbes* dinner. "Of course, afterwards you'll sleep over," she insists. "But don't bother bringing pajamas because Stevie likes to sleep in the nude, so you'll sleep nude too. In the same bedroom. In the same bed. In fact, I'll tuck you boys in so you can cuddle because it's nearly winter and cold. Two handsome boys like you should be roaming your hands all over one another's naked bodies. What's the flesh for if not to enjoy?

"There's nothing homo about that, it's just natural boy-boy exploration, Lord knows, a phase that will pass, but only after you give yourselves over to it. Your phase of wanting to kiss my Stevie will pass, but only after you give into it. I bet my Stevie's a tender kisser. He's got pretty lips, don't you think? Juicy juicy. Then you boys can decide whether you want to room in a dorm at NYU or rent an apartment off campus."

Jake shook his head, practically slapped himself to stop the idiotic fantasy. He smiled at Mrs. Kabakoff as she made her way into the kitchen. She returned with a tray of pigs-in-blanket hors d'oeuvres that she set on the glass coffee table.

Deb looked over at Jake and he knew she was thinking this party strange. Steve picked up the tray to walk it around the room. When he reached Jake, Jake stuck a toothpick into one of the dough-wrapped mini-hotdogs, dipped the hors d'oeuvre in the little cup of mustard. "A really great party, Steve."

Steve winked at him, making Jake think the lie was worth it.

Jake sure was lying a lot these days.

The first day of winter break, Jake sat nervously on his bed while Mom and Dad waited patiently downstairs in the kitchen. Jake's fingers trembled as he opened the envelope that he knew contained his SAT scores. He'd need very high scores—over 700 in each of Math and Verbal—in order to be a serious contender for Princeton.

He tore open the corner of the envelope, stuck index finger inside the top fold, ran it across the top, tearing as he went. He reached in, tugged out the thin slip of paper, read it.

He reread it.

Once more, just to be sure.

He fixed a somber look on his face to tease Mom and Dad, trudged slowly downstairs to the kitchen where they were sitting with forced, casual smiles.

"Look," said Dad. "You did your best, we know you did. If your scores aren't tops and you can't get into…certain schools, then you'll get in elsewhere and do well there. Wherever. The important thing is to get an education. We can't ask more than that you try hard, and we know you've been working your tail off."

"In fact, you've been working too hard," said Mom, shaking a finger. "Remember what Dr. Peril said. Maybe attending an easier school would be a blessing in disguise, better for your health."

"760 Verbal and 740 Math," blurted Jake, beaming. Those scores fit the average of recent Princeton acceptees.

Dad jumped up from the table and hugged him. "Mazel tov!"

"We're so proud," from Mom. "But even so, maybe an easier school would be better. We don't want you to stress yourself too much."

"Nonsense," said Dad. "Jake's a bright boy and should push himself to the max. I knew you could do it, Jake. You'll get into the Ivies for sure. Or NYU that you added to your list—a great school."

"So, with this weight off your shoulders," asked Mom, "what are you going to do to relax? I'm taking Artie to the Franklin Institute during winter break. And the Betsy Ross house and Independence Hall. Want to come?"

"Thanks, Mom, but I've been to all those places like a dozen times already."

"You could go to Echelon Mall with your friends and see movies and eat pizza," said Mom. "You can borrow my car if I don't need it. Or I'll drive you and some friends, or we'll leave you money for a taxi."

"Thanks, but everybody's busy finishing college applications before the New Year's deadline."

"Your reward for getting yours in early is to relax during vacation and read novels," said Dad. "I envy you."

Back upstairs in his room, Jake stretched out on his bed, feeling lighter than he'd felt in months. SATs—over and a success. College applications—done and submitted ahead of time. No school reports to write for the next two weeks, no math problem sets, no French novels to parse. While Dad was at work, Mom would be entertaining Artie in Philly and Jake would have the house to himself...to read...watch TV...eat ice cream any time of the day…lie in bed and think about Steve, imagine Steve knocking on the front door and inviting Jake to play out back in the snow.

Like little boy best buds, they'd build a snow fort together, then have a snowball fight, Steve now ducking inside the fort while Jake hurls snowballs, Jake now running as Steve stands in the fort and hurls snowballs of his own that land smack in Jake's face, covering him with ice-cold white fluff that melts on his eyelashes, turns his cheeks red. Then they build a snowman together, Steve sticking a carrot not where a nose should be, but much much lower. They have a good laugh at that, Jake slapping Steve on the back, Steve grabbing Jake and yanking him in for a deep kiss, Steve's thick tongue a hot wet contrast to his cold chapped lips, his tongue practically lashing at Jake's as Jake wraps his arms around Steve's broad shoulders, the two boys hugging as tight as winter coats permit. Then Steve bursts into tears, admits that since *The Diary of Anne Frank* ended, Steve's been missing Jake to distraction, has constantly been looking for him in the halls between classes. Not seeing Jake these past few weeks, Steve has come to realize something: "I love you," he declares, his words vaporizing into icy steam before he tenderly presses cold lips first against each of Jake's cheeks, then onto Jake's lips. Jake feels that kiss throughout all of him, opens his mouth, feels that tongue, that wet tongue, that warm tongue, that tongue of love just for him—

Jake opened his eyes. Whew. That was amazing. He reached beneath his pillow for tissues, wiped himself and his hand, glanced quickly over at his bedroom door to double check that it was clicked closed.

How stupid Jake was being. How totally stupid. He had to stop these ridiculous fantasies. Steve had a girlfriend. Jake was just being an idiot. An idiot!

In fact, Jake would be better off if he never saw Steve again. Maybe Steve would get into a car accident during winter break.

The roads were slippery, right? Steve was one of the few teenagers Jake knew who had his own car, a used Chevy. Jake pictured Steve driving his *girl*friend to the Echelon Mall. Steve would take his eyes off the road for a moment so he could lean over and give his *girl*friend a kiss. Black ice. Steve would skid, the car would swerve then spin out of control and crash into a pine tree. Both Steve and his *girl*friend would smash their heads into the windshield.

Sirens and flashing red lights. Paramedics rush to revive Steve—a concussion and stitches. "Sorry to tell you, son," one of the paramedics, a gray-haired man with a mustache, says, "but your girlfriend's dead."

"What? Oh my God!"

"What's your number?" the paramedic asks, "I'll call Dispatch to phone your parents so they can meet us at Cherryvale Hospital."

"No, call my best friend Jake. I need him. Only Jake."

After the call, Jake races by taxi to the hospital. He dashes into Steve's hospital room, rushes to his side, grabs his IV-connected hand.

"I knew you'd come." Steve's voice is trembling. "She's dead. My girlfriend's dead."

Jake leans over the bed and hugs him.

Steve grasps him tight. "You'll take care of me, won't you, Jake? You'll stay with me, right?"

"Of course I will."

"I don't mean just tonight, I mean forever."

That's terrible! Jake heard in his head. Not Steve's voice, but God's: *What a terrible thing to wish for—that an innocent girl should die.*

'I didn't actually wish for that, God,' Jake thought. 'It was just my mind wandering. I was dozing. I can't help my thoughts when I'm dozing. Of course I don't want Steve to get hurt. Or his girlfriend.'

Are you envious of Steve's girlfriend because you want to be his girlfriend?

'No! I'm not a girl and I don't want to be one.'

But you want him to love you like one.

'That's not true.'

You see what happens when a boy wants to be with a boy in the wrong way? You see the shameful thoughts that come?

Jake didn't know how to respond.

I expect you to be a yeled tov.

'Yes, Sir.'

Remember—I'm always watching.

A knock on Jake's bedroom door.

"Just a minute." Jake jumped out of bed, pulled up his jeans, zipped, shoved the wet tissue into his pocket, opened his bedroom door.

Dad, his face in a serious sort of sag, walked over to Jake's bed, sat on the rumpled blanket, patted it for Jake to sit beside him.

Did Dad somehow figure out what Jake had just been doing? What he'd been thinking?

"Change of plans for winter break," said Dad. "There's an emergency. The hospital just called. Grandpa's had a gall bladder attack. At first, he thought it was a heart attack, but thank *Hashem* it wasn't. He's going home tomorrow, but will need surgery. They're squeezing him in, in a couple days. Your mother and I've got to be there, so we'll drop you and Artie off in Westchester with Aunt Millie and Uncle Irv. Then your mother and I'll stay at Grandpa's in the city so we can be at the hospital."

"I want to be with Grandpa, too."

Dad patted Jake's face. "You're a good boy. But there's not a lot of room at Grandpa's, and a hospital's no place for you and your brother."

"But Dad, I'm sixteen. Next year I'm going to college. I'm old enough to see Grandpa in the hospital."

"Your brother will need you. After the surgery, once Grandpa's on the mend, I'll pick you boys up to see him. Besides, you'll get to visit with Dave for a few days. Won't you enjoy that?"

Of course Jake would enjoy seeing Dave. Jake always enjoyed seeing Dave. But—hadn't he concluded he'd be better off not seeing Dave again? Not being tempted to touch Dave the way they had the end of the summer? Naked? Naked in bed and touching? While Grandpa's having surgery? While God's watching?

The first night, after word came that surgery had gone well, Uncle Irv and Aunt Flora took all three boys to the movies and for pizza, played Monopoly with them. They put Artie to bed in Dave's room, and sent Jake and Dave with sleeping bags to the basement Uncle Irv had recently refurbished—dark wood paneling similar to that in Jake's den at home, white acoustic ceiling tiles, beige linoleum flooring. Jake washed up, took his nightly antihistamine tablet, then joined Dave on the sleeping bags. "Sorry your grandfather's so sick," said Dave, seated on his bag. "You've always liked him, haven't you?"

"Grandpa's strict with religion, but he's always interested in what I'm doing. Every time he says goodbye, he pats my cheek and says, 'Be a good Jewish boy.' And every time he says hello, he asks me, 'How's my *yeled tov?*'"

"Cool."

"Yeah."

"I guess we should go to sleep," said Dave. "Unless you wanna do something."

"Sleep's good." Jake thought about reaching over from his sleeping bag to Dave's, but how could he do that right after talking about Grandpa, who was lying in a hospital recovering from surgery? The boys fell quickly asleep.

Aunt Flora's French toast the next morning at her square white kitchen table, a snowball fight in the back yard, then hot cocoa back in the kitchen. The phone rang. After a few words and an "Oh, dear," from Aunt Flora, she handed the receiver to Jake.

It was Mom explaining that Grandpa had caught some kind of infection in the hospital. "Endocarditis," she called it, "a heart infection. They've hooked Grandpa up to intravenous antibiotics. Jake, you're old enough to be told—this is a difficult infection to beat. We all need to prepare ourselves, just in case. Do you understand what I'm saying?"

He looked at Aunt Flora, who was offering an I'm-here-if-you-need-me smile. "Yes, Mom."

A quiet afternoon leafing through Dave's *Archie* comic books. Roast beef with boiled potatoes and Uncle Irv telling lame jokes to try to make Jake and Artie smile. Afterwards, a few comedy programs on TV—*The Carol Burnett Show* was Uncle Irv's and Aunt Flora's favorite—then everyone got into their nightclothes and went to bed.

"You worried?" asked Dave when the two boys were alone in the basement.

"Yeah."

"Sorry." With a "vroom," the heating duct sent gusts of hot air blowing right overhead. Dave undid the buttons on his green flannel pajama tops. He was a little pudgier than he'd been a few months before. "Want a distraction?"

Jake knew what Dave meant, but...what with Grandpa so sick.... "I don't know."

"It'd be good to take your mind off things. Worrying won't improve his condition."

"I guess."

Dave pulled a magazine out from under his sleeping bag. "You ever see *Hustler?*"

Jake shook his head.

"It's Dad's. Lots of naked chicks. Not just tits like the other mags, but pussies, too."

The closest Jake had ever gotten to seeing pictures of vaginas was the diagrams in Health class.

Dave lay on his back with his green pajama tops falling open, and gestured for Jake to slide over beside him so they could look together. Jake did so and Dave held up the magazine.

"Look at this one," he said. "Her pussy's hairy. And this one," he flipped a page, "with big lips."

Jake was fascinated. So that was what vaginas looked like. Each one was different.

Dave turned the page to a photo spread of a muscular, naked man lying on top of a naked woman. "It's almost like they're really doing it. Gets me all hot thinking about banging Sheila."

The man's butt was clenched with dimples and a fine coating of hair that Jake wanted to caress.

Still holding up the magazine with one hand, Dave reached over and, seemingly absent-mindedly, rubbed Jake's crotch through his blue flannel pajamas. "Sheila rubs my cock like that when we look at magazines together."

Jake gave a soft moan.

Dave tossed the magazine aside, tugged down Jake's pajama bottoms and squeezed, stroked. Jake reached out to reciprocate for Dave.

They played with each other until—

"Yuck," said Dave, reaching beside his sleeping bag for a washcloth. He plopped onto his own sleeping bag. "Guess we should go to sleep."

Jake rolled onto his side, feeling lousy.

The next day, they didn't refer to their nighttime play—not over Aunt Millie's pancakes, not while shoveling the sidewalk and driveway of snow, not over lunchtime tuna salad on toast with potato chips, not while building a snowman with Artie, not in the dark movie theater during Mel Brooks's horror comedy *Young Frankenstein* (although, when their greasy fingers met in the extra-large popcorn tub, Dave gripped Jake's index finger and moved his own like a piston until Jake yanked his finger away). Nor did they talk about it during split-pea soup and knockwurst dinner, nor during Monopoly again with everybody around the kitchen table and Uncle Irv making Artie laugh with dumb knock-knock jokes.

That night, when the heat vroomed on in the basement, Dave said that his father kept the heat on so high that they'd both be more comfortable without pajamas at all. Even before Jake could untangle his feet from the bottoms, Dave was gripping him.

They rolled on the sleeping bags, hugged one another, pressed hard against one another. "Shit," said Dave, "your body's lean like Sheila's." They rubbed against one another and rubbed until—

"Yuck again," said Dave, again handing Jake a washcloth.

Again Jake felt lousy.

The next morning began another day of non-discussion.

The following night, as they lay side by side pressing against one another, Dave whispered into Jake's ear, "I'm imagining that I'm fucking Sheila right now. She lets me fuck her all the time."

"Really?" asked Jake, a little breathless as he felt Dave's hand squeeze his butt. "You actually go all the way?"

"Yeah, she gets so wet, it feels great."

"Wow," was all Jake could think to say as he pictured Dave naked with a girl like in that *Hustler* photo.

"She also loves to blow me," said Dave. "She says a dick feels great in her mouth and it sure feels great when she does me. Here, let me show you what you're missing. It's amazing." Without another word, Dave slid down and thrust Jake into his mouth.

Jake gasped at the sensation—beyond anything he'd imagined, beyond anything. He looked down at Dave's bobbing head with brownish-red hair, pictured Steve's curly light brown hair. Jake wove his fingers through the hair, shut his eyes, felt more than he'd dreamed of, clutched a shock of hair, flung his eyes open and tried to yank that head up off him, gasping, "Now! Now!"

The head just kept bobbing as Jake flooded into Steve—no no, into Dave.

Jake tingled all over. His head spun. Oh my God, he thought. Oh my God.

Dave lifted his face close to Jake's. "Wasn't that hot?"

"But you...you..."

"Yeah...well...Sheila always says the taste is great, so I thought I'd give it a try. Not so bad. Yummy protein."

"Gross. Go brush your teeth."

Dave pulled on pajamas and tiptoed upstairs.

As Jake was putting on his pajamas, he heard, *While your grandfather's lying ill in the hospital, you're taking this shameful behavior further?*

"I'm sorry," he mumbled out loud.

You think I don't see?

'Once I get started,' he replied to God in thought, 'it's like I can't control myself.'

Then don't start.

'It was Dave who started it. And he seemed to like doing it.'

If he liked hacking people to death, would you hand him a cleaver?

'It's not the same thing. It's not like this is hurting anybody.'

What's wrong is wrong. Haven't you told me you want to be a normal boy?

56

Returning, Dave tiptoed down the gray wooden basement steps, breathed in through his teeth, making a hissing sound. "Minty fresh."

"I want to ask you something," said Jake. "When you visited in August, you said you'd introduce me to Sheila so I could get some experience with a girl."

"It's pathetic that you're still a virgin."

"Is she around this week? Could you introduce me?"

"I, um…" Dave flashed an embarrassed grin. "I'm not sure…" He brought a fist to his mouth, pressed hard.

"What?"

"Before I tell you…. You liked the bj I gave, right?"

Jake just stared.

"Listen," continued Dave, "you're my friend so…don't hate me."

"Hate you? What are you talking about?"

"There is no Sheila. I made her up."

Jake blinked as if not hearing what he'd just heard. "What?"

"I made up Sheila so you'd think I'm straight."

"You made her up? You mean you never…squeezed her breasts or felt her up or…or did anything with her?"

Dave shook his head.

"You lied to me?"

Dave shrugged. "All's fair in love, war, and getting laid. You're young yet. Grow up."

"We're supposed to be friends."

"You can't get more friendly than what we just did."

"You made her up in order…to seduce me?"

"Yeah, and it worked. Although I gotta say, you're one of the easier ones to seduce."

"One of the easier *ones*? You've done this before?"

"There are a few horny guys at school, their girlfriends won't give head, so that's where I come in. Basements, garages. Parents never suspect when it's two dudes hanging out together."

"I can't believe you did this to me," Jake muttered.

"I didn't hear you complaining ten minutes ago."

Jake stared directly into Dave's eyes until Dave's smile faded and he looked away. Jake picked up his sleeping bag and moved to the far end of the basement.

"You'll come back for more," said Dave. "They all do."

/ /

The next morning at the breakfast table, Jake vomited smack onto his plate of lox and eggs.

"Goodness!" cried Aunt Flora in her squeakiest high canary voice, running over with a dish towel and wiping Jake's mouth. "You must have the flu, poor baby." She pressed her hand to his forehead. "You don't feel warm. Better not take any chances. You go right upstairs and get into Dave's bed. Artie, tonight we'll put you in Jake's sleeping bag beside Dave in the basement."

"No!" blurted Jake.

Aunt Flora looked startled.

"I want Artie next to me," said Jake.

"But if you're contagious—"

"I'll feel better if Artie's next to me."

Artie broke into a huge grin and sat up straighter in his chair.

"Fine," said Aunt Flora. "He's probably been exposed by now anyway. We'll put Artie on the floor beside the bed in Dave's room. Dave, you'll continue sleeping in the basement."

"Super," Dave mumbled. After Aunt Flora left the kitchen to look for the thermometer, Dave squinted at Jake and asked, "Are you afraid I'd touch your dumbass little brother? Who's only eleven? Really? Is that what you think of me now?"

"I don't know what to think about you anymore."

Jake played sick the rest of the day, staying in Dave's bed, reading Dave's collection of Superman and Batman comic books, eating Aunt Flora's chicken soup that she sent Dave carrying upstairs on a tray. "You don't look sick to me," Dave said, his eyes looking sad.

"I really am sick to my stomach."

"It's because of me, isn't it?"

"What do you think?"

"I think maybe I fucked up," said Dave. "I think maybe in order to have a little fun, I blew more than a dick—I blew a friendship."

Maybe Jake shouldn't be too tough on Dave. After all, Dave's family wasn't as religious as Jake's, so no wonder Dave didn't obey Torah—he didn't know any better. But Jake did and had to be the strong one. He had to stop the two of them from any more…sinning. That was what it was, Jake should just call it what it was: sinning.

"So I guess you're gonna want to sleep up here with your brother every night instead of in the basement with me."

"Yeah," Jake replied.

Later that night, after Artie crawled into the sleeping bag on the floor, he said up at Jake in bed, "This is fun. Like camping. Do I really make you feel better?"

"Yeah, Artie, you do. Go to sleep now."

Jake flipped onto his belly, pressed quietly against the mattress, probably on the spot where Dave pressed himself every night. Jake vowed never to look at pictures of naked women like the ones in *Hustler* again, pictures showing men's beautiful butts. Jake pressed harder against the mattress. He would never grope Dave's thick body again. Jake pressed against the mattress. He would never grip Dave's hardness in his hand, would never let Dave grab him, would never ever let Dave take him in his mouth. Jake grunted.

"What?" mumbled Artie, half asleep.

"Nothing."

Damn, thought Jake, tugging out a tissue he'd placed under the pillow just in case. Damn. Damn damn damn.

/ /

A knock on the bedroom door woke Jake.

"Boys," said Uncle Irv, stepping into the room and standing tall over the two of them. "Boys, I've got sad news. Your mother just called. You've got to be strong now. It's your grandfather."

At the cemetery, standing in the mud, feeling the cold whirl around him, Jake watched the workmen lower Grandpa's pine casket into the hole, heard the loose lid clatter as the casket hit bottom. Following Dad's lead, Jake tossed two shovelfuls of dirt onto the casket, then stuck the shovel into the dirt mound and placed Artie's hands on the handle. "I can do it!" protested Artie.

Jake watched as Artie tossed two half shovelfuls.

Dad put one arm around each of the boys. He spoke in a start-stop rhythm, obviously struggling to maintain composure: "Your grandpa...asked me to tell you...that you boys...made him... proud." Dad squeezed the boys to his chest. All three embraced.

It was then that tears started their burn down Jake's cheeks. Tears at the thought of never again seeing Grandpa, who thought Jake a good boy. Tears because Jake let Grandpa believe the lie about Jake's true reason for performing in *The Diary of Anne Frank*. Tears because Jake had forgotten to send Grandpa the autographed program from the play like he'd promised. Tears because Jake felt relief that Grandpa would never know the sinful things Jake had done with Dave while Grandpa lay in the hospital, dying.

/ /

That afternoon, Jake and his family returned home to begin sitting *shivah*, the traditional week of mourning when friends and cousins and fellow congregants came to pay respects, to provide the requisite *minyan*, ten adults, for prayer services so that Dad could recite *kaddish*. These visitors, Deb included, offered comfort and brought food to sustain the family and the endless stream of other well-wishers. Uncle Irv, Aunt Flora, and Dave drove all the way down just for a day, refused Mom's invitation to stay over "because we wouldn't think of intruding."

Dave extended his hand to Jake and voiced condolences. Jake shook the hand and thanked him. After an awkward silence, Dave moved into the dining room and fixed himself a plate of whitefish salad and noodle *kugel*.

The boys did not speak again.

PART 3

During winter, Jake particularly enjoyed his English class's focus on the seventeenth- and eighteenth-century writings of New England's Puritans and other Protestant thinkers, which their textbook defined as "the foundation of American literature and culture." Clearly these writers understood sin. Jake read and reread Puritan poetry. He memorized it. He thought of Puritan poetry especially at lunchtime when making small talk with Deb while scanning the cafeteria to locate Steve, to watch him from a distance, to detect whether he was eating Beefaroni or a hot dog or fried fillet of sole or mac 'n cheese. How many girls was Steve sitting with today? How many times did he smile during lunch? How often did he laugh? Was he massaging anyone's shoulders the way he'd massaged Jake's?

Once in a while, Steve stopped by their table "for an *Anne Frank* reunion," sat beside Deb and munched a bag of chips. Jake envied the laughs Steve shared with Deb about rehearsal blunders during their scenes. Jake could barely speak at those times for the shooting of tingles from temples to chest, for the drying of his mouth and the closing of his throat.

"Auditioning for the school musical?" Steve asked them both one lunchtime.

"I can't sing or dance," Deb said, shaking her head. "Besides, my grades slid during *Anne Frank*, so my parents won't let me do any more extra-curricular activities this year."

"I'm auditioning," blurted Jake.

"Cool. If you get a part, I'll come opening night," Steve said.

"You're not auditioning?"

"Nah, I gotta work after school. Saving money for college."

All the air rushed out of Jake's lungs. Without even being consciously aware, he'd been anticipating winter rehearsals with Steve, assuming he'd at least get to watch Steve onstage the way he'd done all fall. To be in Steve's presence, to share an occasional smile. Maybe they'd even be cast in the same scene or two so they'd get to rehearse together. Maybe Steve would suggest that they rehearse privately sometimes, at Steve's house. While his parents were away. They'd run lines in Steve's living room: sensing Jake's nervousness, Steve lays Jake face down on the blue and yellow floral living room sofa to give him a massage. Steve's hands start at Jake's neck, work down Jake's shoulders, massage his back down to his waist. Gradually, Steve's hands slip beneath Jake's belly and up across his chest. Steve lies flat on top of Jake, holds him tight, breathes against the nape of Jake's neck.

"Congratulations!" Deb was hugging Steve.

What had Jake missed?

"How come you didn't tell us the minute you sat down you got in early admission?! Now you can be with your girlfriend. That's terrific."

"Yeah," said Jake, extending his hand for a shake. "Congratulations."

As Steve pumped Jake's hand across the cafeteria table, Jake felt a heat radiate through his fingers and palm up his arm, throughout all of him. Was he blushing?

It was real. Steve would be attending NYU next year. To be with his girlfriend.

Of course he was.

Stupid stupid stupid. Jake was stupid stupid stupid. He better get used to not seeing Steve any more because after graduation, that'll be it. Steve'll spend the summer with his girlfriend, and in the fall he'll be off to NYU and Jake will be at…well, he didn't know, but hopefully at Princeton. Unless…no, if Jake were to go to NYU, he'd make a fool of himself over Steve. No—even if Jake were to get in there, he wouldn't attend. He'd go anywhere else but NYU. He never should even have applied.

Besides, Princeton wasn't all that far from NYU—a train went to New York from Princeton, or some station around there. Close enough for a visit now and— Stop it! Jake screamed in his head. Stop it! Stop being so damn stupid!

In early February, Jake was cast in *Guys and Dolls*, the musical comedy about 1940s gangster gamblers in New York. He'd play Arvide Abernathy, the head of a local Salvation Army unit. "Sorry to typecast you as an old man again," said Mrs. Horowitz, "but you're the only one who can do the part justice."

At least Jake got to do an Irish accent, which was fun. And Arvide had a solo song. Jake found himself enjoying rehearsals with the small Salvation Army band: in Grandpa's shoes that Dad let him keep, Jake clomped around stage thumping a marching bass drum strapped to his chest and summoning gamblers to follow the fold and cease their sinning. During each rehearsal, Jake sang a call to morality at the top of his lungs. Mrs. Horowitz always applauded, remarked how convincing he was as a missionary trying to save souls.

"I'm really into my character," said Jake.

/ /

Rehearsals and homework. A rare Steve sighting in the hallways between classes. Rehearsals and homework. Mom complained that Jake wasn't eating breakfast anymore, just chugging a small glass of milk. "Not hungry," replied Jake day after day. He wasn't that hungry for lunch either, spending the hour in the cafeteria craning his neck to catch glimpses of Steve. Rehearsals kept him late at school, so he'd scarf down half a quick dinner at home before dashing up to his room to spend hours on homework. Already thin, he lost weight.

Jake's nights were spent tossing and turning as he dreamt about falling off a cliff with Steve standing above, reaching out a hand that Jake couldn't grasp. Or about drowning in a lake while Steve waved goodbye from shore. Or about being hit by a truck while dashing across a street to greet Steve.

"**A**re you all right?" asked Mrs. Horowitz after Jake asked to be excused from carrying the marching bass drum during rehearsal. "You're looking gray under the eyes."

"Just a little tired," he said.

During French class the next day, just as Madame Fournier was reciting lines from a Molière play, Jake felt a severe aching pain in his upper back. On the left. The pain continued during English and chemistry. Mrs. Horowitz let him out of rehearsal—"Go home and rest." Jake telephoned Mom, described his symptoms, and asked if she could pick him up.

"Sit near the front office," she said in a clipped voice. "I'll be there in five minutes."

/ /

As he slid into the front passenger seat, Mom said she wasn't driving him home, but to Cherryvale Hospital's emergency room.

"Why?" he asked.

"I telephoned Dr. Peril—he's on vacation for a month, so we're going to the ER." Jake heard the urgency in her voice.

In the ER, Mom explained things to the nurse at the front desk, who ushered Mom and Jake immediately down a short hall into a small examining room, told him to remove his shirt. "Your mother did the right thing. Sometimes a heart attack starts with referred pain—to your upper left shoulder."

Heart attack? Was Jake having a heart attack?

A young ER doctor, a handsome resident with close-cropped black hair, rushed in and pressed a cold stethoscope to Jake's chest, listened, said, "It sounds like metal in there. Have you had chest surgery?"

"Uh, no." Sure, Jake had some hair around his nipples, but not on the rest of his chest. Nothing to obscure any surgical scars. Couldn't the resident see that? How could Jake have gotten metal in his chest?

"It's not a heart attack, but I don't know what it is."

Mom insisted that the resident summon a cardiologist. The young man left, returned a few minutes later with an older woman wearing a gray bun. "I'm Dr. Colman," she said, shaking Mom's hand. "Let's see what we have here."

Dr. Colman pressed a warmer stethoscope against Jake's chest, listened. "Ah...yes...classic pericarditis."

Mom gasped. "My father-in-law died a few months ago from endocarditis. Jake didn't even visit him, he couldn't have caught it from—"

"No no no no," said the doctor, taking Mom's hand. "Your father-in-law had *endo*carditis, a *bacterial* infection of the heart. Your son has *peri*carditis, a *viral* infection of the pericardium, the tissue surrounding the heart. We'll give an electrocardiogram to confirm, but I'm quite sure. Jake has a classic pericardial friction rub—that metallic sound my young resident heard. There's inflammation and pain—but only when his heart beats." Dr. Colman smiled warmly. "Jake, think of it as a cold. But instead of your sinuses swelling, the tissue around your heart is swelling. It will pass." She soothed a hand across Jake's back. "You'll be fine. We'll keep you in the hospital a few days. We'll give you aspirin to reduce the swelling. Muscle relaxants four times a day will reduce your discomfort. After two weeks of rest, you'll be fine."

"A whole two weeks?" exclaimed Jake.

"It's not a serious condition," said Dr. Colman. "But we don't want it to become one. You'll need lots of rest. You can keep up with schoolwork, but from home. You'll be good as new in no time."

Mom called Mrs. Horowitz, who gasped over the phone—"His heart!" Immediately she said that she could rehearse around Jake for the next couple weeks. "Tell him we love him and need him."

/ /

Each day in the hospital, Dr. Colman brought medical students on her rounds so they could "listen to a classic pericardial friction rub," which was more pronounced when Jake lay flat on his back than on his side. "The patient's been tolerant of our daily Frankenstein treatments," she said while squeezing Jake's forearm. He lifted his arms one at a time as if he were Frankenstein walking down a street. Smiling, she explained that she was talking about the daily electrocardiograms—after gobs of cold jelly were placed on Jake's chest, wire-attached sensors were affixed so as to conduct electrical impulses to a portable machine able to record any the heart's electrical activity and detect any abnormalities. He wasn't crazy about the procedure, but did enjoy the notion of looking like Frankenstein. "His EKGs are looking good," said Dr. Colman.

Anxious to return to school and the play as soon as possible, Jake took all his medication on schedule, of course including the bedtime antihistamine that Dr. Peril had been prescribing for allergies since Jake's boyhood. The last thing Jake wanted was to feel lousy because of allergies on top of this heart thing.

/ /

Deb visited the evening of Jake's second day back at home, brought homework from various classes. While Jake lay propped in bed on four pillows, she sat in his desk chair, caught him up on who'd begun dating whom this past week, who'd dumped whom, who was asking about him.

"Nobody's telephoned," he said.

"Because nobody wants to disturb you and your heart. Everyone's asking about you."

"Everyone?"

"You mean Steve, don't you?"

Jake blushed. "Why would you say that? It's a general question."

"Come on, Jake, you're crazy about him."

"I don't know what you're talking about."

"The way you always hunt for him in the cafeteria, stare at him with those moon eyes, and hang on his every word, the way you get all tongue-tied around him. It's obvious. To me, anyway."

Obvious? Jake's feelings were obvious? "He's a nice guy, that's all. What's wrong with enjoying conversation with a nice guy? I don't really have close guy friends at school."

Deb sighed, scooted her chair over to his bed and took his hand. "It's okay, Jake. I don't blame you. I think he's terrific too."

He yanked his hand away. "What are you implying?" He started to sweat. "I thought you were my friend. I never expected you to start nasty gossip about me."

"Gossip? I'm not saying this to anyone else. I'm talking to you."

"Yeah, well, maybe you shouldn't. Maybe you should just go."

"Wow, you're cranky."

"You'd be cranky, too, if people went around making crazy assumptions about you."

"Sorry. My mistake. Calm down. You shouldn't be getting all excited, what with your heart and all."

"You're right. Maybe the muscle relaxants are making me irritable."

"Maybe I'd better let you relax." She stood, gave him a peck on the forehead. "The teachers say there's no rush getting your homework done. Nobody wants to give you a heart attack."

"Thanks. Thanks for stopping by. That's really nice of you."

As she walked out his bedroom door, she turned and said, "A broken heart is painful. I hope yours heals quickly."

Before Jake could respond, she skipped downstairs. What the hell was she talking about a broken heart for? His heart had a virus. And not even his heart, really, but the tissue around the heart. Deb was reading too much poetry or romance novels or something. He'd have to tell Mom not to let Deb visit again while he was sick because all she did was agitate him.

Jake picked up one of the books beside his bed and tried reading a Molière scene. He couldn't concentrate.

Were his feelings for Steve so obvious? They must be if Deb knew. Could Steve tell? When Jake got back to school, he'd have to be more careful.

/ /

"Come in," Jake said groggily.

"Sorry to disturb your nap, honey, but there's a phone call for you," said Mom. "You can take it on the extension in my bedroom. It's that fellow from the *Anne Frank* play."

Jake bounded out of bed.

"Take it easy," said Mom. "Don't over exert."

Although he wanted to sprint, Jake forced himself to walk slowly down the hall to his parents' room.

"Hey there, buddy boy," said Steve in as cheerful a voice as Jake had ever heard. "Deb said it's okay to call."

"Wow, sure."

"Not too taxing for you?"

"No, not at all. I just need a little bed rest. And to take some medicines for a few weeks. Then I'll be good as new."

"So, you're feeling okay?"

"Oh yeah, for sure."

"Good. You gave everybody a real scare. Glad you're getting better. Well, I just wanted to call to check. I'll keep an eye out for you in the cafeteria."

"That'll be great, Steve," Jake said, reminding himself to keep his reaction low key.

"Take care of yourself."

"For sure. And thanks an awful lot for calling."

Jake's imagination went wild. Wow wow wow. Hearing about Jake's illness, Steve suddenly realized the true nature of his feelings, had been sitting at home every evening weeping at the prospect that Jake, his beloved, had fallen ill and would be sequestered for an entire two weeks. No shared glances in the hallway, no brief conversations in the cafeteria, no shared smiles for an entire two weeks. How would Steve survive? Steve purposely refrained from declaring his love over the telephone because he didn't know how Jake felt about him and didn't want to make a fool of himself or upset Jake. Steve hadn't even been sure if he should call, but Deb had probably encouraged him.

Good ol' Deb. Deb who understood things without the need to talk about them. Jake had to be nicer to her. She was a real friend.

Obviously, Steve had played it cool on the phone when what he really longed to do was propose lifelong bonding. Unable to think of anything but Jake's imagined kisses, Steve would soon be flunking classes. Only Jake's return to school could revive him.

The first time Steve saw Jake back at school, he'd throw caution to the winds and give him a bear hug. He'd insist on eating lunch just with Jake and Deb every day from then on, Deb being the cover for their full-fledged boy-boy romance that she didn't find hideous at all. Between classes, Steve would hunt for Jake just to stand for a minute and rest his arm casually around Jake's shoulder and squeeze, a gesture no one else would read correctly because this was Steve, a touchy-feely kind of guy.

Without labeling it a date, Steve would invite Jake for pizza at Scotto's at the Echelon Mall and then a movie where they'd select a seat in the back row where Steve would set his hand on the arm-rest beside Jake's, his index finger stroking the back of Jake's until Jake felt emboldened to flip his hand palm-up, at which point their fingers would intertwine and squeeze and they'd both *know*.

In a telephone call to NYU, Steve would dump his girlfriend, and would then spend weekends taking long walks with Jake on the other side of town where no one knew them, where they could hold hands in the park along the Cooper River, and one day, Steve would turn to Jake and speak the words of love that had been burning within them both. He'd cup Jake's face in his hands, lean in for their first kiss, they'd embrace, then rest heads upon one another's shoulders and softly squeak forever promises. Their future together was assured. This get-well-soon phone call was just the beginning of daily phone calls and a lifetime of togetherness.

Until it wasn't.

Steve didn't call again during the rest of Jake's week and a half at home.

After a follow-up examination, Dr. Colman gave the thumbs-up for Jake to return to school as long as he continued taking the muscle relaxants four times a day, stayed out of gym class, and limited rehearsal time after school. "The hospital will forward my records to Dr. Peril—he's due back from vacation soon, I understand. He'll be the one following up with you from now on. Good luck, my Frankenstein!"

The day Jake returned to school, he scanned the hallways for Steve, and when he saw him, waved, expecting Steve to…to…. Steve sauntered over, clapped Jake on the shoulder, shook his hand. "Glad you're back. Feeling okay?"

"For sure."

"Great. Glad to hear." Winking, Steve said, "See you around."

At lunch in the cafeteria that day, not even a wave from Steve.

"Steve told me he called you," Deb said over her tuna-noodle casserole.

"Yeah," said Jake, without looking up from his.

"It's this thing he has," she said. "He wants to be a doctor. Anytime someone's sick, he calls to say hi. He says it's good for a patient's morale and promotes healing."

Jake lifted his eyes to meet Deb's. "He does that for everyone?"

"Everyone he knows, yes," she said. "I thought you should know that. To avoid any possible misunderstanding. I'm sorry."

"Sorry for what? For him being a nice guy? And anyway, why did you tell him it was okay to call me in the first place? Maybe you should just mind your own business instead of interfering in other people's lives!" Jake lifted his cafeteria tray, took it over to the tray-return conveyer belt, dumped the rest of his meal in the trash, and stomped out.

/ /

For the next two weeks, Jake avoided the cafeteria entirely. He brought a bag of pretzels to school and, lunchtime, ate them in an empty classroom, then sipped from a water fountain to take his midday muscle relaxant. Deb and some others tried talking to him between classes, but Jake kept cutting conversations short, turning his back, or walking away.

During rehearsals, he sat alone at the back of the auditorium when awaiting his turn to perform. Onstage, he recited his lines, followed the prescribed blocking, sang his solo.

"Jake," said Mrs. Horowitz one afternoon, "you're going through the motions of your role, but there's no heart in it anymore."

"Yeah, well, my heart's been damaged," he said. "Nothing I can do about it."

Mrs. Horowitz stared at him, but said nothing further.

/ /

A few days before opening night, Jake had a follow-up visit with Dr. Peril, who put gobs of cold jelly and sensors on Jake's chest and took another EKG. A few minutes later, in his office, he read the results: "Fine and dandy!" he said. "The old ticker's fine and dandy."

"Isn't that good news?" asked Mom, seated beside Jake.

"Yeah," said Jake, looking down at his scuffed black shoes.

"And from the looks of things," Dr. Peril added, "our Jake here has begun shaving since our last visit."

"Twice a week or so. No big deal."

"Yes indeedy, growing right up. Everything back to normal at school?"

"Yeah," said Jake.

"Still doing your school play?"

"Yeah."

"And he gets to carry a big marching band drum," said Mom.

"Drum doesn't hurt your chest?" asked Dr. Peril.

"No."

"He's been at rehearsals every night," said Mom. "Maybe they're tiring him out?"

"They are not!" snapped Jake.

"Millie," asked Dr. Peril. "Our boy seems a little on edge. Glum maybe?"

"Now that you mention it," replied Mom. "He's been a little…I don't know…quiet and…forgive me, Jake…moody."

"I am not!"

"This isn't unusual after a cardiac event," said Dr. Peril. "It's quite a scare. Just keep an eye on him, and Jake, if you or your Mom are feeling depressed, you can call me and I'll see what I can do, okay?"

"Yeah, fine."

"Jake, listen to me," said Dr. Peril, his face turning unusually serious. "Your heart was never at risk here. Let me assure you, you've recovered extremely quickly from the infection. You're absolutely fine. There'll be no permanent effects. You don't have to worry about your heart, not now or ever. You'll live a long healthy life, okay?"

Jake shrugged.

"Call me if you need me, Millie."

/ /

Throughout the week, Jake went from classes to rehearsal to bed as if walking through a thickening fog. He told himself he was exhausted from dress rehearsals and struggling to squeeze in time for homework and from eating less and less.

By Friday's opening night, he didn't feel the excitement he'd felt last fall when *Anne Frank* was opening. He didn't feel much of anything. The play was just an obligation to get through.

"Even though it's *Shabbes*," said Dad as Jake headed out the front door, "your mother and I will be at your performance. We're proud of you, son."

As Jake watched himself nod at Dad, he thought that Dad's remark should have made him feel good. But Jake felt nothing.

Makeup. Costume. Standing offstage in the wings.

Overture. Opening number. Act I. Intermission.

Early in Act II, Jake-as-Arvide began singing his one solo, the tender "More I Cannot Wish You," to the character of Arvide's granddaughter. Jake began the song normally, as he'd rehearsed it dozens of times, gazing down with an adoring look at his lovesick granddaughter in her navy blue Salvation Army uniform with red piping trim. But as the song progressed, as he truly heard the song's words wishing for this heartbroken girl to find her own true love, Jake pictured himself singing to himself, as if he were the one listening to words of advice about the crucial importance of finding one's true love.

A moment of silence throughout the auditorium. Then, much to Jake's confusion, the audience rose in thunderous applause. Thunderous. They jumped to their feet and applauded and applauded and applauded.

Looking out at the house seats through the glare of the spotlight, Jake saw several people dabbing eyes and noses with tissues.

In the dressing room after the show, Mrs. Horowitz shoved her way through the excited crowd to Jake. "You've never sold your solo with as much heart as you did tonight. You brought new meaning to that number. And you brought me to tears."

As she hugged him, Jake gave a wan smile. Shouldn't this hug make him feel good?

The next morning, Dad knocked on Jake's bedroom door to wake him for services.

No response.

"Jake?" Dad asked through the door.

No response.

"I'm coming in," said Dad, rattling the black doorknob and opening the white door. He looked at Jake bundled up in bed.

"Time to get ready for *shul*."

Jake just stared.

"You feeling all right?" asked Dad. "Is something wrong with your heart?"

Jake just stared.

"Maybe you're exhausted. All right. Stay home this morning and rest. You've got another performance tonight, so take it easy today, just *daven* when you get up. Your mother, brother and I'll be back in a few hours, then we'll have lunch together."

Dad left the room and shut the bedroom door.

Jake shoved aside his covers. Had they always been so heavy? Had he always had such a difficult time moving his arms and legs? He felt like the universe had turned into a big bowl of pudding to slog through.

He collapsed onto his royal blue wall-to-wall carpet. He stroked it. "You're my best and only friend," he whispered, his body stretched out and pressed close. "You're the only one I can talk to, the only one who understands." He caressed the carpet, brushed palm and cheek against the soft, compact fibers.

Jake knew he was addressing his carpet, understood that this sudden "best and only friend" was an inanimate genderless thing. He harbored no delusion of it being anything else. But he suddenly felt an intimate closeness to his carpet, not that he ever had before, not that he'd previously noticed it as anything other than a blue surface forever showing lint from white socks like a sky chock-full of stars for Mom to vacuum away.

Of all the objects in his bedroom, why was it the carpet that drew his affection? Why not the L-shaped plywood desk Dad had knocked together when Jake was a little boy, replete with drawers and cabinet? Why not the oak dresser or the white-painted walls or posters of Elton John or Sonny and Cher, or the black bookcase crammed with science fiction novels and Westerns? For that matter, why not the gold-trimmed ceiling light fixture, or windows or blinds?

Did the "blue" of the carpet unconsciously echo his mood? Did the carpet remind of pubic fuzz he'd been noticing on other sixteen-year-old boys in the gym class locker room and, more recently, in the Drama Department dressing room? Blue pubic fuzz? Although he'd be considered incredibly strange if anyone were to see him, he couldn't be condemned as immoral for caressing a carpet.

Jake crawled across the carpet to his closet, crawled deep inside, pulled the white wooden folding doors shut. Bunching up his knees, he wrapped his arms around them. How safe there in the dark beneath shirts and slacks, jackets and ties. He recalled the words of the Puritan poet Jonathan Edwards: "It is true, that judgment against your evil work has not been executed hitherto; the floods of God's vengeance have been withheld; but your guilt the meantime is constantly increasing, and you are every day treasuring up more wrath;…" And couldn't Anne Bradstreet's self-definition have doubled for Jake's own?: "…this sinful creature, frail and vain, / This lump of wretchedness, of sin and sorrow, / This weather-beaten vessel racked with pain,…" Maybe if Jake spent the rest of his life deep in his closet, God wouldn't be able to find him or clearly see the horrible person he was becoming. True, hiding their nakedness hadn't worked for Adam and Eve after they ate the forbidden fruit—God spotted them in the Garden of Eden anyway. But they only had trees to hide them, not a whole closet.

You think I can't see you? There God was, right smack in Jake's head.

Jake shrugged.

Of course I can see you. Foolish child. I can even see your thoughts: you're still desiring that innocent boy, Steve.

Jake covered his face with his hands.

You're still refusing to be a yeled tov.

Jake buried face against knees, covered head with hands.

Mildly nauseated by the stifling fragrances of fabric softeners and dry-cleaner sizing, Jake creaked the closet doors open, crawled out across the carpet—still his best and only friend—and up into bed, pulled the yellow-and-blue-striped blanket to his neck.

A knock on the clicked-closed bedroom door. "Jake?" It was Dad, back from *shul.* "Jake?"

Supine in bed, Jake stared at the door.

"Jake, I'm coming in."

Once again, the black doorknob rattled, the white door opened, and in came Dad with that look of forced cheer he slapped on whenever Jake was ill. "How're you feeling, son? Better than before I left?"

Unable to define his feelings even to himself, Jake simply stared.

Dad touched palm to Jake's head to feel for fever, grabbed Jake's wrist and checked his pulse. "Are you angry at something? Your mother and I told you last night how wonderful your performance was. We didn't know you had such maturity and depth inside. You were amazing. We told you. So, what could you be angry at?"

Jake just stared.

Dad sat on the foot of Jake's bed. "Would you like to come downstairs for something to eat?"

Jake wanted to say "No," but lacked a derrick with which to haul the lead-brick word up from his belly. Never before had language felt so impossible to voice. Never before had he felt so far removed from the least possibility of communicating. He was hearing Dad and understanding him, yet unable — physically unable — to let him know. All he could do was meet Dad's eyes with an unbroken stare.

"Please talk to me," said Dad, his tone laced with pathetic pleading.

Jake continued just to stare.

Dad sighed, squeezed Jake's foot through the blanket, left and clicked the door closed.

Jake felt badly for Dad's sadness while at the same time not caring all that much.

Fifteen minutes later, Dad burst into Jake's room without even knocking. "Stop taking the muscle relaxants! They're interacting with your antihistamines and causing depression."

In a light-bulb moment, Dad had called Dr. Peril to ask whether Jake's depression could possibly have been medically induced. Alarmed at hearing of the muscle relaxants — "The hospital still hasn't sent me Jake's records, so I didn't know he's been taking them"—Dr. Peril ordered Dad immediately to stop the relaxants.

"Muscle relaxants and antihistamines both act as depressants," Dad explained to Jake, "and have been compounding one another's side effects. Antihistamine is what's in over-the-counter sleeping pills—they knock you out. You poor kid. As if you haven't been through enough lately. Now listen: Dr. Peril's encouraging you to go through with tonight's performance. He says it's import-ant to force yourself to get out of bed and back to normal activity right away. That will help the depression clear."

Jake just stared.

"You didn't take the lunchtime relaxant yet, did you?"

Jake barely shook his head.

"Okay. You're going to come downstairs—I'll drag you by the hair if I have to—and you're going to spend the next few hours drinking as much water as your belly can hold. We've got to flush your system. And of course you're done with the relaxants for good. Your mother will make you soup. You might need to spend every offstage moment peeing, but you're going to that show tonight, and you're going to perform, and you're going to get better."

Jake just stared.

Dad gave Jake a tight embrace. With a glimmer of hope that maybe his own weirdness might actually pass, Jake managed to lift one arm and wrap it around Dad.

"You surprised me again," said Mrs. Horowitz after the evening's performance. "You took everything more slowly tonight, even more in character for an old man than last night. Well done. Very well done."

Jake mustered enough energy to offer another wan smile, then excused himself to the restroom.

At home, Dad insisted that Jake join him and the rest of the family in the kitchen for Mom's famous chocolate-chip cake, Jake's favorite. She'd baked it while he was performing.

"Thanks, Mom," Jake said, feeling genuine appreciation. "You're too good to me."

"Nothing's too good for you."

"Or for me!" piped in Artie, his cheeks smeared with chocolate icing.

"Or for you," added Mom, pouring him a second glass of milk.

Dad teased conversation out of Jake, about how it felt to perform tonight ("It was hard to carry the drum, but I remembered all my lines"), how his solo went ("The audience still seemed to like it even though I took everything slower"), how he was feeling overall ("Not as heavy as before, and it's a lot easier to talk").

"Thank goodness you're a medical librarian," Mom said to Dad, "and knew enough to call Dr. Peril."

That night in bed—having missed a third dose of muscle relaxants, and having skipped his nightly antihistamine for good measure—Jake looked down at the blue carpet and thought himself an idiot for his earlier behavior. Of course the carpet wasn't his friend: the carpet had witnessed Jake's shameful fantasizing in bed, his playing with Dave at the end of last summer. The carpet knew who Jake was, his inner self, his worst and most obscene behaviors—so why on earth would the carpet want to be his friend?

PART 4

As soon as they set down their trays of turkey tetrazzini in the cafeteria, Jake showed Princeton's acceptance letter to Deb, but said nothing about also having been accepted to NYU.

"Princeton! Your first choice—mazel tov! And I got into Penn's architecture program!" They slapped high-fives. "My folks are thrilled because I'll be just across the river. And you'll be only an hour from here."

"Yep. Mom's ecstatic." As Jake craned his neck, Deb said, "You're wasting your time."

"What?"

"You're wasting your time looking for Steve. He's skipping lunch and taking an independent study project in the library so he can leave early every day and put in extra hours at McDonald's. He really needs the money for NYU next fall."

"What's any of that to me?" asked Jake. He didn't want Deb to see his disappointment. She saw too much as it was. He asked her, "Did you tell Noah yet? About Penn, I mean."

Deb's face took on a dreamy cast. "Not yet. We've only been on two dates, so I don't want to be pushy."

"It's not pushy to tell the Penn freshman you're dating that you'll be going to Penn next year."

"I don't want to scare him off."

"You think he likes you only because you live way across a bridge in New Jersey?"

"I guess I'm being silly. I'll tell him Sunday. He invited me to the Rodin Museum."

"Sophisticated."

"He says my mind is as attractive as the rest of me."

"What a sap. Does he know about your monster fetish?"

"Stop it—it's not a fetish. It's just a soap opera."

"But you watch it five days a week. All those re-runs. You're obsessed."

"I'm not obsessed, I just like it, that's all. *Dark Shadows* is incredibly romantic and sad. Everyone on the show has a secret love. Half the characters are supernatural beings that have to hide their true selves or else they could be killed."

"Sounds dumb," Jake said while thinking he should give the show a try. He could relate to those kinds of issues.

That very afternoon at home, he watched one of the re-runs. As the final credits rolled, Jake felt an excitement—he couldn't wait until the next day's episode to know if the witch Angelique, who loved Barnabas the vampire, would find his coffin's hiding place. And what would the Stoddard family do if they realized Barnabas wasn't a contemporary relative from England but a centuries-old vampire? Would he be able to control his nature and stop drinking the blood of unsuspecting young women? Poor Barnabas, a freak of nature, a hideous monster who struggled to control unnatural impulses that he had to hide all the time.

Jake watched the show day after day, and each time a romantic male lead leaned in to kiss a pretty young woman, Jake pictured the man as Steve leaning in to kiss him.

Mom watched once to see what about the show fascinated Jake so much. "Do you think it's good for you to watch something so gloomy and depressing?" she asked.

"It's not depressing," he replied. "It's exciting."

"How about you get out of the house a little and enjoy the beginning of spring? Take my Oldsmobile and drive into the Pine Barrens. Enjoy nature. Or go to the movies. Here, take the newspaper and see if anything interests you."

He took it and leafed through. On the movie page, he noticed a listing for the Liberty Theater. Each of its movie titles was followed by three X's. What was with the logo depicting a woman's wide-open mouth?

As if a flashlight turned on, Jake realized this to be an ad for a cinema showing x-rated films.

Right there in suburban New Jersey. Not across the Delaware River in Philadelphia, but at the Liberty Theater smack in a neighboring town. Should Jake go?

In bed every night that week, hands beneath the covers, he wondered what a porn movie would be like. Would they actually show naked bodies? Completely naked bodies? No way. Naked men's bodies? Too risky. No briefs or anything? You're not going. How much would he be able to see while the actors were doing it? What could you be thinking? Or were pretending to be doing it—they were actors, right, so they wouldn't actually be having sex, would they? You, a good Jewish boy nerd at a porno movie? You? Jake thought of blankets pulled down to reveal torsos "making the beast with two backs" (they'd read *Othello* in English class last year), then blankets tossed boldly aside to reveal butts, naked butts, naked men's butts hairy and muscular, all sweaty and jiggling up and down how incredible.

On Sunday, he told his parents he was going to spend the afternoon at the Echelon Mall. Sin number one, he thought—lying; sin number two—disrespecting father and mother. The list was just beginning.

It took less than fifteen minutes to find the Liberty Theater, which was on a main street. He parked Mom's gray Oldsmobile sedan three blocks away on a narrow side road, out of view of passersby who might just know Mom and recognize her car. He sauntered casually but quickly to the theater's entrance.

Realizing he was underage, he feared being humiliated and turned away at the ticket booth. But he had to try. If he could just get in, if he could really get in, if he could only get in, maybe, maybe if the camera angle was right or a sheet slipped for a second, maybe he could actually catch a fleeting glimpse of...an adult man's erection. The fact that the man would be having sex with a woman didn't matter—an erection was an erection.

"One, please," he said in his deepest teenage bass, chin pressed hard against chest (he'd practiced at home in front of the bathroom mirror). The jowly woman in the ticket booth didn't raise either of her purple-shadowed eyebrows, didn't even look into Jake's face, just grabbed his money, ripped a ticket in half and handed over the stub. Whew!

Jake noticed the lobby's tattered gray carpet, the snot-colored paint peeling from the walls, the odor of stale smoke. In the auditorium, he saw a dozen or so old men scattered in isolated seats throughout. They, he was certain, were all there to see the naked women.

He slunk into a seat at the far end of an empty row and waited for the film to begin. What if Dad were to walk in and see him, not that Jake had any reason to think Dad frequented such a venue, but still? Would Dad just wink and slap Jake's shoulder? Or would he somehow be able to figure out that Jake was planning to look at naked men, then crumple in shame? Or worse: what if some of the men in the theater were actually undercover cops preparing to raid the place? Taken away in handcuffs, Jake would be the face of dinnertime's Action News: The Perverted (Underage) Jew. Neighbors would stone their house, and they'd be forced to move. Maybe Dad would be fired from his job. All because of Jake.

The houselights went down, the movie began.

From what Jake could tell from the minimal dialogue, the opening scene involved a husband and wife. They, fully dressed, were smoking cigarettes. Then they argued over money. He threw her down onto the bed in a rage. For some reason Jake missed, this violence excited her. She ripped off her dress—no bra, no panties—and started displaying her body, fondling her own breasts and then—Jake couldn't believe it—playing with herself, between her legs, right on camera. Although not excited, Jake was totally intrigued. Was this what married women did?... Mom?!

Then the porn husband removed his clothes: his shirt—skinny chest, pot belly—and his pants. Apparently, thought Jake with a quiet snicker, this family did not believe in underwear.

The man's erection. Jake wanted to cry. He'd never considered the possibility of one being so large. His own erection, although harder now in the theater than the actor's in the film, couldn't have been more than half the size. Jake wanted him.

Husband initiated sex with wife. His titty licks and pussy laps did nothing for Jake, but when she lay back and he straddled her, positioning his erection over her face, when he did push-ups into and out of her mouth, well...Jake was alone in his aisle...so... without moving his shoulder in any way potentially discernible to any of the respectable patrons in the theater, and relying upon the experience he'd gained in *shul* on Yom Kippur last fall, he moved his hand discreetly over the surface of his zipped jeans... gently back and forth.

He watched the porn star's push-ups, thought what a shame there was no Academy Award for this category of expertise, and imagined Steve doing push-ups into Jake's mouth. Jake's mouth. Oh, how terrible. Oh, how awful. Oh how shameful. Oh how wonderful how incredibly wonderful. Gurgle gurgle gurgle. Shuddering and sighing ever so softly, Jake then looked around to check that no one had noticed his moment of ecstasy, returned to watching the film in the hopes of achieving another such moment.

Husband and wife engaged in intercourse in various positions, then the wife went shopping. At that point another woman showed up. She looked the same age as the man, but he called her "Daughter," so Jake figured his own perceptions were the ones out of synch with reality. "You're late!" said naked father to dressed daughter, "And must be spanked." Off with the dress (no underwear here either). Naked daughter over naked daddy's knees. Gee, she seemed awfully willing. He spanked her and this, oddly enough, turned her on. He did various things to her and then she knelt and sucked him. Jake's hand moved into position again, and rubbed. Suck suck. Jake shuddered and sighed softly a second time. His Jockeys and pants were soaked.

Then the wife returned home, and the three of them did weird things together. But Jake was too drained to get involved. He watched to see how the story would end and to let his pants dry a bit before he walked out in public. Although feeling deeply ashamed, he also felt wildly free: here was a place he could come and live his (horrible) secret fantasies in a whole new way.

Mother took daughter to bed—now that was something Jake had never imagined, how interesting, what clever script-writers they had…while the father, down to his last pack, went out to buy more cigarettes. Realism.

On a dark street corner, a stranger approached him to bum a smoke. The porn hero reached into his pocket. At that exact moment, the stranger pulled out a huge butcher knife from within his trousers and thrust it deep into the porn hero's gut. The stabber, saying nothing, stealing nothing, ran quickly away. Apparently, his only goal had been to stab.

The porn hero doubled over and collapsed, and the film, this hour-and-a-half of sex, ended with thirty seconds of the camera panning a man dying in the gutter, blood spurting into the street, a huge butcher knife sticking out of his belly. He hadn't been shot or strangled or hit by a car. He'd been stabbed. Stabbed by another man. Symbolically fucked to death by another man, thought Jake. The ultimate horrific punishment, right?

The film ended, Jake stole out of the theater, avoiding the eyes of everyone else who was stealing out while avoiding eyes. He walked quickly to Mom's Oldsmobile, drove slowly home, his hands shaking on the steering wheel the entire way.

At home, Jake darted upstairs, peeled off jeans and briefs and dropped them into the laundry hamper, wash-clothed himself, slunk to his room.

Lying all curled up in bed, he felt not only shame, but fear. Not just the usual fear of being discovered, but a new terror.

You understand the director's message? Jake heard God ask him.
'Yes, Sir.'
Think about that.
The director's message was clear: perverts should be executed.

"**K**eep your eyes open when you're around real actors," cautioned Dad. "They're libertines."

"What's that?" asked Jake.

"People with loose morals."

"Sol," said Mom. "What an old-fashioned stereotype. Jake, pay no attention to your father. It sounds like a fun opportunity."

"And I assume you'll have to work on *Shabbes*? You think that's okay?"

Jake had known this was coming. "Yes, it's a job, Dad, but I'll be having fun. It's not like it's really forbidden 'work.'"

"Are they paying you for being there on Friday nights and Saturday afternoons?"

"Yes."

"Then it's 'work.' Prohibited on *Shabbes*. But you've graduated high school and are about to go off to college. You're old enough to make your own decisions, even if they're wrong."

Jake called Mrs. Horowitz back and told her he'd love to take the summer job. What a surprise that their town's Tip Top Club, the largest nightclub between Philadelphia and Atlantic City, needed a stagehand for the summer. Their usual entertainment consisted of stand-up comics, bands, and singers; but this summer, they were trying something new—dinner theater. Management had booked a touring company of *Hello, Dolly!* for the summer, and needed local teens to work as stage crew. After filling three of the four slots, they called Mrs. Horowitz, the high school drama teacher, for a referral for the last one. She recommended Jake.

Even though it didn't pay all that well, Jake would need the spending money for college, for books, movies, snacks, the occasional dinner in town. Besides, the job would be fun.

At the Tip Top Club, the stage manager, a skinny man named Louie who wore jeans so low they revealed the top of his hairy butt crack, assigned Jake to repaint scenery that had gotten damaged in transit, make sure the dressing room water pitchers were always full during rehearsal afternoons, operate a side curtain downstage left during performances, and to Coke the stage.

Jake liked that part of his job most of all because it put him in charge of something. Given that the nightclub had not been designed for dancers, the floor's polish was too slick. Jake had to mop the stage with Coca-Cola every afternoon to give it just a tad of stickiness. After Jake's mopping, the lead dancer, Carl, came onstage, did a few leaps and pirouettes to test the stickiness, explained to Jake whether he needed to re-Coke slick spots or mop overly sticky spots with plain water.

Jake liked Carl, a short stocky dancer with thin black hair. Whereas the other performers pretty much ignored Jake and the rest of the stage crew, Carl always thanked him for mopping the stage, always engaged him in chit-chat about school, told stories of what it was like to be a professional dancer.

One day, after approving the stage for the evening's performance, Carl casually said, "So, tell me—you haven't mentioned a girlfriend."

Jake blushed and shook his head.

"A handsome boy like you and no girlfriend?" Carl motioned one of the women dancers over from doing her stretches in the wings. "Maureen, can you believe it? Our boy Jake here doesn't have a girlfriend."

"No?" asked Maureen, tall with curly red hair. She put an arm around Jake's shoulder, brought her face close to his and blew hot air into his ear.

When Jake pulled back, she winked and asked, "Still a virgin, right?"

Jake blushed again.

"Maureen, don't make fun," said Carl. "Virginity's serious business for a boy about to go off to college."

"If I don't turn you on, I'm sure I could find one of the other girls to oblige. We can't let you start college as a virgin."

Gosh, thought Jake. Dad was right. These actors really are libertines.

"No thanks," he muttered. "I'm okay."

"How insulting!" exclaimed Maureen in an exaggerated huff as she strode off stage. Just before she flitted behind a teaser panel, she turned and said, "Or maybe Carl's more to your liking?"

"Shoo," said Carl. "You're scaring the poor boy with your hussy ways." Carl turned to Jake. "Don't mind her, she's just teasing. Besides, you don't like boys, do you?"

"Uh, no," stammered Jake. "No, of course I don't."

"I didn't think so. That's too bad. You see, I like boys, so I was going to suggest that maybe, if you wanted...well, never mind."

What? Carl was a homosexual? And he talked about it openly just like that? Like saying he had black hair or was short?

"You're probably underage anyway," added Carl, patting Jake on the cheek. "Are you eighteen yet?"

"I'm turning seventeen in the fall. I skipped third grade."

"Well, that explains why you're so cute." Carl planted a kiss on Jake's left cheek, then twirled himself off stage.

Leaning on his mop, Jake couldn't believe what had just happened. A grown man, an admitted homosexual, had just called Jake "cute." And he also implied that Jake didn't look homosexual. All Jake's practice standing and walking in front of the mirror had paid off.

He wanted to ask Carl questions, but couldn't figure out how to raise them without bringing suspicion upon himself: was life for a homosexual really as sad and creepy as Jake imagined? Did people spit at Carl on the street or beat him up? Had he been arrested lots of times? Did his parents know? Had they disowned him? Did landlords keep evicting him from apartments? Did he ever get fired from a dancing gig because of who he was? Did he have any friends? Was Carl lonely? What did Carl think God thought about him?

During that night's performance, Jake stared at Carl whenever he was onstage, watched his every taut muscle, his pointed toes, his erect posture, the graceful lifts of his arms, the strong curve of his buttocks, the fullness of his...bulge.

Night after night, Jake watched Carl.

And, before each performance, when Carl tested the slipperiness of the stage and chitchatted with Jake, Jake noticed how large Carl's blue eyes were, stood a little closer to Carl each time, practically tilted his cheek toward Carl just as Carl was about to leave the stage so that Carl could give Jake's cheek a kiss, which he always did—their new ritual. Afterwards, the spot on Jake's cheek felt warm the entire evening, as if radioactive and glowing.

What are you doing? God asked Jake one night in bed.

'Going to sleep, that's all.'

Why are you flirting with Carl?

'Flirting? I'm not flirting. What are you talking about?'

You're flirting with a known homosexual.

'Mind Your own business.'

You are my business. Boys who play with fire get burned.

'I don't know what You're talking about.'

Really? All of a sudden, you're stupid?

After the following night's show, while the cast was removing makeup and changing into street clothes, Jake and the other stage hands did the usual post-show backstage rearrangement of scenery for the following day's performance: stacking the shelves used in the general store scenes, carefully propping up the fake train the actors "rode" during one of their songs, folding the chairs from the fancy restaurant scene. Then Jake went into the male dancers' dressing room to grab their water pitcher and wash it.

"Hey, buddy boy." It was Carl, seated on a folding chair at the makeup counter beneath a mirror that ran the length of the wall. He was dabbing cotton and cold cream to remove eye makeup. Naked but for white jockeys. Thick-bodied and muscular, just the way Jake had pictured him. With a few sprigs of hair smack in the center of his chest. Pointy nipples. Thin black hair protruding from under each arm. So masculine.

"Am I in your way here?" asked Carl. "Do you need to sweep or something?"

"Uh, no. I just came for the water pitcher."

"Be a good boy and bring me a sip? I'm parched."

Jake stepped to the far end of the counter, poured the last bit of water into a paper cup and brought it over to seated Carl. As he handed it to him, their fingers touched, and Jake felt a fire race through his hand, up his arm, through his center. He gasped.

"You okay?" asked Carl after guzzling the water.

Jake just stared.

"Oh, my," said Carl, "look at you." He winked at Jake's crotch, now bulging at Carl's eye level.

Betrayed by his own body, Jake was mortified.

Carl stood, stepped to within an inch of Jake's face. Jake smelled Carl's pungent sweat mixed with the residue of pancake makeup.

"So maybe you do like boys, after all?" whispered Carl.

Jake didn't move, couldn't move.

"Jake," Carl said, raising a hand to Jake's cheek. "Jake, you're a sweet boy." Carl leaned in and kissed Jake lightly on the lips.

At the cool moist touch, Jake shuddered, spasmed, groaned, "Oh, God," and fell onto Carl's shoulder.

"My goodness!" exclaimed Carl. "Did you just come? From that little brush of my lips?"

Jake pulled back. "I'm so sorry. I…I…"

Carl grabbed him by the shoulders. "Jake, listen. You're young. You're very very young. I'd adore initiating you, but…too young. Find someone your own age. My kiss was just…I don't know…. Friendship tenderness, an older gay man showing a younger one that he's not alone."

"I'm not gay!" Jake knocked Carl's hands off him and stepped back. "I'm not a homosexual!"

"Sorry," said Carl, also taking a step back. "But your reaction made me think—"

"I'm not a faggot!" Jake blasted into Carl's face.

"Okay," said Carl, putting up both hands like stop signs. "I get it. Sorry."

"I'm not a faggot!" yelled Jake, turning and running out the dressing room. "I'm not a faggot! I'm not! I'm not!"

Jake fled the nightclub, ran the three blocks to the bus stop, paced and stomped and mumbled "I'm not! I'm not! I'm not!" until the bus came, then strode down the aisle past the single other passenger, a heavy woman dozing against a window. He slumped low into a seat at the very back, pummeled fists against thighs over and over, mumbling, "I'm not! I'm not! I'm not!"

As he slipped his key into the front door, Mom called out from the kitchen, "That you, Jake?"

"Yeah."

"I just finished baking brownies. Fresh out of the oven. Would you like—?"

Before she could finish the question, Jake had already darted upstairs to the bathroom and shut the door. Dropping jeans and briefs, he looked in disgust at his genitals covered with a thin crust of his body's own shame, got into the shower and scrubbed and scrubbed and scrubbed. He rubbed the loofah sponge hard against that spot on his cheek that Carl liked to kiss, and against his lips until they stung.

Wrapped in an orange towel, he cracked the bathroom door open, listened and heard TV voices drifting up from the den—some father scolding a child in a movie-of-the-week. Jake called downstairs, "Really bushed. Going to sleep early."

"Okay, Jake, nighty-night," called Mom, then Dad, then Artie.

In his room, Jake shut the door, pulled on heavy, flannel pajamas even though it was summer, crawled into bed, yanked the blanket high, covered his head with his pillow.

Jake! came God's muffled voice.

"Sleeping," Jake mumbled out loud.

You think because you've got a pillow over your head, I can't see you?

"Leave me alone!" Jake whispered.

Shame on you! came the voice.

Jake yanked the pillow off. "You were right, okay? I was flirting. I'm sorry. Maybe I am a faggot, after all. Maybe I am. But I don't want to be. I don't. I want to be good. Why'd You make me this way?"

You blame Me for your lack of self-control? You don't know right from wrong?

"Of course I do."

Then show it.

"Yes, Sir," Jake mumbled beneath the pillow.

/ /

After a fitful night's sleep—pillow and blanket ended up on the floor—Jake showered again in the morning, put chapstick on his peeling lips, then telephoned Louie the stage manager, said that he'd come down with pericarditis ("a terrible heart infection") and wouldn't be able to work for the remaining four weeks of the show's run.

"Fuck!" replied Louie. "Now what the hell am I going to do?"

Jake hung up the kitchen phone, and when Dad came in for breakfast, Jake said, "Don't tell Mom because I don't want her to get upset, but you were right, Dad. Those actors are…libertines." He explained how Maureen had tried to seduce him.

"That whore!" Dad exclaimed. "Excuse my language. You're not going back to that nightclub. I'll give you whatever spending money you need for college, but you're not setting foot in that club again. The job's over."

"Okay, Dad, whatever you say. I'll call them after breakfast and quit."

"You're a good boy, Jake. A good boy."

Jake felt awful.

"**H**ow's your architecture internship going?" Jake had waited three days, until Sunday, to telephone Deb. Sunday afternoons were her only free time; even then she was too exhausted to get together and do anything. At least they could talk on the phone. "I'm learning so much," she said. "Still enjoying the nightclub?"

"Dad made me quit."

"He did? Why?"

"He didn't like the moral atmosphere there."

"The moral—? Well, he's awfully religious. Probably didn't like you working on *Shabbes* in the first place."

"You got it. And there was this woman."

"A woman?"

"A dancer. She kept trying to have sex with me. Kept running her hands all over me every chance she got. Tongue-kissed me before I could stop her. Grabbed my crotch. Dragged me into the woman's dressing room and practically raped me."

"What?!"

"Yeah. I'm lucky I got away. Really creepy."

"I'll say. Are you okay?"

"Yeah."

"Good. So what are you going to do the rest of the summer?"

"Too late to find another job or sign up for camp. Maybe I'll get a head-start for college. I'm going to start studying Russian in college, so maybe I should learn the alphabet. And there's the swim club."

"That sounds thrilling."

"Dad's taking us on a family vacation to Atlantic City at the end of the summer."

"Fun with Mommy and Daddy."

"Yeah."

"If you're bored and lonely, you could always call Steve."

"What?" Jake's head snapped as if slapped.

"Just kidding. He's already moved up to New York. He and his girlfriend are living together in an apartment. And guess what—they got engaged!"

"Engaged? So soon?" Jake's heart sank. "But he hasn't even started college yet. That's crazy."

"He told me his girlfriend proposed to him."

"That's weird." Steve was getting married? Actually married?

"Can't blame her. Steve's totally dreamy. I guess she wanted to be sure to lock him up before some other woman got him."

"That must be it." Jake heard a crashing in his head—the sound of dreams plummeting to Earth from thirty thousand feet up. "I'm happy for them," he said with the biggest lilt he could force into his voice. "You don't have his address in New York, do you?"

/ /

Jake bought a card congratulating Steve on his engagement. It had silver sparkly champagne glasses on the cover and lots of little lovebirds flitting about. "Wishing you both endless happiness together," Jake wrote.

He fantasized that under the guise of a thank you note, Steve would write back questioning his decision to marry so young, and asking if he could see Jake for help clarifying his thinking. Jake would reply immediately and Steve would take the bus home to Cherryvale the very next weekend.

The minute Steve saw Jake at the bus station, he'd embrace him. "As soon as I saw your signature on the card, I felt a pang in my heart and knew I'd made a terrible mistake."

Steve would drop to one knee and ask Jake to be his boyfriend. "NYU and Princeton aren't all that far from one another," Steve would say. "We could take the train and visit every single weekend, spend all weekend in bed, hugging and kissing and sharing ourselves like with nobody else. And I'll try transferring to Princeton for sophomore year so we could really be together. Permanently."

Jake would shout "yes!" and they'd live happily ever after.

Day after day, Jake watched for the postman around 3:00 and ran to the mailbox at the front of their yard as soon as the blond postman slipped the mail in.

Day after day.

Nothing from Steve.

Not a thank you card, not a note, nothing. Not even a phone call.

Of course not, thought Jake. Of course not, you stupid idiot!

Who the hell sends a congratulations engagement card to someone who never even told you he was engaged in the first place? An idiot, that's who. Steve must think Jake an idiot. Because that's exactly what he was.

Jake had to acknowledge the foolishness of his fantasy. Of all his Steve fantasies.

Deep inside, he knew he'd never hear from Steve again.

Because Steve was normal.

/ /

The rest of the summer progressed uneventfully. From time to time, Jake studied the Russian alphabet from a book he checked out of the Cherryvale Library. When Mom let him have the car, he went to the movies—legitimate movies—on his own or with Artie. And of course there were *Shabbes* services in *shul* with the family.

A week before heading to Atlantic City at the end of August, Dad invited Uncle Irv, Aunt Flora, and Dave to join them—"It's a pre-birthday celebration for Jake because he'll be away at school on his actual birthday," Dad explained over the phone.

But they made their apologies because Dave was apparently so involved with theater at his sleep-away camp in the Poconos, he just couldn't take the time.

Just as well, thought Jake. He didn't want to see Dave, the way he'd lied about Sheila who didn't even exist. Just to seduce Jake. Maybe all Jake's problems were Dave's fault. Better stay away from him.

"You know who I haven't seen in the longest time?" Mom asked while washing the lunch dishes. "Your sweet friend Deb. Would you like to invite her to join us in Atlantic City?"

"Deb?" asked Jake, genuinely puzzled. "Bring her on a family vacation?"

"Well, you're such good friends, that's all, and she's such a nice girl." Mom dried her hands on a red plaid dish towel, leaned against the kitchen sink. "You haven't really seen her this summer, have you?"

"Her internship in Philly's keeping her super busy. I don't think she'd be able to get away for *our* family vacation."

"Is there any problem between you two?"

"No, Mom," said Jake, deciding not to correct Mom's obvious impression that he and Deb were more than just friends. "No problem between us."

"Princeton and Penn aren't all that far from one another," Mom added. "And we're right in between. You could come home weekends and she could take the High Speedline train in from Philly to visit her folks, and the two of you could see each other."

"Yeah, Mom, sure."

"And there'll be holidays, of course."

"Mom, stop. We're fine."

"Okay, no more matchmaking from me. For today at least." Mom gave Jake a sheepish grin.

/ /

Dad booked the family a kosher hotel in Atlantic City. Actually, it was an old Victorian house whose widowed owner rented bedrooms to observant Jews and served kosher, family-style suppers in her dining room. "The rabbi told your father about it," Mom explained to Jake. "I said it sounds a little too *frum* for us, too religious, but your father wanted to give it a try. How bad can it be?"

Their first morning there, as Mom headed down the stairs in sandals and an open, knee-length terry-cloth robe that revealed a bathing suit, Mrs. Krulewitz, wearing a floor-length floral housecoat, asked, "You going to sit on the beach in a bathing suit? In front of strange men?"

"It's a one-piece suit," Mom replied, opening her robe wider. "With a knee-length skirt. Quite modest."

"This is proper behavior for a Jewish woman?" asked Mrs. Krulewitz as she tugged at her gray wig. "A *married* Jewish woman?"

"My husband and boys will be with me."

"In front of your children, you flaunt yourself before strangers? How can your husband permit this?"

"I don't need his permission to dress the way I choose," said Mom. "Nor do I need yours."

Mom spun around, climbed back upstairs, told the rest of the family what had just transpired and ordered them to pack. "We'll have tuna sandwiches for lunches and broiled fish in local restaurants for dinners. Or plain spaghetti in tomato sauce. Or we'll go hungry. But we'll enjoy our vacation without some busybody judging me and making snide remarks."

"She means well," said Dad. "She's extremely religious, that's all. She's trying to protect your dignity."

"You've seen me wear this bathing suit at the swim club dozens of times. Are you calling me a hussy now?"

Dad gave a chuckle. "Calm down, Millie. Nobody's calling you a hussy. You're a perfect lady. I'm be proud to be seen on the beach with you. Even if you want to go naked."

Jake and Artie's eyes bugged out.

"Naked?!" Mom reached for a pillow and swatted Dad across the chest.

"Let's go to the beach naked!" exclaimed Artie with an evil grin.

"Nobody's going to the beach naked," said Dad, laughing together with Mom. "We're a respectable Jewish family. Boys, pack your things."

They left, then checked into a Holiday Inn down the block. The hotel coffee shop served tuna sandwiches, egg salad sandwiches, even peanut butter and jelly—all kosher things they could eat for lunch. "We won't starve," Mom told Dad.

Throughout the week, Jake actually enjoyed dodging waves with Dad and Artie, strolling the boardwalk with Mom and poking into little stores. At a novelty shop, he bought mirrored sunglasses that prevented anyone from seeing where his eyes were looking. Now Jake could relax and enjoy the best part of the trip—staring at all the bare-chested men on the beach. There's nothing wrong with looking, he told himself. Everybody looked at everybody on a beach. It was like the beach was one giant gift shop—look, but don't touch. Everybody did it. Besides, the more Jake looked at half-naked men, the more normal their bodies would seem, right? Maybe he only wanted to see men's bodies because they were usually covered up all the time. Didn't he hear that people in nudist camps stopped getting excited at seeing one another because they grew so accustomed to nakedness? That was all Jake was really trying to do—to get himself so accustomed to men's nakedness, or half-nakedness, that eventually he wouldn't even notice at all. A wholesome objective.

Jake looked to his heart's content at thick chests and flat ones, hairy chests and smooth, at firm bubble butts and jiggly ones, at husky men in boxer bathing suits (like the ones Jake, Dad, and Artie wore), at lean men in bikini bathing suits revealing more than Jake thought any respectable man should reveal in public although he was glad they did, at bathing suit points and bulges in crotches wet with sea water. And every night in bed, after checking that Artie in the bed beside his had fallen asleep, Jake reached beneath his own covers, touched himself and fantasized, imagining this man approaching him and begging for a kiss, that one slipping Jake's hand into his swim trunks, another using his mouth on Jake in ways that made Jake nearly scream in ecstasy... before he returned the joyful favor...and dropped off to sleep.

Each morning, as Jake put on *tefillin* and *davened*, he prayed for forgiveness for the prior night's shameful fantasies and misbehavior. He prayed that today would be the day he'd grow so accustomed to men's near nakedness that he'd stop noticing. That this cruel phase of attraction for men—he had to admit he did feel attraction—passed. And he prayed that college would cram his mind full of so many important ideas there'd be no space left for all the perverse imaginings that so filled his head right now they nearly leaked out his ears.

College couldn't come soon enough.

PART 5

"Too bad you didn't place out of the freshman writing course requirement," said Ted from the bottom bunk.

Having arrived on campus and their room before Jake this morning, Ted took the lower bunk. Just as well, thought Jake — what with Ted being so tall and muscular, he might have crashed through the top bunk smack onto Jake some night if he'd taken that one. Besides, Jake would rather not stare up every night at a mattress holding such a hunky guy. Too distracting.

"Yeah, well," replied Jake, lying on his back, staring at the white ceiling with white-painted pipes running a couple feet from his face. "It won't hurt me to take an English composition course spring semester — it'll focus on American literature, and we spent so much time on the Puritans in high school, that I missed out on lots of other authors. You must be a good writer to place out."

"I want to be a novelist. I love French novels — in the original, of course."

"Of course."

"And German ones."

"In the original?"

"Definitely."

"Wow."

"I'm studying Arabic this year so I can read Arabic poetry. I want to become a professor to support my novel-writing habit."

"I'm starting Russian. It's the era of Détente, you know. Everyone expects trade between the U.S. and the Soviet Union to pick up. I want to be an international lawyer."

"Sounds exciting. What exactly does an international lawyer do?"

"Business contracts between countries, I guess. I've got time to figure it out."

"I hear Russian 101 here is as hard as organic chemistry."

A trickle of water echoed from above their ceiling.

"A woman peeing," said Ted.

"Not a man?"

"I've got three sisters. It's a woman. The women's room must be right overhead."

A loud whoosh of water rushed through the ceiling pipes. The distinct sound of muffled shower spray followed. Then the bass boom of rock music thumped through the wall from the dormitory's lounge next door.

"We sure got a plum room," said Ted.

Jake pulled his pillow over his head. So this was college life: noisy neighbors and a gorgeous roommate Jake would love to spend hours staring at—wavy brown hair down to his shoulders, deep green eyes, square jaw, smooth pink complexion without the mild acne that Jake had just started to develop, and an athlete's physique. Jake would need to make sure his eyes never lingered on Ted nor moved inappropriately along various body parts, and although Jake really wanted to see Ted naked, he'd have to do his utmost to avoid that or else he might give himself away and Ted would get so insulted and angry he'd pummel Jake to a pulp or curse at him loudly so that others would hear and come in from the lounge and laugh at the faggot, and everyone on campus would know and students would throw stones at him as he walked to classes and teachers would seat him in the back of every lecture to avoid meeting his eye and the administration would eventually expel him for corrupting the campus.

A difficult first night's sleep.

Their dorm telephone wouldn't be hooked up for a couple more days, but Jake's parents had asked him to call and let them know how his first night went. So, early in the morning, he walked down University Place to the Dinky station, a small train depot for a spur line that took commuters to the main station in Princeton Junction where commuters could catch trains to New York or Philadelphia. Jake figured they had to have pay phones there. He entered the high-ceilinged, cavernous room, empty but for long wooden benches facing tall grimy windows, found the pay phones and called home. He reassured Mom that Ted was a nice guy.

The next couple days Jake wandered around grassy campus squares bounded by gray-stoned neo-Gothic buildings with concrete casement windows, occasional turrets, even gargoyles. He attended orientation meetings, registered for classes, found Stevenson Hall, the kosher dining hall where he'd signed up to eat, a fifteen-minute walk way across campus beyond Firestone Library, and way down Prospect Avenue. The very last of the eating clubs at the campus's farthest end. Having a place to eat kosher food—the first at any Ivy League university—had added to Princeton's appeal. Jake looked forward to being able to eat whatever was served, not having to limit himself to certain "safe" foods the way the family had to do in Atlantic City. "And there'll be lots of Jewish *maidlach*," added Dad with a wink, not that Jake had given any thought to meeting available young women.

The dining room of this converted old house felt incredibly cozy despite the many tables for four or eight. And Jake certainly was impressed by the food: bagels and cream cheese and gefilte fish and eggs for breakfast. Dairy lunches of blintzes and kugels, egg salad sandwiches and tuna sandwiches, or meat lunches of burgers and hot dogs and fries. Dinners of chicken schnitzel or pot roast, roast beef or fried liver and onions. Potatoes, knishes, rice. Always an abundance of fruit and desserts.

Then there were the other students. Jake ate by himself the first couple days, but during dinner the third night, two seniors sat with him.

"You're wearing a *yarmulke* during dinner," said one of them—with a cute fuzzy beard—as he pointed to Jake's black cloth skullcap. "Do you wear one all the time, even to classes, the way I do?"

"No, only when I eat or *daven*," replied Jake.

Look of disapproval from Fuzzy Beard.

"Have you ever tasted *traif*?" asked Horn-rimmed Glasses Guy beside him.

"No. Never any pork products, no shellfish. Only kosher meat."

Approving nods of the head.

"Do you work on *Shabbes*?" asked Fuzzy Guy.

"No."

Approving nods of the head.

"Do you turn the lights on, on *Shabbes*?" asked Horn-rimmed Glasses Guy.

"Yes."

Looks of disapproval.

Fuzzy: "Do you lay *tefillin* every day?"

Jake: "Yes, but not on *Shabbes*, of course."

Fuzzy: "Of course."

Horn-rimmed: "Do you wear *tzitzit* all day?"

Jake: "I wear a *tallit* when I *daven* in the morning." Dad never required him to wear the fringed undergarment that Orthodox boys did throughout the day.

"Well," said Fuzzy, sharing frowns with Horn-rimmed, "can we count on you to attend daily *minyan* services here on weekdays with the other guys before breakfast?"

Jake and Dad never went to morning services at *shul* until Grandpa died. After that, Dad went every morning before work so he could say mourner's *kaddish* with a *minyan*, a group of ten congregants, but didn't make Jake go. "Only the son, not the grandson, needs to say *kaddish*," Dad explained. "Grandpa's soul won't rest unless I do it daily for eleven months. A pain, I've got to admit, but anybody can be religious when it's easy."

"We don't always get the ten men we need for morning *minyan*," Fuzzy Beard added, "so we need you to sign up. You'll be coming here for breakfast anyway, so you might as well."

"I'll probably be skipping breakfast," said Jake, irritated by the pressure. "My dorm's the other side of campus, and according to my schedule, Russian classes are early."

"And you wouldn't want to inconvenience yourself for *Hashem*," said Fuzzy, shoving back his chair and standing.

"I'd inconvenience myself for God," replied Jake. "But not for you."

Both Fuzzy and Horn-rimmed left the table, grumbling things like, "Only here for the good food" and "Pretend Jew."

"Don't mind them," said a chunky young woman in tight jeans, loose green blouse, and with thick wavy black hair. "I'm Dora." She extended a hand, which Jake shook. Dora sat in Fuzzy's spot. "Not everybody here's a police-rabbi-in-training."

"Thanks," said Jake, smiling.

"It's nice to have a Jewish place to sit and schmooze, right? Just to hang out during meals and socialize. And you know you can date anybody here without worrying if some cute guy or girl is Jewish or not. And the *shiddachs* we upperclassmen make for you young ones!"

What? They were going to do matchmaking?

"Look at that shock on your face!" Dora said. "Just kidding. Or maybe not. Sit with me and a friend for dinner tomorrow night?"

/ /

The next evening, as he looked around the dining room for Dora, he caught Fuzzy's eye. Fuzzy poked Horn-rimmed in the side, they both scowled at Jake, then turned away.

From a far corner, Dora waved. Jake went over and joined her at a table with another woman, slim with fluffy light brown hair.

"This is Marla Kaufman, another freshman," said Dora. "She broke up with her boyfriend months ago, so she's totally available."

"Dora!" scolded Marla.

"What? I'm lying? She refuses to discuss details of the break-up, which shows you what a discreet and sensitive woman she is."

Marla blushed.

"Marla," continued Dora, "this is my old friend, Jake Stein."

"Old friend?" asked Jake.

"We've known each other a whole twenty-four hours," said Dora, slurping her split-pea soup. "But I've done my investigating and I know all about you."

"You do?"

"You're from Cherryvale, across the river from Philly. And you come from a good Jewish family and are living in Lockhart Hall and are signed up to take Russian."

"How you do you know all that?" asked Jake.

Dora raised and dropped her eyebrows a couple times as if to say, 'Aren't I something?' "A friend works part time in the Registrar's office. Marla here grew up on the Philly mainline, the opposite side of Philly as you—you're practically *landsleit*, Jewish immigrants from the same region. Maybe you both should come to our *Shabbes oneg* together? We've always got great cookies." Marla darted a timid glance at Jake, then looked down to concentrate on her pot roast. "You freshmen are so shy," said Dora. "Oh, excuse me. There's somebody I need to see." She left the table and went to chat with other women across the room.

"I didn't know she was going to do that," said Marla, taking a sip from her water glass.

"Kind of heavy-handed."

"A real *yenta*." Marla ate a couple string beans. "So, you like languages?"

"Yes," said Jake, relieved to be talking about a safe subject. "How about you?"

"I'm going to be a Near Eastern Studies major. So I'll continue with Hebrew and start Arabic."

"My roommate's starting Arabic, too. You'll probably meet him. Ted, nice guy."

She nodded. "I hear Russian's hard here."

"I hear that too. I'm kind of nervous. Is Arabic hard?"

"Not if you know Hebrew. They're both Semitic languages."

They chatted about other courses, about shared intentions to attend law school, about differences between living on the mainline side of Philly versus the New Jersey side, about plans for Yom Kippur starting in just a few days. "I'll stay on campus," said Marla. "And attend Hillel services. I hear that Princeton's Hillel is a nice one. They've got their own rabbi, hold all kinds of services, holiday parties, study sessions, and stuff."

"Sounds cool, I should definitely check it out," said Jake. "But my Dad's coming to pick me up and take me home for Yom Kippur. It means *shlepping* back to campus Monday night right after breaking the fast because classes start Tuesday morning, but the folks want me there."

"You're a good son."

"I try," said Jake. A nice person, this Marla.

As he was getting ready to head out to his dorm, Marla said she'd hang back at Stevenson to talk with Dora some more. "I'll probably be at the *oneg* after *Shabbes* services tomorrow night," she said. "Maybe I'll see you there."

"Maybe," said Jake. "Not sure yet what my plans are."

"Of course. 'Bye."

Walking down tree-lined Prospect Avenue, Jake thought about attending the *oneg* the following night so as to talk more with Marla. But what if Marla misinterpreted Jake's interest? Dora had obviously been trying to set them up. If he showed at the *oneg*, Marla might think he wanted to date her, which he didn't.

Better not go to the *oneg*. Of course, he could talk to Marla if he saw her at Stevenson Hall for meals. Those would just be meals, not dates. Maybe they could become friends.

On Sunday morning, Dad drove the hour to campus to get Jake, then drove them the hour home. Yom Kippur was to begin at sundown. Jake would fast from then until sundown Monday—no food or drink—attending services that evening and all day Monday.

Jake wasn't looking forward to Yom Kippur, remembering the previous year's "Leviticus passage" Torah reading and the way he'd lost control and touched himself in *shul* beside Dad. He still couldn't understand how he could have done such a thing, even if his unconscious were hoping Dad would notice and intervene and save Jake from himself. What twisted, idiotic reasoning even for an unconscious.

Sitting in *shul* beside Dad this Yom Kippur Monday, Jake made it through all the prayers of atonement for sin, some of which he mumbled, others of which he did not. Then came the Torah reading with the Leviticus passage, and then the rabbi's sermon.

On the raised *bimah* in front of the congregation, stood their tall, mustachioed rabbi in his white Yom Kippur caftan of purity. He lifted from the lectern and flapped a flimsy newspaper clipping, which he explained to be from *The Village Voice*. How surprising that their socially conservative rabbi was reading a progressive newspaper. *"The Village Voice*, right?" the rabbi said in a tone of nasal mockery. Ah, he was about to poke fun.

"An advertisement from a so-called 'congregation.'" He proceeded to read the clipping's advertisement aloud—an announcement of gay Jewish holiday services ending with: "'Everyone's welcome.'" The rabbi then crumpled the clipping, hurled it to the blue-carpeted floor, slammed his palm down onto the lectern and yelled, "But it says right here in the Torah that they are abomination!" Scolding finger pointed out at everyone: "You can't be homosexual and Jew at the same time." Finger now pointed to the ark holding the Torah scrolls: "It says so right in the Torah! How dare they! They're not Jews! How dare they!"

His stare was not directed at Jake, but might as well have been. Jake's entire body went cold.

"They're not Jews! How dare they!"

Jake wanted to vomit.

A fear that had been lurking just below Jake's consciousness for a long time, now sprang out and slapped him across the face: these persistent feelings...these feelings that made him an abomination...if Jake's obscene phase didn't pass, if he continued to be one of those abominations, then—was it true that Jake couldn't be both Jewish and...? Their rabbi had just said so, and he knew way more about being Jewish than Jake ever would. The rabbi who had presided over Jake's bar mitzvah years ago, thereby officially welcoming him into the Jewish fold, had just threatened to expel him.... Unless Jake grew out of it and became normal.

/ /

At home after services, he barely ate the boiled chicken and rice Mom reheated for them all. But he forced himself to eat a slice of the *parve* chocolate pre-birthday cake Mom had baked.

"We'll miss you on your birthday," said Mom, visibly suppressing tears.

During the drive to campus, Dad observed, "You're awfully quiet. Looks like you took Yom Kippur very seriously this year."

"It's a solemn holiday," said Jake. "Gets you thinking about who you are."

"That's the whole point," replied Dad, reaching over and patting Jake on the knee. "To remind us to try harder to be better Jews."

"Yeah," muttered Jake. "I got that."

"**Z**dravstvuite!" said the energetic white-haired teacher as she bustled into the classroom. "At least that's one word everyone knows."

Uh-oh, thought Jake, who didn't recognize that word at all.

"Welcome to class. I am Mrs. Polenko," she said, adjusting her black-framed glasses.

"If you tink my class easy 'A,' please exit door right now. You are here to work and to learn. If dis not hardest class you have, you doing it wrong. Understand?"

Jake and the thirty-some-odd other students nodded.

"How many studied Russian in high school?"

Half the hands in the class went up. But this was Russian 101, thought Jake, the beginners' course.

"You tink you learned Russian in high school, but you are wrong. High school teachers do not know how to teach Russian. You not learn correctly."

A student with long brown hair raised her hand.

"Yes?" asked Mrs. Polenko.

"I studied Russian for four years in high school," the student said, "from an extremely competent teacher."

"Really?" asked Mrs. Polenko, "four years?" She then launched into a rapid-fire series of questions. In Russian.

The student turned beet red.

"You cannot answer, can you?" asked Mrs. Polenko.

Looking down at her lap, the student shook her head.

"Did you even understand all my questions?"

Again the student shook her head.

"You see? I told you. But don't embarrass. Not your fault. Fault of stupid shithead high school teacher."

All the students giggled, including the embarrassed student.

"Much better," said Mrs. Polenko. "Listen, everyone: I am strict and very difficult teacher. But I love you all because you are my babies. You don't know how to speak—you are babies. Understand?"

Some students looked at one another, but Jake nodded.

"You," she said, pointing at Jake. "You also studied Russian in high school?"

He shook his head.

"You mute?" asked Mrs. Polenko.

"I don't know how to say 'no' in Russian."

"So you prefer silence?"

"Uh, yes Ma'am."

"So…'yes' you will say in English, but not 'no'? Very strange boy."

Jake didn't know how to respond.

"Russian word is *nyet*. *Nyet* means 'no.' *Nyet*. Can you say?"

"*Nyet*," said Jake.

"*Nyet*, you cannot say word? Or *nyet*, you are repeating word for practice?"

"I'm…I'm…" Jake stammered.

"I joking," said Mrs. Polenko, who walked over to Jake, bent down nearly to the floor, grabbed hold of his left ankle and yanked. "I pulling your leg. You understand?"

This woman's a lunatic, thought Jake, smiling uneasily as the rest of the class giggled.

"All right, my babies. We will learn together five mornings a week. Two of those days, we will study a second time in afternoons. Plus one day a week you will study alone in language lab listening to my beautiful Russian voice on tape recorder. Understand?"

Everyone nodded.

"Good. Today we study alphabet. You will know it please by tomorrow."

Thank goodness Jake had studied the alphabet this summer when it took him weeks to be able to recognize and write all the letters with any degree of comfort.

After class, he left East Pyne Hall for Corwin Hall where he attended the first lecture of a course on international relations. In English. He understood every word.

Then it was time for lunch. Jake hadn't needed to go to Stevenson for breakfast, given that Mom sent him back to campus with a dozen brownies last night. Jake shared them with Ted this morning, of course.

Now he hesitated, sat down on Corwin's steps. It'd be easy to walk down the block and get a kosher lunch. He'd have plenty of time before needing to reach his first American lit class.

But ever since the rabbi's sermon yesterday, hearing the rabbi declare that homosexuals weren't real Jews, Jake had been questioning whether he belonged in a Jewish environment like Stevenson Hall, at least while this disturbing phase lasted. Marla and the other young women were all looking for Jewish husbands, weren't they? It wasn't like he could avoid them at Stevenson, such an intimate place, or at campus Hillel services and events.

Even if Jake tried to be just friends, what if one of those women asked him out on a date? Hadn't Marla already hinted? He didn't feel like dating. If they asked him out, he'd just have to turn them down. But then they'd feel all hurt. He didn't want to hurt anybody's feelings. And it wasn't like he could explain.

Jake decided to avoid the problem entirely by eating at Commons, the main cafeteria on campus that would accept his Stevenson Hall dining card. Ted had complained that Commons was so large "you could drop dead in there and nobody'd find your body for a week." Anonymity would be perfect. Besides, it was close to their dorm, which would be a plus in bad weather.

Jake stood, walked through the plaza in the opposite direction of Stevenson Hall, and crossed Washington Road. No, he wouldn't be able to eat meat or chicken at Commons because it wouldn't be kosher, but he could eat cheese and eggs and peanut butter and salads and potatoes and rice—lots of stuff. Besides, by eating alone, he could get through his meals quickly then get back to studying, which was the real reason he was at Princeton, right?

In his room, he finished up the phone conversation of Mom and Dad's birthday congratulations—"No, not doing anything special except studying," Jake replied. "And yes, if I find time, I'll call McCosh Infirmary to get my annual physical." He knew he wouldn't bother, but Mom needed reassurance.

Hunching over his desk, he immersed himself deep in thought over page 152 of the *History of the Cuban Missile Crisis* until he heard Ted's key in their dorm door. Damn it, he thought, not again. Every night this week, Ted and his new pal, Sheldon from Arabic class, interrupted Jake's evening reading to hang out and smoke pot. They couldn't very well smoke in the dorm's public lounge, Jake understood that. And Sheldon was rooming with three other guys, each of whom brought girlfriends to their room—no privacy there. But did they have to come to Jake and Ted's room? What was Jake supposed to do? He had to read a book a week for his international relations course and turn in a written summary; for his microeconomics course, he had to read a dense textbook chapter every week, parse out all sorts of graphs and charts; Russian demanded at least five hours a day memorizing vocabulary and grammar rules and writing pages of homework. For his psych course, he had to read complex theoretical chapters.

There weren't enough hours in a week, especially considering that Jake couldn't do any writing on Shabbes. He needed every spare hour of every evening. Yet Ted and Sheldon kept showing up around 10:00 PM.

"Hey, Jakeroo," said Sheldon as he sauntered into the room, tucking a shock of thin greasy blond hair behind his ear. "I've got some primo weed tonight."

Was he mocking Jake? By now Sheldon had to know that Jake wouldn't partake.

"Cut it out, dufus," Ted told Sheldon. "You know smoking's against his religion."

Jake had told them that as a way of avoiding smoking without looking lame. "I really admire your conviction, man," Ted said to Jake. "Standing by your principles, and all. I'm an atheist so this is new to me. But it's way cool."

"Thanks." Jake shut his book, turned off his desk lamp, weighed going to Firestone Library now. It was already 10:30, Jake wouldn't get there until 10:45. It'd be 11:00 before he found a free carrel and settled in, and the library closed at midnight. Was it worth trudging out for an hour of reading?

Ted and Sheldon kicked back on Ted's lower bunk, Sheldon rolled a joint and lit it. The two passed it back and forth, inhaling deeply, as Jake shut his nose and breathed through his mouth. He hated the smell of pot.

"Wish you had more of your Mom's brownies," said Ted.

"All gone, but I've got some cookies." Jake pulled a half-empty box of Entenmann's chocolate chip cookies from his top dresser drawer.

"Good man," said Sheldon, reaching for the box.

Through a mouthful, Ted said, "Jake, show Sheldon those leather straps you put on every morning."

"Nah, it's not interesting."

"Leather straps?" asked Sheldon. "Sounds kinky. Show!"

"It's religious, dufus, not kinky. Jake needs to wear them when he prays every morning."

"You pray every morning?" asked Sheldon. "Hail Mary full of grace."

"You could use some of Jake's self-discipline," said Ted. "He's way cool." Ted gave Jake a wink.

"Thanks." Maybe Jake could skip one evening of reading, he thought. He'd read extra fast tomorrow.

"At least have some cookies with us," said Ted, holding out the box. "They're yours, after all."

Jake did. He had to admit that he liked the way Ted and Sheldon laughed so easily, the way Ted winked at Jake from time to time, as if sharing something private. He didn't quite understand why they found the chocolate chips so hysterical, or what Sheldon meant by repeating, "It's for the goof, man, for the goof." But, okay, the study break was kind of pleasant.

"Did you catch a look at her tits, man?" Sheldon asked.

"Yeah." Ted explained to Jake—"our Arabic TA's got great tits. Like the biggest jugs."

"Wow." This was Jake's standard response when pretending to be impressed by a woman's body.

"Yeah," added Sheldon. "I'd love to rub my dick between those bazongas and come all over her fucking face."

"Don't be gross," said Ted.

"Watch her lap up every drop."

Ted took the joint from Sheldon. "No more for you."

Jake didn't know what to say. He sat quietly as the two others talked about groping this part of the TA's body and that, slipping off her panties, then their own briefs, then…

As they egged one another on, Jake noticed that both young men were now sporting erections tenting their jeans.

"Fuck!" said Sheldon, grabbing his own. "You've given me a hard-on."

"Me?" asked Ted. "You're the one with all the gross fantasies."

"Maybe we should cruise on down to the Dinky station for a homo bj."

"What are you talking about?" asked Ted.

"You haven't heard those rumors? Fags hang out at the Dinky station and blow anyone with a hard on."

"You saying you want sex with a dude?" asked Ted.

"Any port in a storm. A mouth's a mouth."

"You're disgusting."

"Think so?"

"Yes I do."

"How about you, Jake?" asked Sheldon.

"What?" What exactly did Sheldon mean about the Dinky station? Jake had been there a few weeks ago—it was just a train station. One big room with some tracks behind it. How on earth could anyone have sex there? Sheldon was full of baloney.

"How about you, Jake?" Sheldon repeated.

"How about me…what?"

"Do you think I'm disgusting?" asked Sheldon.

"Uh…well…"

"Of course he thinks you're disgusting," said Ted. "Jake's religious. Cut it out, Sheldon. Stop talking shit."

"It's okay," said Jake, "I don't believe in imposing my religious beliefs on anyone else."

"You're a cool dude, Jakeroo," said Sheldon.

"Thanks. I've got to go shower, anyway. Got an early Russian class tomorrow."

"You shower at night, man?" asked Sheldon. "Like a girl?"

"Cut it out, dufus," said Ted. "He showers when he wants to shower. None of your goddamn business."

Jake usually showered at night because most of the men in the dorm showered in the morning. At night, there was less risk of seeing another man naked and embarrassing himself with an inopportune erection.

"We should follow his example," added Ted, "and go to sleep. We've got an Arabic quiz first thing tomorrow."

Jake grabbed his blue terry-cloth robe from the closet, slipped off shoes and socks and put on flip-flops, left the room. He hoped Sheldon would be gone by the time he returned, although he knew there was no guarantee.

After an uneventful shower, he returned in his robe, clothes in his arms. Sheldon was gone and Ted was already under the covers. "Night, man," he murmured, his eyes closed.

How handsome Ted's face looked, his long hair in disarray on the white pillow, his square chin propped on the edge of the red wool blanket. His lips were puckered as if poised for a joint. Jake wanted to…maybe Jake could just wait until he was sound asleep…after all, Ted was so stoned he might not notice, and… Jake could lean down and give those full lips a light kiss. Ted would never know, but Jake would have a memory—

Stop! What the hell was Jake thinking? Shame on him. Jake had been trying to avoid precisely this sort of feeling. Whenever Ted came into the room smelling sweaty and musky after a game of basketball, Jake opened the window and breathed the fresh air deeply. After Ted showered and smelled of herbal shampoo, Jake forced himself to imagine being alone in an orchard with just trees. When Ted's rich baritone voice made Jake think of dark chocolate pudding on a spoon sliding into Jake's mouth, onto Jake's tongue, down Jake's throat, Jake bit his cheek so the twinge and metallic taste of blood would mask all other thoughts.

He turned his back to the now sleeping Ted, pulled green striped pajama bottoms from his dresser, slipped them on under his bathrobe, removed the robe and quickly pulled on matching pajama tops, hung up the bathrobe in their closet, then climbed to his bunk. He lay listening to Ted's breathing grow more steady, a light snoring, but not grating. Intimate even. The breathing of a nice guy, one who defended Jake, who respected him, who maybe even admired him a little. A friend, that's all. A friend whom Jake needed to keep at a distance.

For both their sakes.

Walking into class for the first day of psych lab, Jake spotted, on each lab table, a wire cage holding a gray pigeon. He stopped still just inside the door. No, he thought, not again.

"Here for the Psych 101 lab?" asked the TA, the graduate student teaching assistant, at the blackboard.

Jake gave a tentative nod.

"Come on in! Pick any lab table."

Jake went to the back row, sat on a metal stool and stared at the gray pigeon caged on the table. Gray with black and white wing feathers. It kept turning its head at Jake, first goggling one eye, then the other.

Jake raised his hand and, as other students continued sauntering in, the TA came over. "I'm Fernando," he said, extending a thick hand. Jake shook it, gazed into Fernando's smiley dark brown eyes, thought how handsome he was with that tawny complexion and thick curly black hair. "Question?"

"Um...yeah." Concentrate, jackass, Jake told himself. Concentrate. "The pigeons—we're not going to kill them, are we?"

"Whoa," said Fernando. "Dark imagination."

No, thought Jake, not imagination—experience. Jake flashed back to his high school biology class three years before. They'd spent most of that year—Jake was fourteen then—studying photosynthesis, DNA, ways of defining genus and species, and other harmless subjects. Then they moved on to anatomy. When they walked into class that first Monday of June, Ms. Hodges announced that their final project would be dissection of live frogs. "Isn't that an exciting surprise?" She grinned so widely her freckles nearly popped off her face. "Take your seats and let's jump in—get it? Frogs…jump in? Ha ha."

"Shouldn't we talk about this first?" asked Jake.

"Don't tell me you're squeamish," she said, fluttering her long fake blond eyelashes.

"I don't want to hurt a frog."

"It won't feel a thing," she said, then added with a wink, "as long as you do it right. So let's leap right in—get the pun, everybody? Frogs…leaping in…ha, ha. Here, let me show you how it's done."

At her desk, she tugged on surgical gloves, then picked a live frog out of a glass tank that had been empty up to this point in the year. "Here's how you pith one." She proceeded to demonstrate: holding the frog in one hand and a long pin glued into a wooden handle in the other, she stuck the pin down the back of the wriggling frog's neck and straight through its spinal column, stirred the pin as if it were a straw in a milkshake. The frog went limp. "See?" She then laid the frog on its back on a waxy tray, stuck push-pins through its wrists and ankles, and sliced open its belly. "It can't feel a thing because I've destroyed its central nervous system with the pin. We can see the heart pumping, the blood flowing, everything. How cool is that?"

Jake was horrified. What if he didn't get the pin perfectly down the frog's spinal column to destroy its nervous system? Then he'd be inflicting excruciating agony.

Skinny Marie, at the lab table to Jake's left, giggled uncomfortably, and Harold on his right looked like he was going to upchuck through his braces any minute.

Ms. Hodges handed each student a frog, which they held in their left gloved hands as instructed. They lifted the wood-handled pins in their right hands. After whispering a prayer of apology (at least Jake did), they simultaneously thrust pins down the center of their frogs' backs and jiggered. Jake's frog went limp in his hand. He breathed a sigh of relief because limpness indicated that the nervous system connection between spine and rest of body had indeed been severed. His victim truly wouldn't feel a thing.

He laid the frog on its back on the waxy tray, dutifully pierced wrists and ankles with pins. As did Harold on his right with his frog, as did Marie on his left with hers. Then, following further instructions, they slit open the skin of their frogs' bellies, making two horizontal cuts connected by a vertical one, like a sideways letter "H," so they could open the abdominal skin flaps and look inside. Everything was going smoothly until Marie screamed.

Jake looked over.

Her frog, its abdomen having been slit open, was yanking out the pins holding down its left wrist and ankle. Ms. Hodges ran over, scissors in hand, stuck one blade of the scissors through the frog's mouth and the other onto its skull, squeezed hard through bone, and cut the frog's head off. Crunch crunch crunch. "You didn't pith it right," she explained to Marie. Ms. Hodges was sweating like crazy and her black eye liner was running down her cheeks, making her look as if she were crying ink. "Its nervous system was still intact, and it was feeling everything."

"Oh," was Marie's only reaction.

Ms. Hodges ran to the sink at the back of the room, spit up.

Jake's mouth dropped in a silent scream. Marie's frog had felt everything—the pin down its back, the pin crucifixions into its wrists and ankles? THE SLICES INTO ITS ABDOMEN?

Jake stopped breathing. He'd been complicit. He wanted to flee the room, the school, the planet. Come to think of it: even if his own frog didn't feel physical pain, wouldn't it be aware that some monster had numbed its body, was now poking around in it while the frog was paralyzed and unable to flee? Wouldn't it be terrified out of its mind?

Quietly, Jake stood and, saying not a single word, left the class and the school, walked the forty-five minutes home, explained tearily to Mom. Mom and Dad both wrote notes to Ms. Hodges asking for Jake to be excused from the final project. Without objection, Ms. Hodges permitted Jake to write a report about amphibian anatomy instead.

That was when Jake decided not to go to medical school, but to law school.

"Why would you think we're going to kill the pigeons?" It was Fernando, the TA. Jake shook his head to erase the high school frog memory.

"We won't even touch them," Fernando continued. "Our treatment will be totally humane. We're going to observe how they learn."

The first two weeks, their lab work involved positive reinforcement, their goal being to teach each caged pigeon to peck at a green tab instead of a red one. Jake didn't like experimenting on caged pigeons at all, but at least if his pecked a green tab, Jake would reward it with a food pellet. The pigeon—Jake secretly nicknamed him Pecker—received no reward for pecking the red tab. Clever experiment, thought Jake, and all he was doing was feeding a pigeon and teaching him something.

But then began a negative reinforcement experiment requiring Jake to give Pecker an electric shock each time he pecked the very same green tab. And no food. Now, only when Pecker pecked the red tab would he receive a food pellet. This struck Jake as inherently unfair. "First we reward him for doing something and then we punish him for doing the very same thing?" he asked Fernando.

"Yep, that's the experiment. To see how they'll react."

Jake looked around the room for support, but none of his fellow students seemed perturbed.

"But electric shocks—that's cruel," said Jake.

"Nah, they're nothing, very mild."

If the shocks were nothing, then how could they be effective in the first place?

Jake performed the experiment, cringed each time Pecker leapt backward after receiving an electric shock. How could Jake do that to him? "Could I just write up a paper speculating on various possible experimental outcomes?" asked Jake.

"The experiment and lab report are your mid-term. You don't complete both—you get a failing midterm grade," replied Fernando. "Your choice."

The next couple weeks, Jake participated, hating himself each time he pressed the shock button and watched Pecker recoil. Finally, Pecker figured out that he now needed to avoid the green tab and peck at the red tab in order to earn food. Jake sighed relief.

Then, the Wednesday before midterm week, came the last experiment, when they changed procedures yet again in order to explore the effects of random reinforcement, both positive and negative: Jake had to reward Pecker with a food pellet randomly, now after pecking the red tab, now after pecking the green; likewise, he had to shock Pecker randomly, now after he pecked the green tab, now after he pecked the red. In other words, Pecker was expected to disregard all prior learning, never knowing whether he would receive food or shock no matter what he did.

After an hour of receiving random rewards and shocks, Pecker stood stock still, stepped away from the red and green tabs, began twirling in circles, his eyes rolling around in his head.

"Shit!" exclaimed Fernando. "He's having a nervous breakdown."

"I've completed the experiment and will turn in the lab report next week on time," declared Jake, yanking his jeans jacket on, picking up his backpack of books, and storming out of Green Hall, across Washington Road, down the path between Firestone Library and the neo-Gothic chapel. He strode across campus to his dorm room, dumped his backpack, climbed face down onto his upper bunk, covered head with pillow, pounded his bed and yelled, "Fucking goddamn fuck fuck!" over and over and over until, eventually, he exhausted himself and drifted to sleep.

"Hey, Jake, it's dinner time."

What? Jake tugged off the pillow. It was Ted.

"Want to come to dinner with Sheldon and me?"

Jake wasn't hungry, but didn't wish to be alone.

The three walked to Commons. At the serving line just inside the enormous vault-ceilinged, brown wainscoted hall, Ted and Sheldon each took servings of minute steak and mashed potatoes. Jake took just the potatoes, then fixed himself a large salad at the salad bar.

He followed Sheldon and Ted to empty spots at one of the dozens of long, dark brown wooden tables filling the hall in two parallel sets of evenly spaced rows. "The tables look like train tracks," said Jake. "Tracks of railroad ties without the rails."

"Cool imagination," said Sheldon, pulling out a heavy, brown wooden chair opposite Jake. "No meat?"

"You know he can't because it's not kosher," said Ted, taking the chair beside Jake. "He's religious, remember? How much did you smoke today?"

"Every man's gotta do his own thing," Sheldon replied, shoving an extra large slice of rare steak into his mouth. "Hey, Ted, did you get a load of what the TA was wearing today?"

Amid the din of the filled dining hall, the two of them chatted about her while Jake's mind drifted back to the experiment.

"Hey, you okay?" asked Ted.

"Yeah, sure," Jake said.

"Your face is all scrunched like you're upset."

"It's my damn psych lab." Jake explained the experiment and Pecker's reaction.

"Sounds kind of Nazi," said Sheldon.

"Exactly," said Jake. "How can we do that to an innocent animal?"

Ted reached his arm around Jake's shoulders and gave a little squeeze. "Just be glad it's over. Maybe you could write an ethics section into the lab report. Sort of a protest."

Jake loved that idea, but while Ted elaborated about what Jake could write, all Jake could think about was the feel of Ted's arm around his shoulder. Jake leaned to his side a bit, as if preparing to rest his shoulder in the crook of Ted's arm and his head on Ted's shoulder. But he caught himself—of course Ted wasn't giving him *that* kind of hug!

Jake leaned forward over his plate so that Ted's arm would naturally slide off. Obviously, Jake couldn't trust himself around Ted because he was growing to like him too much.

After dinner, back in their dorm room, Jake picked up his backpack and headed off to the library. He left Ted and Sheldon to their evening smoke.

The following day, Friday, Jake spent the afternoon alone in his room typing up his psych lab report mid-term. As Ted had suggested, Jake inserted final paragraphs of protest:

> Having completed the assigned lab, I must in good conscience protest the experiment. The positive reinforcement section — rewarding a pigeon with food — is not problematic (unless one finds caging animals and using them to advance scientific knowledge as problematic under all circumstances). However, shocking a pigeon — inflicting pain upon it — is inhumane. The final phase of the experiment — randomly inflicting electric shocks in a process that undermined all that my pigeon had been learning — distressed my pigeon to such an extent that he suffered a nervous breakdown. This constitutes out-and-out cruelty.
>
> Why does a pigeon, or any other of God's creatures (or "living being" if "God's creatures" is too unscientific a phrase) deserve to suffer for the sake of human knowledge? What right do humans have

to hurt less intelligent species? Yes, we kill animals in order to eat them and survive, but there's a difference between humane killing (e.g., kosher butchering) and torturing an animal by inflicting electric shocks to satisfy our own intellectual curiosity. At the very least, if one deems such experiments absolutely necessary in order to further human medical knowledge, then such experiments should be conducted only by graduate students pursuing careers as researchers or therapists working to help humankind. There's no reason for pigeons to suffer in order to teach undergrads like me, who are taking the class merely to fulfill a science course requirement.

Rereading the text, Jake felt a modest easing of guilt.

5:00—time to rush to Commons just after it opened. Without even removing his brown, hooded Mighty Mac coat, he sat by himself in a far corner of the hall, gobbled a meal of fish and chips. Thank goodness they served fish on Fridays, the only dinner during the week when Jake got to eat protein other than processed cheese shreds, peanut butter, or eggs.

From Commons, he strode down University Place in the cold drizzle, passed his dorm and a couple other gray neo-Gothic ones, then the white triangular columns rising like irradiated versions of Lego construction—Spelman dorms. Across the street, McCarter Theatre loomed like a large and brooding conscience.

Jake continued past the stone-fronted Dinky station—glancing into the huge filthy windows, he saw a few commuters sitting on the long benches—and went into the Wawa convenience store where he bought a fresh box of Entenmann's chocolate chip cookies, a large box to last the whole weekend. He hastened back up the street, noticed a bearded man in a forest-green parka standing outside the Dinky station, but not on the platform behind it; rather, the man was hovering by the outdoor entrance to the men's room. Must be waiting for a friend in there. Unless... unless that rumor Sheldon had mentioned weeks back about men meeting for sex there.... No, that was crazy. Jake had been in the Dinky station to use the telephone and there was no place to have sex—it was one big open cave-like room. Where would men do it, on the train tracks? That Sheldon was a nutcase.

In his room, Jake hung his drizzle-damp coat on the back of his wooden desk chair, set the box of Entenmann's on his desk corner for the positive-reinforcement study program he'd concocted for himself: each time he finished redoing a week's worth of Russian exercises, he'd reward himself with two chocolate chip cookies. That way, he (a) would have something to look forward to all evening, (b) would take in enough sugar to keep himself alert for studying, (c) wouldn't grow hungry during the evening, (d) would have built-in study breaks, which were important for maximizing efficiency, and (e) would show solidarity with Pecker, the pigeon he'd driven insane.

Jake figured he'd have the room to himself all evening because Ted and Sheldon typically went to dinner around 6:00, and then, according to Ted, they were going to see some movie on campus. Jake opened his purple-covered Russian textbook. Only this weekend before the Russian midterm and Jake still found the noun case endings confusing: three genders, six cases...how on Earth could anyone keep all the noun endings straight? Book...*kniga*. I read the book...*knigu*. To the book...*knige*. In the book...*v knige*. Of the book...*knigi*. With the book...*c knigoi*. That was a feminine noun. Then there were masculine nouns. And neuter ones. And plurals. And adjectives. And verb declensions. And all the vocabulary. And everything was written in this crazy alphabet Jake still had trouble reading and pronouncing.

"Practice practice practice," Mrs. Polenko had said earlier today. "Only way to prepare for midterm—practice. Practice when in class, practice when walking to class, practice when eating, practice when sleeping. One hundred times—repeat every word and grammar exercise. One hundred times. Practice practice practice. You are babies learning to speak."

Jake couldn't practice everything one hundred times, but he'd do it as many repetitions as he could. He'd devote the entire weekend to Russian. Only after Monday's exam would he start studying for his econ and international relations exams by reviewing all the lecture notes and underlinings in the books he'd read.

His review of Chapter 1 went well—he remembered all the new vocabulary, and the grammar exercises were simple. Study break of two chocolate cookies.

Just as Jake started in on Chapter 2, Ted and Sheldon walkd in.

"Hey, Jakeroo," said Sheldon.

"Hi. You guys back from dinner so soon?"

"I hate fish," said Sheldon. "We took the burger option, but they ran out of fries, can you believe it? So I shouted 'Down with common Commons!'"

"And I hustled him out of there," said Ted. "Seemed like a good idea to leave before they called the proctors on us."

"If you're hungry, you could have a couple cookies," said Jake, shutting his Russian book and slipping it into his backpack.

"You don't have to leave just because we're here," said Ted.

"That's okay. I was getting ready to go to Firestone anyway."

"Sure you don't want to come see *Cabaret* with us? It starts in an hour."

"No. Too much studying to do." Jake pulled on his coat, took his backpack and umbrella, and left.

Damn. The drizzle had switched to cold rain. He zipped his coat higher to his neck. Dark now. Jake sloshed through puddles and small piles of brown wet fallen leaves. Inside Firestone Library, he heard a light hum of conversation that he wasn't accustomed to. He walked down to A-floor, the Reserve room where professors placed special books students could check out for a couple hours and read right there. That was a cozy study space, well-lit with lots of carrels. Jake walked to the far end of the room where he usually sat. Every carrel was occupied.

Jake checked out the library's upper floors, but each carrel up there was occupied, too. He then walked down to underground B-floor and C-floor, snaking through stacks he'd never before visited, discovered carrels in corners and along walls—wow, he thought, these are great for studying, so secluded. But none were vacant. He couldn't find a single vacant study carrel anywhere in the library.

Midterms.

He looked at his watch. He'd now wasted a full forty-five minutes that he should have spent studying. Well, if he returned to his room now, Ted and Sheldon would be gone, off to the movie.

Back across campus.

As he approached his dorm room, he shook his head and thought, no, please don't let that pot smoke be coming from my room.

He opened the door. The room stank.

Ted and Sheldon were sitting on Ted's bed, smoking and giggling.

"Aren't you going to be late for the movie?" asked Jake.

"Who wants to see a bunch of Nazis?" said Sheldon. "And I hear one of the characters in that film is queer. I don't need to see that shit. Have a puff." Sheldon held out a half-smoked joint.

Ted took it from him. "Cut it out. You know Jake doesn't smoke."

"Thanks for the cookies," said Sheldon, pointing his chin to the empty Entenmann's box on Jake's desk.

"You ate them all?" asked Jake.

"Sorry," said Ted, looking down sheepishly.

"You know how it is, man," said Sheldon. "The munchies."

"But, all of them? I said you could have *a couple*. You ate all of them?"

"Hey, man, chill. They're just cookies."

"They were *my* cookies. Mine. You had no right to eat them all. You, you potheads!"

Jake spun and left, slamming the door behind him. He stormed to University Place, heading back down toward Wawa to buy another box of cookies, one he'd eat all by himself. In fact, he'd buy two boxes and hide one in his dresser drawer beneath his underwear.

Then what was he going to do? He had to study.

Where could he study? Not on any bench under a street lamp somewhere because of the rain. And now a cold wind was kicking up. Firestone Library didn't have a single free space. His room was not an option. What was he to do? Where could he go?

As he passed the Dinky station, he again glanced through the tall grimy windows. This time, he didn't see anyone. A huge empty room. Maybe there weren't any more trains this late, so nobody was there. That was it—this was where he could study, right in the Dinky station. Plus there was a men's room outside if he needed it. The perfect place to study. He'd buy cookies afterward, as a reward.

He pulled open the heavy door and stepped inside, folded his umbrella. The room wasn't heated, but at least it was dry and shielded from the wind. Okay. After having wasted an hour and a half, he could now sit and study undisturbed for hours. Unzipping his brown Mighty Mac coat, he sat at the end of a long wooden bench facing the trackside windows, dropped his umbrella onto the floor, opened the purple Russian book on his lap. The bench felt hard against back and thighs—the discomfort would keep him alert, as would the chill. He blew on his fingers, examined sample declensions of masculine nouns, now and then looking up away from the book to mumble aloud and test himself.

Two pages in, when he looked up, he gave a start: through one of the large grimy windows, Jake spotted the bearded man he'd seen standing outside the men's room earlier in the evening. In a forest-green parka. Standing on the platform. Looking in through the window. Looking directly at Jake.

Their eyes met.

Jake glanced quickly down at his book, but couldn't read what now appeared to be one big blur. His stomach clutched and his breathing nearly halted. Streams of perspiration jetted out under his arms. He looked up to see the bearded man pacing back and forth in front of the large window, all the while peering in. At Jake.

Jake was there to study, he reminded himself, that's all, just to study. Nothing wrong with finding a quiet place to study. Admirable, in fact. None of his business if some guy wanted to hang out at the train station when it seemed too late for any trains to show up.

With peripheral vision, Jake saw the man open the station door and step inside.

Oh no, thought Jake. Oh no. Please, God, don't let him walk over to me. Please God, let him walk over to me.

Jake continued staring down at his book. Down at his book. If he stared hard enough down at his book, the man would go away. But if Jake stared hard enough down at his book...the man would go away.

Jake looked up.

The bearded man approached, stood directly in front of Jake, unzipped his parka, rocked back and forth, his jeans-covered crotch mere inches from Jake's face. Looking straight ahead, Jake stared at the man's bulge. Jake lifted his eyes. The man was probably in his mid-twenties, thin, bearded, acne-pocked cheeks, but not unattractive. Continuing to rock back and forth, to bring his bulging crotch closer to Jake's face, the man asked, "Watcha up to?"

"Studying Russian." Jake held up his book as proof of innocence, and to serve as barrier between Jake's face and the man's crotch.

The man sat beside Jake on the bench, close enough so his thigh touched Jake's. "Let's see your book," he said and grabbed it, lifting it off Jake's lap, setting it on the bench on his other side. "Now," said the man, staring at Jake's crotch, "I get a clearer view of the scenery." This wasn't happening. This couldn't be happening. This was impossible. Things like this just didn't happen. The stranger reached over and cupped Jake's crotch. "Want some?" he asked.

"Sure." Who said that? Had Jake said that? What was he telling this man he wanted?

You know, Jake heard God say.

'No, I don't,' Jake silently replied.

Get out of here now, before you do something you'll regret.

'I don't know what You're talking about,' answered Jake.

"The men's room entrance is outside," said the bearded stranger. "But that's locked at night. The ladies' room entrance is indoors and open." He gestured his nose toward a side of the waiting room with a sign marked "Ladies."

A ladies' room? Jake had never been in a ladies' room, except maybe as a toddler with Mom. He didn't belong in a ladies' room. Jake was a man. He was. A man a man a man.

He wanted to dart away like the cartoon Road Runner, leaving nothing in his wake but dust. He wanted to flee to his dorm room, climb into his upper bunk, cover his head with the blanket and not peep out all weekend.

But Jake didn't flee. Instead, he followed the bearded stranger into the gray-painted ladies' room. "We can't turn on the lights," the man said, "because the police might see and investigate."

Even if Jake slipped through a policeman's grasp and escaped
scoldings, handcuffs, maybe even a pistol-whipping—he'd left
his Russian book on the bench. What if the police kept it for
evidence? It had all Jake's notes. He'd fail his midterm for sure.
And he'd written his name on the inside cover, so the police
would surely find him. Jake would flunk out *and* go to prison
at the same time.

This stranger led him into a stall and latched the door.

Are you really doing this? Jake heard God's voice in his head.
Really?

'Shut up,' Jake thought. 'Just leave me alone.'

Inhaling the stale urine air, Jake looked up at the man, a few
inches taller than him. The man grabbed Jake's shoulders, pressed
his lips to Jake's and shoved his tongue into Jake's mouth.

Smelling the beard's rainy evening dampness, Jake shut his eyes,
his lips surrounded this stranger's tongue, automatically sucked it
in. Jake felt chills run throughout him. How good the man's strong
tongue felt in Jake's mouth, how good it tasted—minty.

The man's tongue swirled beneath Jake's upper lip, tingled his
gums, filled his mouth as it probed. Jake liked the feel of the soft
bristly mustache. Jake's arms reached around the man and Jake
pictured Dad walking in, standing just behind the bearded man,
peering over his left shoulder. Was that a smile because Dad's boy
was finally about to experience adult sex and become a man? No,
Dad was shaking his head, hanging it in shame.

The guy yanked off Jake's Mighty Mac and tugged Jake's blue
flannel shirttails out of his jeans, unbuttoned Jake's shirt. He ran
his hands up and down Jake's chest.

The man's hands were icy cold. Jake shivered.

The man sucked on Jake's nipples.

Jake murmured at this new sensation. "Oh."

The man bit Jake's nipples, and Jake jerked back in pain.

The man undid Jake's belt and zipper, shoved his pants down, crouched and took Jake into his mouth. The sparks and shivers felt even better than when Dave had done that to him nearly a year ago. Jake concentrated on the sensation, the trembling of his thighs, the tightening of every muscle in his body. Despite his efforts to be silent, an "Ahhh!" shot from his mouth as he fell back against the plastic stall wall.

The man swallowed, licked his lips, stood, dropped his own pants, grabbed Jake's shoulders, shoved Jake down to his knees, rubbed Jake's face against him. The man's pubic hairs tickled Jake's nose. Jake smelled Dial soap, and as he did his awkward best to return the rendered favor, he kept picturing Dad beside them there in the stall—eyes bugging out, fist beating against chest in High Holiday repentance prayer ritual while muttering, "*Ashamnu, bagadnu*" "We have sinned, we have betrayed…"

After the man spasmed, Jake coughed, coughed again, spat the lightly salty mouthful into his fist as discreetly as he could, wiped palm against jeans, stood.

They zipped up. Jake buttoned and tucked in his shirt, suddenly feeling the cold.

"I want to see you again," said the man.

"Um, I'm not sure."

"That's what all you students say."

All us students?

"Let me check no one's out front," said the man, exiting the stall, stepping to the ladies' room door and poking his head out. "Oh, my God!" he exclaimed. "A fat lady in a red dress is heading right toward the ladies' room!"

Jake's face twisted into all the horror he felt at that moment.

The man laughed. "Gotcha!"

Jake rushed past him out of the ladies' room, grabbed his Russian book and umbrella, jogged, under what was now a heavy rain, back to the dorm.

Ted wasn't there, thank goodness.

Jake stripped, pulled on his terry-cloth bathrobe, hurried to the men's room, brushed his teeth twice with globs of Crest, gargled over and over with Scope, then showered and scrubbed. Back in his room, he slipped into his flannel pajamas, climbed up into bed where he lay picturing what he'd just experienced, alternately enjoying the memory and cringing at his own enjoyment. *Is this whom you've become?* he heard God ask. *Someone who has sex with strangers in public toilets?*

Maybe Jake didn't belong kneeling *beside* a toilet but actually *in* one. Maybe he deserved to be flushed away with other pieces of shit.

After tossing and turning all night, Jake woke in the morning to see that Ted's bunk had not been slept in.

Jake washed, then davened the *Shabbes* morning service, added High Holiday prayers of atonement as well as promises to God that he would never ever again do anything as disgusting as what he'd done the night before. And he asked God's help on his midterms, "because I know that no matter how much I study, it's up to You whether or not I do well on the exams."

We'll see, came God's reply.

Jake took his backpack to Commons and scarfed a breakfast of eggs, toast, and potatoes, then walked through the sunny, post-rain blue-sky campus and reached Firestone Library by 8:00 AM, just as the heavyset guard in crisp blue shirt and navy-blue pants unlocked the glass doors. Jake was the first to enter.

He descended to C-floor, the lowest of the three underground levels, to a row of secluded wooden carrels he'd noticed the evening before, as far from elevators and stairs as possible, extremely quiet. He found himself with an abundance of study spots to choose from. Was this God's response to Jake's remorseful atonement?

Jake selected a carrel at the row's far end, beside a door marked "Electrical Utility Room." Setting his Russian textbook on the desk, Jake read the various graffiti scrawled onto the carrel sides with sharp-nosed pens. One line in particular stood out, a plea: "Dear God, why can't I be the best *something* here at Princeton?" Exactly, thought Jake.

As he tested himself on vocabulary lists in Chapters 1 and 2, his mind started drifting to the prior night's experiences.

No!

It was a mistake, a terrible mistake. Lesson learned. No need to dwell on it. He wouldn't think about the softness of the stranger's beard brushing his upper lip.

He wouldn't think about the warm fullness of the stranger's tongue in his mouth.

He wouldn't think about—no! No no no!

He forced himself to concentrate on vocabulary…

…until he began picturing the stranger dropping to his knees—the man's cute little bald spot that Jake hadn't noticed but remembered now. And the shockingly wonderful sensation of being taken deeply into the stranger's warm wet mouth. How amazing that was, the man's tongue, the feel of the stranger filling Jake's own mouth…how incredi—No! Stop!

Studying was impossible, so he got up and took to wandering the stacks, distracting himself with eighteenth-century diaries in heavy leather bindings. Here he was, in one of the world's greatest university libraries with books on nearly every subject, yet he hadn't taken advantage of it. Any subject he wanted to learn about was right here at his fingertips for gosh sakes, any subject at all, like…. Why hadn't this occurred to him before?

He knew he shouldn't spend time doing personal research now, but he wasn't fully in the frame of mind for studying, so he might as well do something productive, right? And if he found a book that provided answers, he'd be able to relax more and focus on his actual studies.

So, he darted two flights upstairs, forced himself to walk casually into the main floor's card catalogue room with all those cabinets holding seemingly hundreds of drawers. He sauntered to the "H" section, glanced around to make certain nobody was observing him, then found the "Ho" drawer, opened it, and sifted through the index cards. Not a lot of listings, but a good half-dozen with disparate Dewey Decimal System classification numbers. Jake memorized the first two call numbers, shut the drawer and sauntered down one flight.

He hunted through the stacks until he found the first section of noted books, those categorized as 132.2 with titles like *Mental Derangements, Psychopathic Behaviors*, and *The Criminally Insane*. No, those books wouldn't hold any of the answers he was seeking. He moved on to the 159.9's with books like *Abnormal Psychology* and *Perverse Sexual Behaviors*. Quickly scanning two chapters of the latter book, Jake learned how typical it was for homosexuals to tryst in furtive places like men's rooms. That meant Jake's experience at the Dinky station was actually typical. He felt momentary relief that at least he'd engaged in aberrant behavior in the normal way. At least *something* about him was normal, even if it was his perversion.

But did this mean he'd have to spend his life having sex in public restrooms?

He continued reading: "Homosexuals are hopeless narcissists incapable of love." That couldn't possibly describe Jake because he was capable of love. Hadn't he felt love for Steve? Did this mean that Jake was not a true homosexual? That there was hope for him? Or was he an aberration among aberrations—the only homosexual actually capable of love? How strange was he?

He pulled out *Guide to Treating the Sexually Perverse*, and flipped through. His skin crawled as he read about psychiatric treatments "to cure homosexuals" by means of electroshock therapy to the brain. And lobotomies whereby part of the brain was cut. He snapped the book shut. He couldn't bear reading details. He slipped the book back into its place on the shelf, picturing himself in a mad scientist's laboratory, harnessed onto a metal table by leather straps holding down ankles, wrists, and waist. Some cackling nurse with an evil grin walks in and attaches electrodes to his forehead and temples, then shoves a mouth guard into his mouth so he won't swallow his own tongue during convulsions. A Dr. Frankenstein-wannabe rubs palms together and flips a giant wall switch, sending lightning-like bolts of electricity zig-zagging around the room and into Jake's head where they sizzle, sending smoke to the ceiling. Or the doctor withdraws an enormous needle from a tool chest, lances it through one of Jake's temples and rattles it around the way Jake had pithed the frog's spinal column. Jake will be a zombie with no will of his own.

Was this what lay in store for him? Genuinely frightened, he returned to his carrel, packed up, and went for an early dinner at Commons to clear his head. After finishing his salad and rolls, just as he was heading out of the dining hall, he literally bumped into Ted, who was about to walk in with Sheldon. "Sorry," mumbled Jake.

"No, *I'm* sorry," said Ted, looking into Jake's eyes. Ted clasped a hand on Jake's shoulder. "Really sorry for eating all your cookies last night."

How good that hand felt on Jake's shoulder, radiating warmth throughout his chest. Jake needed that warmth right then, that gesture of normal friendship. "No big deal," Jake said, meaning it, "just cookies. Sorry I overreacted. Stress, I guess."

"And we were stoned." With a wry smile, Ted added, "We should have left you at least one cookie."

Jake grinned back.

They shook hands—how firm Ted's handshake was, thought Jake—and continued smiling.

"Hey, lovebirds, I'm famished," interrupted Sheldon.

Jake yanked his hand to his side. "So, I'll see you in the room tonight?" Jake asked.

"Yeah, I was too embarrassed to see you last night. Crashed on Sheldon's floor."

"Crashed is the right word," Sheldon added. "Can you say te-qui-la?"

"Shut up, dufus." To Jake, Ted said, "I'll see you later. I'm hoping this one here—" Ted pointed his elbow at Sheldon, "—lets me actually get some studying done for Monday morning's Arabic midterm."

On his way back to Firestone Library, Jake felt a lightness in his chest. Maybe things would work out, after all. He had a normal friend in Ted. Jake wouldn't give in to that abnormal behavior garbage. He had self-discipline. He'd be okay.

He held a good study session all evening, his mind drifting only to the friendly interaction with Ted. The shoulder clasp. Their handshake. Their shared smiles.

/ /

The next morning, Sunday, he saw that Ted's blanket had fallen off. How innocent and childlike Ted looked there curled up on his side in t-shirt and sweatpants, fine brown hair strewn over his forehead, his thick lower lip moist with a thin coating of drool. Jake covered him gently, so as not to wake him, then left to go study.

Jake might not get the best grades, but he was showing God his efforts to be a decent friend and a good student. To do the right thing.

Late Sunday night, Jake returned to his room from the library to find Ted lying naked—completely naked—half in his bed and half out: apparently, he'd been sitting and then just keeled over, falling back onto the bed while his thighs and bent knees remained jutted off the edge, propped up by feet planted firmly on the floor. An empty tequila bottle remained clutched in Ted's hand.

Never before had Jake seen Ted completely naked. How beautiful his hairless, muscular chest and small nipples, lean waist, fuzzy brown pubic hair and thick...thick and long...with those big spherical...

Jake felt nearly overwhelming desire to drop to his knees and gently take Ted into his mouth. Maybe Ted was so drunk he wouldn't notice?

Are you out of your mind? resounded God's voice in Jake's head. *Just this morning you covered your friend, but now you would take advantage of him?*

Jake shut his eyes, gulped his own saliva, swallowing his desire.

Jake pulled the crumpled red blanket off the foot of the bed, and with lips pressed tightly together, he lifted Ted's naked legs onto the bed. Not a murmur from Ted. Jake covered him with the blanket, pried the tequila bottle loose from his hand and set it on the floor.

Then Jake went to the men's room and showered, returned and changed into his pajamas, climbed to his upper bunk, and set his alarm clock for the usual 6:00 AM. Both he and Ted had midterms in the morning.

/ /

"Shut that damn alarm, would ya?" mumbled Ted. "My damn head."

Jake jumped off his upper bunk and stood over Ted, who was sitting up now, blanket across his lap, and holding his head. "What happened?" asked Ted.

"I found you passed out naked with the bottle in your hand."

"Naked? You found me naked?"

Jake nodded.

"You didn't molest me, did you?" mumbled Ted with a weak grin.

"Nah," said Jake, controlling both his fear and wishing, "you're not my type."

Ted grinned again. "I feel like shit. I'm going back to sleep."

"Don't you have a midterm this morning?"

"Shit! Of course! Oh, shit. Sheldon said a couple shots would help us concentrate, but a couple led to a couple more and… damn. I didn't study shit. And I feel like shit."

"A shower might help." Jake tossed Ted's robe from the closet and turned his back to give Ted privacy.

Ted donned the robe, opened their dorm door. "Fucking shit!"

Jake spun around and ran over: in the hallway at their threshold lay Sheldon, passed out on his back, his face eggplant purple.

"I bet he took speed to help him study after the Tequila," Ted said. "What do we do?"

Jake dashed to the telephone on his desk, dialed zero for the campus operator. "Our friend's passed out on the hallway floor. His face is purple. Possible drug overdose." Listening to instructions, Jake set down the phone receiver, ran over to Sheldon, checked his pulse, ran back to the phone. "Yes, he's got a pulse." He gave their dorm name and room number, then hung up. "Proctors will be here in a minute," he said.

Two men in ties. Ambulance. Stretcher.

Other students from the dorm hovered outside in the cold with Ted and Jake, everyone shivering in an assortment of pajamas, robes, flip-flops, shoes.

"We'll take him to McCosh Infirmary," stated one of the proctors. "Every exam period, the same damn thing." After climbing into the ambulance beside Sheldon, but before shutting the back doors, he looked out at the crowd of students. "They're just grades, people — nothing to kill yourselves over." Off they went.

Ted gazed after the ambulance careening up University Place. "Should I have gone with him?"

"To do what? He needs doctors now, not friends. You can visit later. Now you've got to take your midterm."

"Fuck it," said Ted, forehead in hand. "How am I supposed to concentrate on an exam now?"

"You've got to. You can do it. You're smart."

Ted looked into Jake's eyes. "Thanks for believing in me."

"Go shower and we'll have breakfast. And lots of coffee."

While Ted showered, Jake put on *tefillin* and *davened*, asking God to take care of Sheldon and help Jake and Ted on their midterms.

You performed a mitzvah this morning, came God's reply, *a very good deed. Maybe you even saved a life. You deserve My help.*

Over breakfast of oatmeal and coffee, Ted asked, "Will you walk me to class? I feel stupid asking, but I'm real shaky and I don't want to turn chickenshit and bail. If you're with me, I'll make it."

"Sure," answered Jake, thrilled at being needed by Ted.

"You're someone I can count on," said Ted between sips of coffee. "Not like Sheldon." Ted nodded to himself as if coming to a realization.

After breakfast, they headed silently in the direction of Jones Hall. On the way, as they reached East Pyne Hall with its intricately ornamented sandstone façade, Ted said, "This is where your Russian exam is; you should stop here. I'll be okay."

"I can walk five minutes out of my way to your building."

Ted nodded.

When they reached Jones Hall, Ted said, "You don't need to go in with me. I'm okay now."

"Sure?"

"Yeah. You really think I can pass?"

"Absolutely."

Ted gave a firm nod and a wave. Jake watched him enter the building, then waited a few minutes to make sure Ted didn't slip out. After all, Ted was counting on him.

J ake felt that his Russian midterm went well, and was ecstatic
when he learned a week later that he'd earned a "B+." He
wasn't flunking out of Princeton! He could do it! Maybe God
really did help those who helped themselves. Maybe all Jake's
davening and other praying had helped. Maybe this was God's
sign that He forgave Jake for...everything.

Ted got a "C" on his Arabic midterm. "I was damn lucky," he
told Jake. "From now on, I want to study like you." Jake received
an "A-" on the econ midterm, "A-" on the international relations
mid-term, and an "A+" on his psych lab report "because of the
quality of your analysis of the experiment as well as your contem-
plation of ethical considerations involved in experimentation on
animals," scribbled the professor on Jake's lab report. "You're the
only one in class to raise ethical concerns."

"You're a star," said Ted while reading those remarks.

"I just said what I thought," replied Jake, "like you encouraged
me to do."

"I went to see Sheldon again today."

"Is he out of his coma?"

"Yeah. But he's gone. His parents transferred him to a hospital
near their home in Connecticut. After talking with one of the

deans, they decided to withdraw him from the university. It was
that or risk getting expelled because he was dealing drugs, too. I
never knew that."

"Wow, I'm really sorry. I'm sure you'll miss him."

"Yeah, but…I'm being selfish, but maybe it's better for me he's
not around anymore."

"I'm here if you get lonely," said Jake, hoping Ted couldn't
detect his burning blush.

"You'll be a good influence."

Next morning, and each morning after that, Ted asked to eat
breakfast with Jake before the two walked off to their respective
language classes together. They looked for one another in Commons at lunchtime on those days when class schedules freed them
at the same time, and again for dinner. Occasionally, a couple of
Ted's friends joined them, but Ted always sat directly beside Jake.
After dinner, the two took to studying quietly together in their dorm
room, each at his own desk on opposite sides of the room. They
went to bed at the same time, both woke at Jake's alarm. On weekends, they walked to Firestone together, Jake studying at "his" carrel
on C-Floor while Ted studied in the Reserve Room on A-Floor "so
I can chat with some friends, but just during study breaks."

After a bit of cajoling—"Your studying will be more effective if
you give your brain a break sometimes"—Ted finally persuaded
Jake to go out with him on Saturday nights; they'd go to a campus
movie together or a student play at Theatre Intime, and then eat
ice cream at the Student Union where some of Ted's friends typically squeezed around their small square table. Everyone took to
asking them which movie or show "you guys saw," just assuming
that Jake and Ted had gone out together.

Ted loved to explore ethical questions with Jake, like whether it
was okay to steal if you didn't get caught. "What difference does it
make if I steal an umbrella from the U-store? They won't miss it."

"Somebody's got to pay for it," argued Jake.

"The corporation that manufactures it—big deal."

"Your stealing would make their costs go up. They'd pay workers less to compensate or raise prices for everyone else. Some poor person who can barely afford an umbrella as it is might be priced out of the market entirely and end up forced to walk in the rain. All because you stole an umbrella."

Ted grinned at that, or rather half-grinned, raising his right cheek higher than his left. He said he loved intellectual sparring, "especially with you because you're so religious, you always find an ethical reason for social rules. I really respect that."

The weeks between midterms and Thanksgiving were the happiest Jake could ever remember.

/ /

During his few days at home during Thanksgiving break, he wondered what time Ted's mother served Thanksgiving dinner, whether Ted preferred white meat or dark, whether Ted was drinking beer with dinner, whether he was using the weekend to catch up on class reading the way Jake was doing and had advised. At night, Jake had difficulty falling asleep alone in his room until he imagined Ted in a bunk below him. Then Jake slept well.

"Missed ya," said Ted when they returned to campus after the four days.

"Same," replied Jake, purposely avoiding Ted's eyes and downplaying his excitement. Their shared routine resumed...

Until two weeks later when, on the way to dinner at Commons,
... Ted said, "This woman keeps coming over to my carrel every
afternoon and interrupting my reading."

"Tell her to stop."

"I would, except she's kind of cute." Ted's face lit up in a grin.
"Long brown hair to her waist. Wide smile. She laughs really
loudly at just about everything I say."

Jake weighed his response carefully. He couldn't very well
express the first thought that came to him — "Tell her not to get any
ideas because you're mine." If Jake tried to prevent Ted from dating
girls, Ted would get suspicious, would stop wanting to eat with him
or do anything with him. Maybe Ted would even move out of their
room. Besides, if he wanted to be a good friend, shouldn't Jake
encourage Ted to live a normal life? Normal meant dating girls.
"Maybe," said Jake, "she keeps bothering you because she likes you."

"You think?"

"Maybe you should ask her to dinner and find out."

"You wouldn't mind if she joined us one night?"

"Joined us?" Jake was surprised to be giving another guy dating
advice. "Listen, dufus," he said, using that affectionate jab for
the first time, "your first dinner invitation should be for just the

two of you. Even I know that. Find a spot in Commons where nobody else is sitting."

Ted patted Jake's back, said, "Thanks, pal."

As they continued walking, Jake's back tingled and his stomach felt hollow.

/ /

First it was just dinner. Then Ted and Nancy went to the movies on a Saturday night.

"I've got lots of reading to catch up on, anyway," said Jake.

"Thanks, pal."

When Ted returned to their room late Saturday night, he talked about how funny Nancy was, how warm and genuine.

"She sounds really great," said Jake, admitting to himself that he'd hoped Ted would tire of her quickly.

"She wants to meet you. I told her how amazingly disciplined you are, with your prayers and studying and everything. She respects that."

"Sounds nice."

"She suggested that she and I study together some evenings. In her room, not here—I told her I'd never interfere with your studying or kick you out of the room."

"Gee, thanks. But, doesn't she have a roommate, too?"

"Her roommate's boyfriend is an upperclassman with a single, so she spends every night in his room. Nancy's alone most of the time."

Jake just nodded, suspecting what was to come.

And he was right: the following Saturday night, Ted didn't return to their room before Jake went to sleep. And when Jake awoke at 6:00 AM on Sunday as usual, Ted wasn't in his bed, which clearly hadn't been slept in.

Jake looked for Ted at Commons for breakfast. No sign of him.

/ /

At lunch, just as Jake was about to set his tray down in an isolated corner spot, he heard Ted call his name. Jake turned to see Ted and a grinning young woman each holding trays. "Can we join you?"

Jake plastered on an immediate smile. "Of course. You must be Nancy. I'm so glad to meet you!"

"Me, too!" While setting her tray down beside Jake's — Ted sat opposite both her and Jake — she said how much she admired him for protesting the unethical treatment of pigeons in his psych class. "When Ted told me that, I knew I'd like you. I work summers in a wholesale pet import store; we sell to pet shops and even small zoos. I get in trouble for letting lovebirds out of their cages." Giggle giggle. "Just to fly around the shop, you know? I feel sad for them being all cooped up."

"Cool," replied Jake. As much as he wanted to dislike her, he couldn't. She was bouncy and friendly, telling stories about chimps reaching through their cage bars to hug her — giggle giggle — about baby leopards loving their tummies stroked — giggle giggle — about flying squirrels gliding around the store "when I let them out of their cages, too." Giggle giggle giggle giggle.

After lunch, she and Ted hugged goodbye. She gave Jake a quick hug, too.

"She's incredibly nice," Jake said on the way to their room.

"I'm glad you like her."

Once inside, Ted sat on his lower bunk and said, "I need to tell you something. I'm kind of worried."

"Tell me."

"You know I didn't come home last night."

"Right."

"I spent the night with Nancy."

"I figured."

"I didn't plan on it. We were kissing, which we've done before, and hugging, but then…we got carried away, and…next thing I know, I was waking up naked beside her."

"That's normal," said Jake, meaning it. Isn't that what normal young men did—sleep naked with girlfriends? If Jake had a girl-friend…that's what he'd do.

"You don't think it's immoral?" asked Ted. "Having sex with someone you don't know really well? I like her a whole lot, more than any other girl I've ever met, but it's not like we're in love. That could happen, but not yet. You're a religious person; what do you think? Did I do a bad thing?"

Ted sounded like a little boy. Yet how well Jake understood the look in Ted's eye, one of worry at having fallen below one's own standards of decency. Jake wanted to blurt out about the Dinky incident, to reassure Ted that whatever Ted did paled in comparison to Jake's immorality. As if it were a competition. As if confessing Jake's own sin would address Ted's worry. As if, after hearing about the Dinky incident, Ted would say something like, "You idiot! If you wanted sex with a man, why didn't you turn to me? I'm right here. I spend every night staring up at your mattress and I just want to climb up there and snuggle close."

If Jake told Ted about his own sex with a stranger, Ted would be disgusted and horrified and surely move out.

"I might be religious," said Jake, "but I'm human, too."

"What are you saying? That you had sex with a woman?"

"I'm just saying I understand the urges. The need. It's over-whelming sometimes."

"Tell me about it."

"It seems to me that sex is normal." Normal sex is normal, he thought, not perverted sex. "As long as you both want to do it, you should. Just remember my father's advice—'Never hurt the girl.'"

"Your father's a wise man, not that I'm surprised. The apple doesn't fall far from the tree."

"Thanks."

Ted still looked worried.

"Is there more?" asked Jake.

"Well…I didn't expect to…to go all the way, so I didn't have… you know."

"Protection?"

"Right."

"And did you…inside her? I'm sorry, that's too personal a question."

"No, it's okay. That's what's worrying me. I can't remember. When I woke up, I couldn't remember if I'd…you know."

"That means you probably did. You probably did…then fell right to sleep."

"Shit."

"She didn't say anything this morning?"

"No. We were both kind of embarrassed. It was the first time for both of us."

How vulnerable Ted seemed at this moment, how trusting. This truly was best-friend conversation. Jake wished he could preserve this closeness forever. "I know it's awkward, but you really should discuss it, the two of you. If *you're* scared, just imagine how *she* feels. Maybe you should call her."

"Now? But I just left her."

"She's probably having an identical conversation with her roommate, except that she might remember what happened and could be super worried. I'll leave the room so you can have privacy."

"No, stay." Ted dialed Nancy's room. She answered. Jake listened as Ted broached the subject, asking if Nancy felt okay about what had happened last night. "I want you to know," said Ted, "that

I really enjoyed it." He gave a nervous laugh. "But we don't have to do that every time we get together. I just like being with you."

Jake gave a thumbs up.

Ted continued, "And in the future...I mean, if you want to and we...do that again—not that we have to—but if we do, I'll bring protection.... Actually, I've been wondering...I know, I guess I just passed out from the total ecstasy of it all." He gave a nervous chuckle. "I figured you might be worried, but listen: just in case...if anything happens...we'll figure it out. Together. I'm not someone who'll just walk away and leave you with a problem. You won't be alone. So don't worry about that, okay?"

What a good man he is, thought Jake. What an incredibly decent guy. No wonder I love him.

Jake caught himself articulating that thought. "No wonder I love him." Love. Yes. Jake couldn't deny it. The feeling Jake had for Ted was precisely that. Love. Nothing else. Way more powerful than what Jake had felt for Steve last year.

Jake's love for Ted would forever remain unrequited, but at least they were friends. At least, for now, they shared a room together, a life together, their deepest secrets. Well...at least Ted was sharing his deepest secrets. Jake would keep his own to himself. Forever.

"Don't cry," Ted said into the phone. "I'm glad you're relieved. But please don't cry. And don't worry. Odds are that nothing'll happen from just one time.... Okay, dinner at 6:00. 'Bye."

After hanging up the telephone, Ted stepped over to Jake and gave him a full body hug for the first time, whispered, "Thanks for encouraging me to talk to her. She's really scared. And thanks for being here."

Jake allowed himself to reach around Ted and return the hug, perhaps the only one they would ever share. He felt the power of Ted's muscular arms around him, the strength of Ted's chest, the boniness of Ted's square chin as it rested on the top of Jake's shoulder, the warmth of Ted's soft breath when repeating his appreciation, the faint herbal fragrance of shampoo on Ted's fine brown hair against Jake's cheek, the light scent of lunch's tuna fish sandwich lingering on Ted's breath. The way Ted whistled a loud "Whew!" after pulling back from that embrace, his "I feel so much better now."

An embrace to last Jake a lifetime.

/ /

Jake felt proud at having been able to help his friend, even though the help led to more evenings of Ted being out with Nancy. The rest of the quarter, any time they coincided at Commons, Ted invited Jake to join them, as did Nancy. Yet as warm as they both were, Jake felt himself an intruder, a proverbial third wheel. Besides, he felt jealous and knew it.

So, whenever possible, he went to Commons just at opening time when few people were there, ate as quickly as he could and rushed out. Or, if unable to get there early, he'd spy where Ted and Nancy were already sitting, then choose a seat as far away as possible, a spot just beyond their line of sight, from where Jake could, if twisting his head around this group of diners and that, catch a glimpse of Ted and see him raise fork to mouth, grin, peck Nancy on the cheek. Occasionally, Ted noticed Jake glance at him and wave him over, but Jake just shook his head, mouthed "thanks," then picked up his tray and left Commons in an exaggerated hurry, as if his refusal to join Ted and Nancy were because of some pressing engagement with a textbook.

At home during the winter break, Jake gorged on Mom's cooking, especially her meat dishes—flanken, roast beef, steaks, burgers, lamb chops, chili, fried chicken, roast turkey. One afternoon, as Mom set a brisket sandwich on the round white kitchen table, she asked, "Don't they feed you at Stevenson Hall?"

Jake didn't want to tell his parents he'd stopped eating there because they'd worry that either he was eating non-kosher food or wasn't getting sufficient nutrition. At the same time, he certainly didn't want to lie. "At Stevenson Hall, they don't cook as well as you do."

"Flatterer." With her back to him as she hand-washed plates at the sink, she added, "I worry about you."

"Why, Mom?" He chomped into the sandwich.

"You seem a little nervous since you came home. I thought I saw it on Thanksgiving, and now I'm sure."

"School's intense, that's for sure. Lots of work, especially with Russian. And finals are after winter break, so I've got tons of studying."

"I don't like all this pressure you're under. Are you doing anything at school besides studying? Maybe you should do something extracurricular."

"No time."

"Like theater. You loved doing theater in high school."

"I said, I don't have time."

"No need to get testy."

With a loud "Mmmm," Jake softened his tone, said, "there's nothing like your brisket."

"It's the onions. I always add lots of extra onions."

"Yes, I remember you telling me once."

Mom dried a couple of dishes. "Are you seeing Deb this break?"

"She and her boyfriend are spending their break in Florida. She sent me a postcard the first day."

"Boyfriend?" Mom said. She turned to face Jake—or was it to observe his face? "Deb has a boyfriend? I'm so sorry."

"Why would you be sorry?"

"Because…weren't you and she sort of…special friends?"

"We're good friends, yes, but that's it. Can't two people be good friends?"

"Of course they can, I just thought—"

"Obviously, you thought wrong."

"Fine, my mistake. There's no need to be rude. Goodness, I forgot the potato salad." Mom pulled a bowl from the refrigerator, scooped a mound onto Jake's plate. "You talk about your classes, but you don't talk about friends."

"I talk about Ted. He and I are friends."

"Of course you are. He sounds like a very nice boy. But what about young ladies? Aren't there any nice young ladies at Princeton?"

Jake wanted to reply, "No. There are no nice young ladies at Princeton. All the young ladies at Princeton are gross, so don't ever ask that stupid question again." Instead, he replied, "There's one really nice girl. But Ted's dating her."

Mom placed hand on hip. "Are you telling me there's only one nice girl in the entire university?"

"You sure have gotten nosy since I've been away."

"Stop being rude, mister." Mom wagged a finger at him. "For seventeen years I knew every single thing about your life, now all of a sudden you're away and I haven't a clue. So you'll forgive my curiosity and put up with a few harmless questions."

"Okay, okay. Ted's girlfriend isn't the only nice young lady in the entire university. But most aren't Jewish, you know. You wouldn't want me dating a non-Jewish girl, would you?"

"That's not at all what I'm suggesting. Don't any nice Jewish girls eat at Stevenson Hall?"

"Sure, Mom. And some of the senior ones are into matchmaking."

"How cute!" Mom grinned broadly. "Have they done any matchmaking for you? Not that I'm being nosy, just curious."

What could he say to make Mom drop the subject without making her suspicious that he wanted her to? "I had a particularly interesting conversation with one freshman girl there named Marla."

"That's a nice name. Where's she from?"

"Main Line Philly."

"The Main Line? Just across the river? We're practically neighbors. If you'd like, your father and I could drive you there this winter break. It wouldn't take but an hour, if that. While you and Marla visit, we could get to know her parents. Better yet, maybe I should invite them all to dinner."

"Mom! *Genug!* Enough!" said Jake, walking over and hugging her. "I said Marla and I had an interesting conversation, that's all."

"Do you have a picture of her?"

"Mom! She and I had *one* conversation!"

"Fine, I'll stop."

He pecked her on the cheek and went upstairs to his room, shut the door.

So, you're lying to your mother now. That was God's voice.

'I didn't lie,' he replied in his head. 'All I said was that Marla and I had a good conversation. That's true.'

You misled. Intentionally. Is this how you obey the Fifth Com-mandment and honor thy father and mother?

'Maybe I've been thinking about dating her but haven't said anything out loud yet.'

This big-deal conversation you had with her—when was that?

'Mid-September.'

And now it's late December. So just when are you planning to ask her out on a date?

'I don't want to pressure her.'

If that's your objective, you're doing a super job.

'I've got studying to do. Leave me alone.'

Just listen how you address Me.

Jake's stomach knotted up. He'd better focus on studying.

Two days after New Year's, Dad drove Jake back to campus for the ten-day reading period, the official study period. Having gotten a head-start during winter break, Jake felt much less pressured than he had before midterms.

Now that Ted was practically living with Nancy, Jake basically had their room to himself.

But soon other students' reading-period tension releases became too distracting: super loud music blaring from the lounge next door and battling with music from half a dozen rooms, clouds of marijuana smoke billowing through the halls, students darting in and out of the dorm slamming doors, whooping and screaming at the top of their lungs. The only calm and quiet place would be the library (or the Dinky station, which Jake ruled out completely).

The first morning he set out before 8:00 AM, his stomach began knotting up the way it had that one day at home. He massaged it while walking. The knotting subsided once he reached "his" carrel on Firestone's C-floor. After a couple hours of studying, the knotting returned, so he stood, hung a left through the stacks, walked past a row of locked cubicles assigned to seniors working on theses, and reached the small men's room he'd found, one with only two sinks, two urinals, two stalls. Private.

While finishing up quietly in a stall, he heard the men's room door creak open. Two pairs of footsteps clomped in and stopped by the two urinals. Jake heard two zippers open. But the sounds that followed were not the expected ones of water splashing onto porcelain. Rather, he heard wet thurping sounds. Grunting. Moaning.

From the limited angle afforded by his frozen-stiff seated position, he could see, beneath the partition, that one man had dropped to his knees. He was wearing black socks and blue suede shoes with black laces. Jake heard slurping and gagging as well as louder moans than before, and then a single, protracted really loud moan.

He couldn't believe it. Right here in a men's room?

What—they should go to a ladies' room maybe like some people have been known to do? Jake heard God echo in a derisive tone.

Blue Shoes stood and Jake heard a spit into a urinal. "Now me." Another knee drop (ordinary black penny loafers), repetition of those sounds except with a slightly higher pitched moan. Another spit into a urinal. Zippers up.

Apparently, it then occurred to one of them to check if anybody were there. A sliver of face peaked through the crack beside Jake's stall door hinges—half an eye, sideburn on smooth cheek, a shock of stringy black hair.

Jake panicked. Would those guys get so angry at his having semi-witnessed them that they'd jump over the plastic stall partition and beat him into silence? His stomach clenched as if he'd been the one doing that dirty, filthy, disgusting, amazingly thrilling deed.

The two darted out of the men's room fast.

Although he wanted to rush out to see the fleeing men's faces, Jake dared not. He sat until the shock glided into fantasy—what if Jake were to find those guys and tell them their secret was safe with him because he was just like them, wanted the same thing,

had even done it once. Yes, he started to picture the conversation
with one of them:

"Hi, are you the guy who likes oral sex in library bathrooms?"

"Why, yes, that's me. Thank you for noticing."

"Those blue suede shoes are hot, especially with those black
laces and your black socks."

"Are you into feet?"

"Not particularly, but I couldn't help noticing those cool shoes."

"What a nice thing to say. How's about I lead you by the hand
into the C-floor men's room and we'll hug and kiss and I'll give
you the best orgasm of your life and then you'll become the man
of my dreams and next year we'll room together, and I'll give you
sex any way you want as many times a day as you want if only
you'll be my secret boyfriend please please please."

/ /

Lonely evening walks through Prospect Garden at the heart
of campus, its evergreen shrubs covered in clumps of wet snow,
pruned rose-bush stalks sticking up like shards of broken bones,
flower beds barren and hard, icy gravel crunching underfoot.
Could just as well be a graveyard as a garden, he thought.

More study alone. Sleep alone. Eat alone.

Day after day. Night after night.

Jake imagined Ted showing up at their dorm room holding
red roses meant for him. "As wonderful as my Nancy is, Jake,
she isn't as amazing as you." Ted spreads his arms, beckons Jake
into an embrace and—*shame! You let your mind wander and look
where it leads.*

His stomach clenched. Was Jake destined to a life of loneliness? In high school he was crazy about Steve, but would never
see him again because Steve was marrying his girlfriend. Now

Ted had found Nancy. They were normal guys, so of course they chose to be with women. Any man to whom Jake would grow attached would leave him for a woman because that was the normal way of things.

I created woman as companion for man, Jake heard echo overhead.

'But…but God—what if I don't want to be with a woman?'

How do you know if you've never tried?

'Most men know they don't want to be with other men even though they've never tried it.'

That's because their desires are normal. Have you ever given a woman a chance?

Jake thought about this. Maybe sex with a woman would be truly wonderful if only he tried it. Maybe all he needed was a good woman's love.

He thought about each of the various women in his classes. None of them appealed. But then he thought about Marla from Stevenson Hall. She'd been pleasant. She'd even kind of suggested meeting at a *Shabbes oneg,* but he never followed up. He wondered if Marla were dating anyone. Or might be interested in giving him a try after all this time.

After finals. After finals, Jake would do himself the favor of asking her out and seeing what would happen. This might be his only chance.

PART 6

Finals went well—challenging, but without surprises. The Monday after, Jake headed to Stevenson Hall for lunch, hoping to run into Marla. Feeling jittery, he massaged his stomach all the way down Prospect Avenue, which was slippery from the morning's light snowfall. He took a few deep breaths at the front door, went in. There she was, alone at a small table, looking pretty, he thought, with her fluffy brown hair and large brown eyes.

After making his way through the food line, he brought his plate of hamburger and fries over to her. "Okay if I join you?"

"Sure." She sat up straighter. "Haven't seen you here for ages."

"Yeah, I've been trying out being vegetarian. They've got a great salad bar at Commons." He took a huge bite of his hamburger.

"Looks like celery sticks left you hungry," she said with a teasing grin.

"I guess I miss a good ol' burger."

"I've been keeping tabs on you, you know," said Marla. "Your roommate's in my Arabic class."

Wow, thought Jake. She's been thinking about him. "Ted's an awfully nice guy."

"He says you're brilliant."

"Me?"

"Ted says you study all the time."

"I guess I do."

"I admire that," she said.

This felt easier than Jake had expected. Marla was really friendly. He remembered her as having been somewhat shy when they first met. Maybe that was just new-freshman nervousness.

They chatted about their fall semesters, about finals. "I could have spent more time with my econ textbook," he said. "But Russian took over."

"Same for me with Arabic."

They moved on to their winter-spring courses, Jake mentioning he had to take the American composition course.

"I'm sure it'll be interesting," she said.

"Do you have to take it?"

She shook her head, munched a fry.

She's too considerate to tell me she placed out of the requirement, Jake thought. That's really nice.

"I asked Ted if you ever take a study break. He said sometimes you go to a play or movie."

Was she hinting about going out with him? Could that be possible?

"I sometimes go see a movie, or a play at Theatre Intime or McCarter Theatre," he replied. "If it's good."

"I like plays and movies, too. But only if they're good."

This was an opening if ever he heard one. "Marla, would you maybe like to go to a play together on Saturday night? If there's a good one at McCarter."

"Sure, I'd like that," she said, setting down her fork, appearing to suppress a grin. "I'd like that a lot."

/ /

Although he tried paying attention to the actors, Jake could focus only on Marla's hand lying unobtrusively on the armrest between them: long graceful fingers, short manicured nails catching an occasional glint of stage-lighting. With peripheral vision, he watched Marla slide her hand forward so it jutted off the armrest's end. Another few minutes into Act I of *The Glass Menagerie*, and she casually pivoted her elbow just a tad; now her hand dangled nearly over his thigh. Jake strained to detect, from the corner of his eye, if Marla were turning her head toward him. No. Not a bit. Was this all his imagination, or was she genuinely hinting for him to take hold of her hand? What was he supposed to do?

During intermission, they stood at their seats, talked about how good the performances were, "Especially the actress playing Laura," said Jake. "She's pretty. But not as pretty as you."

Marla leaned forward and gave him a peck on the cheek. "Sweet talker."

House lights dimmed. They sat as Act II began.

Marla again laid her hand on the armrest between their seats, extended it over the edge, over his knee. Of course she wanted him to take her hand, Jake thought. Of course she did. But should he just reach up and cup it? Should he intertwine fingers? Should he bring her hand over and rest it on his lap? Heavens no, that would be gross, almost like suggesting he wanted her to touch him *there*, which he certainly didn't want her to do. Nor would he rest his hand in her lap because he didn't want her to think he was trying to touch her *there*. She'd haul back and smack him across the face. Right there in the theater. With hundreds of people watching. That'd be awful.

No, he'd have to hold her hand on the armrest. Neutral space. But for how long? Would she expect him to hold it during the entire rest of the play? What if he needed to scratch his nose? Well, he could use his other hand for that. Or what if his hand got hot and sweaty? The theater was awfully warm—way too much heat even though it was early February. He wouldn't want her to feel him all hot and sweaty, that'd be gross. But if he pulled away because he was sweaty, she might misunderstand and think he lost interest in holding her hand, and get offended. Oh, God, what was he to do?

Curtain. Applause.

Whew, all Jake had to do now was use both hands to clap.

As they stepped out of the theater and onto University Place, Jake glanced quickly across the street at the Dinky station. He saw a man hovering outside near the locked men's room. A man with a beard and in a forest-green parka. Yes, it was him, the guy who'd taken Jake into the ladies' room.

"Are you okay?" asked Marla. "You went suddenly pale."

"I'm fine," he said, pulling on the hood of his coat so that, if the man looked over, he wouldn't recognize Jake. "Just cold, that's all."

"We can't have that," said Marla, reaching over and tying the laces on the bottom of his hood. Then she reached into his coat's deep pockets, took out his leather gloves, and slid them first onto one of his hands, then the other, just the way Mom used to do when he was little, the kind of care-taking girlfriends did for their boyfriends. He reached out his gloved hand for hers, which he held tight. And if my hand or hers gets sweaty, he thought, it won't matter because we're wearing gloves.

She lowered her eyes, gripped his hand tight.

They walked a little ways up University Place, then took a side path toward their dorms.

"Did you like the play?" she asked.

"Very interesting. Great blocking. Really good characterizations." Jake said this automatically, not really remembering the play he'd just been pretending to watch, but jumping for joy inside, thinking: I'm holding a girl's hand! I took her hand spontaneously and she held mine back and now I'm walking while holding a girl's hand!

"I've never seen sneakers like yours before," she said, looking down at his purple Keds.

"Me neither. That's why I got them. Great traction on slippery sidewalks, too."

"I like a man who's comfortable being an individual."

Marla was perfect.

When they reached her entryway at Henry Hall, Marla tilted her head slightly up, keeping her eyes fixed on Jake's. She was obviously expecting a kiss. Even he recognized that. Sweat shot out under each of his arms. He'd gone this far, so he could take things the next step. He leaned forward and kissed Marla on her forehead. "I'll call you," he mumbled as he raced away, not even looking to see which expression might be filling her face.

He'd done it. He'd held a girl's hand and given her a kiss. The evening was a total success.

/ /

Lying in bed later, Jake thought: 'I went on a proper date, God. With a nice Jewish girl.'

I saw. You held her hand even. And gave her a Glinda-the-Good-Witch forehead kiss. Very gallant. But you also noticed that horrible man at the Dinky station, didn't you? Did you feel an urge to abandon your young lady and go to him? Drop to your knees in front of him again?

'I didn't abandon her. I didn't go to the Dinky station. I haven't been back there since that one time. Just once. Once!'

So, you enjoyed your date with the young lady?

'Sure I did. She's nice.'

Maybe there's hope for you yet.

Entering Firestone Library's microfilm room, setting his Mighty Mac coat on the back of a study carrel's wooden chair and his backpack on the carrel desk, Jake oriented himself among the open stacks. Mrs. Polenko had assigned them to skim through back issues of the Soviet newspaper *Pravda* to find a few headlines they could understand, and then print them out for class.

Scanning the "P" shelves, Jake immediately noticed...*Playboy*. Hah! Some old letch of a librarian had ordered heaven knows how many years' worth of back issues of *Playboy* with all those photos of nude women. Oh, for the articles, surely. Scholarship, not prurience. Hah hah. Jake nearly laughed out loud at the vision of some sex-starved Ichabod Crane-like professor hunched over a microfilm reader masturbating beneath a carrel desk. Then he noticed something that gave him pause: beside the stack of *Playboy* microfilm boxes stood a solitary white box labeled *Playgirl*.

He'd heard of *Playgirl*, not that he'd ever seen an actual copy, and knew it was supposed to contain pictures of naked men. Standing before that box, Jake looked from side to side—the only other person in the microfilm room was the librarian, a woman Mom's age with black hair pinned against the sides the sides of her head. She was studying something in her office way down near the "A" shelves.

Jake grabbed the *Playgirl* box, opened it, removed the black roll, unfurled the film a good six inches, and held the celluloid up to the ceiling fluorescent lights. Sure enough: chockfull of quarter-page, half-page, full-page photos of nude men. Struggling to catch his breath, he quickly rolled the film tight, inserted it back into its box and, holding it against the side of his thigh, sauntered casually back to his carrel.

Should he do it? He'd never stolen anything before. But this wouldn't be stealing, he reasoned, because he'd certainly return it in a couple days. Wasn't that what a library was for—borrowing materials? And he could skip the official check-out process designed to make sure borrowers returned their materials; after all, Jake fully intended to return the microfilm so why go through the embarrassment of letting some student check-out clerk snicker and then gossip?

Removing gloves from coat pockets, he shoved them into his backpack, then thrust the *Playgirl* box deep inside a newly empty pocket. He slung backpack over shoulder and again sauntered casually, this time out of the microfilm room to the library lobby. Quick glance at the front desk where a small line of students waited to check out books. Jake walked past them and headed directly to the fat bored security guard who'd inspected his backpack a hundred times this year already. Jake opened all the zippers of his backpack, displayed the open sections. The guard nodded, said, "Put on those gloves, it's cold."

"Thanks," said Jake, pulling them out of the backpack and feeling like a criminal.

He zipped the backpack closed, stepped out into the cold late afternoon wind.

He couldn't believe he'd made it.

And he promised himself to return the microfilm in a day or two after examining all the photographs, the only treasure trove of nude men he'd ever likely have the chance to see. He race-clomped through the slush and muck. The instant he shut his dorm room door behind himself, he shed his clothes, climbed into bed, held the microfilm up toward the ceiling light, unfurled the roll with his left hand to examine the stolen booty while putting his right hand to work beneath the covers. Every single one of those gorgeous virile sexy, buck-naked men was smiling directly at him.

After Jake finished, he felt absolutely giddy and ready to start again. He even felt the thrill and joy of his first Dr. Seuss book encounter:

Big chests, tan chests, smooth chests, hairy.

Muscled arms, ripped abs, narrow hips, curvy.

Thick thighs, taut thighs, bubble butts, dimpled.

Big balls, fuzzy balls, long dicks, juicy.

He didn't leave his room for dinner that evening, spent the night in a state of fantasy delirium. The next morning, he skipped breakfast and raced to Firestone to complete his Russian assignment before class. He brought in three *Pravda* headlines, and Mrs. Polenko was pleased. After his day of classes, Jake rushed back to his room to play with his harem of men.

/ /

The following afternoon, Jake's first semester grades arrived in the mail: Russian "A"; Psychology "A+"; International Relations "A-"; Economics "B+". Jake was thrilled.

'Thank you, God, for helping me. I know I couldn't have done so well without You.'

Remember that and behave yourself.

E very night, Jake fantasized about all those *Playgirl* men, but he reminded himself that he was dating a real live woman. Fantasy didn't count; only reality did. Come to think of it, he mustn't forget to call Marla and ask her out on another date.

The semester got off to a good start with his American lit class's opening lecture on Walt Whitman—the professor acknowledged many allusions in Whitman's work to male-male love. The professor even called him, "a great American poet despite his moral failings." Was there a chance Jake could become a great something-or-other despite his own moral failings?

Jake chose to write his first composition about sexual imagery in Herman Melville's novella, *Benito Cereno*. His was an objective analysis including citation of images of men pricking one another with knives. "Interesting," said Jhumpa, the TA in charge of their small group discussion section. From New Delhi, with pointed nose and long, jet-black hair, Jhumpa amazed Jake with her wealthy knowledge of American literature. Speaking from the head of their class's seminar table, she mentioned the examples Jake raised in his paper and asked the group what they thought.

"Really offensive," said Ricky, fingering both her stringy blond ponytail and the huge gold cross over her white, buttoned-to-the-collar blouse. "I can't stand this forced way of reading everything. Just because the professor made that outrageous remark about Walt Whitman, you want to turn every other great author of ours into a homo."

"Now now," said Jhumpa. "One must respect all opinions."

"Including mine," said Ricky. "And the Lord's. An abomination is an abomination."

"Maybe you could write a composition about that topic sometime during the course," suggested Jhumpa.

"Maybe I will. Just maybe I will."

Jhumpa handed Jake's composition back to him, then moved on to discuss the next one in her pile. Jake didn't look up from his notebook the entire rest of the class, slunk out as soon as Jhumpa dismissed them. He hadn't thought of that word Ricky used—abomination—for a while now. The word was so harsh. Besides, his paper was good—Jhumpa had given him an "A" for "creative thinking, abundant textual citations, and clear organization of argument."

After class, Jake headed towards Commons for lunch, but his stomach rumbled so much he hunched over more than usual, felt he couldn't eat, and returned to his dorm room. Inside, in the warmth, he massaged his stomach, picked up the telephone, and dialed. Marla was delighted to hear from him and would love to go to the movies on Friday night. "If there's something good," she said, her voice smiling.

Jake felt better already. Maybe all he needed was the love of a good woman.

/ /

When he stopped by to pick her up on Friday evening after dinner, Marla, in knee-length black wool skirt and loose white sweater, invited him into the suite she shared with two others, a living room and two bedrooms. Whereas Jake and Ted hadn't added any decorations to their room, Marla's living room walls were covered in museum posters from Israel, Greece, and Turkey. Gold and blue striped curtains hung over the window; an over-stuffed gray sofa covered with a rust-colored crocheted blanket dominated the center of the room together with a low wooden coffee table. "Wow," said Jake, "this is really nice. So cozy."

"Glad you like it." She hung his coat on a rack beside the door. "Come." She took his hand, led him to the sofa and sat. Two tall brass candlesticks with *Shabbes* candles in them stood on the coffee table, two filled liqueur glasses at their side. "We already made *Shabbes* at Stevenson, of course, but I thought you might like to do it together before we go to the movies."

"That's really thoughtful," he said, genuinely touched. He hadn't shared making *Shabbes* on campus at all.

She struck a match, lit the candles, covered her eyes, then waved hands gently over the flames, reciting the familiar *brachah*, blessing.

"Have you ever had Greek ouzo? One of my roommates is a Classics major and she spent winter break in Athens. She brought it back. It's made from grapes, so we can say *kiddush* over it. Would you like to?"

"Sure." Jake recited the *kiddush*, the traditional *Shabbes* blessing over wine.

They each took a sip—ugh, anise. Jake hated anise, but he swallowed, disgusting as it was.

"Like it?" she asked.

"It's wonderful." He forced a second sip and got a scary thought: "Gosh, I didn't think to ask—are you okay going to the movies on *Shabbes*?"

"Oh sure, I'm not that religious. I keep kosher and don't work on *Shabbes*, but I use electricity."

"I'm the same."

"Another sip before we go?"

Jake forced himself to take one more sip, as much to bolster his courage as to be polite. Then off they went to see *Harold and Maude*, a big hit a couple years before about a depressed teenage boy who falls in love with a really old woman. During one of Harold's prank suicide attempts (pretend self-immolation), Jake boldly reached over and set his hand atop Marla's. She intertwined their fingers, and Jake sighed, not in excitement, but in relief at having taken another step toward normalcy.

Throughout the movie, he turned his head ever so slightly to see if Marla were looking at him (she was not), but noticed the faintest of smiles on her lips. Maybe she was reacting to the film's irony, but Jake preferred to think she was smiling at holding his hand. He nearly burst with pride. Not only could he could perform heterosexual hand-holding, but he intuitively knew how to do it well enough to please the woman. Without so much as breaking a sweat, he maintained enough stamina to keep up the hand-holding during the entire film, during their entire walk afterward through campus (with gloves on, but still) and during the slow climb up the narrow stairs to her second-floor suite. Maybe there was hope for him, hot hetero stud that he was now turning out to be.

Marla again invited him into her suite. Mysteriously, the candlesticks had been removed from the coffee table and the glasses of ouzo had been refilled.

"I guess one of my roommates expected us to come back," Marla said innocently. "May I take your coat?"

As Jake slid his arms out of his Mighty Mac, his stomach seized with suspicion. Not only was he expected to drink more of that horrible stuff, but clearly Marla's roommate expected something to happen. Had they set him up? Was Marla trying to get him drunk in order to have her way with him?

Marla sat on the sofa, but after lifting his glass, Jake walked across the room and stood with his back stiff against the door. Sofa spelled kissing; hard-wood floor spelled talking. Not questioning him, Marla walked over, clinked glasses. Jake drained the liqueur glass. *Dreck!*

Marla pressed her back against the wall beside him and slid down to the floor, knees up beneath her long black skirt. He slid down too. He spoke about this new concept they were discussing in psych class—the approach-avoidance conflict. "Picture a thirsty dog sitting across the room from a water bowl. He wants the water, but every time he approaches it, he gets an electric shock. He wants to approach, but he's afraid to. A tension with no solution."

Marla listened politely, then said, "It's such a coincidence— both my roommates are spending the night with their boyfriends." She smiled up at him.

An exit cue if ever he heard one.

Jake gave her a quick peck on the cheek and stood. "Gotta hit the library first thing in the morning," he said, grabbing his coat. "Thanks for a really nice evening."

As he was half-way down the hall stairs, Marla called out, "How about *Shabbes* dinner at Stevenson next Friday?"

She wanted to see him again? Even after he was so obviously running out on her implicit invitation to…well, he wasn't exactly sure, but he had ideas. "Uh, sure," he said. "That'll be nice."

As he exited to the courtyard of Henry Hall, he felt even more light-headed than he had during the movie. Must be the ouzo. That goddamn shit. Jake snickered at the foulness of his thoughts. Was this what it was to be drunk? Drunk on a drink he'd said the *kiddush* over. How hilarious was that?! Naughty naughty naughty.

Hey, he thought to himself as he turned right—this isn't the way back to my room. Lockhart Hall's up to the left. If I keep going down this path, I'll end up.... He stopped. He turned around, determined to head back to his dorm, even took a few strides.

Then he turned around again, continued in his original direction.

What are you doing? he heard God ask.

'None of Your fucking business.'

What a horrid pisk *on you, such a foul mouth. I don't know you anymore.*

'Welcome to the goddamn club.'

Jake slowed as he approached the Dinky station. In the shadows, he made out the shape of a man slowly pacing outside the men's room. A familiar, bearded shape in a forest green parka. Was this guy prowling here every damn night?

Taking a deep breath, Jake walked over to him, slurred, "Hi."

"It's you," said the man with a grin. "I wondered if you'd be back for more."

Without responding, Jake walked past the stranger into the Dinky station, checking over his shoulder to make sure the man was following. Jake flung the ladies' room door open, heard it bang against the wall. He stepped into "their" stall. The man followed and shut the stall door. Jake tilted up his head, looked into the man's eyes, opened his mouth, welcomed the man's lips and tongue.

During all Jake's masturbatory fantasies of the microfilm men, he'd never let himself transpose Ted for any of them. But now, tonight, here, as his mind fogged over, Jake imagined himself making love with Ted, thrust his tongue deep into the stranger's mouth, clutched him tight as he could, groped him, moaned aloud, readily dropped to his knees and took Ted deeply inside without hearing God, without picturing Dad, just concentrating on pleasuring Ted and pleasuring himself and giving himself to Ted, proving to Ted that he, Jake, was the one Ted should be coming home to night after night after night, until—

"Whew! That sure was something. You're a real firecracker," said the stranger. "You weren't this good last time—what happened?"

"Ouzo," mumbled Jake, wiping his mouth with the back of his hand, pulling up his jeans.

"Find me again sometime," said the man as he reached around Jake for a goodbye hug.

Jake stood limply in the embrace, said nothing, grabbed his coat and without even putting it on, strode back to his dorm room, allowing the cold to beat against face and chest. Then he stripped, showered, climbed up into bed.

Passed out.

Sunday morning, he woke with a light headache, dry mouth, growling stomach. The big bowl of oatmeal and two cups of coffee at Commons didn't help much, which suited Jake just fine. "I deserve to feel lousy," he mumbled while leaving Commons.

You said it, I didn't, echoed in his head.

He forced himself to go to Firestone where his C-floor carrel was available. He studied an article by a Princeton professor who was completing a book on what he called "the bicameral mind." Some of the hypotheses disturbed Jake, especially speculation that when biblical prophets thought they were hearing God, maybe they were actually hearing one hemisphere of their brain talk to the other hemisphere. Weren't such notions blasphemous? Jake made a note for himself on the top of his Xerox copy: "interesting but not worth dwelling on."

Next, Jake had to start reading a Faulkner novel for English, but needed to use the men's room, so he meandered through the stacks to the small one he always used. As he shoved open the swinging door, he froze, stared for a moment, then backed out.

What? Could he just have seen what he thought he'd seen?: a totally young naked man—lean with straight blond hair, erection in hand—dashed from the urinals into a stall. What had that guy been doing there buck naked with an erection? Masturbating into a urinal? Why on earth would he do that in a public restroom when anyone could walk right in and catch him? Unless—could that be the very point?

Jake told himself he should just walk away. Wasn't it bad enough he'd had sex twice now in a ladies' room at the Dinky station? The last thing he needed to do was pursue the possibility of sex in a library men's room.

But how could he walk away from a naked man exposing an erection? Maybe the guy didn't want anything at all. Maybe Jake was just projecting his own perversions onto the guy. Maybe the guy was heterosexual and standing naked in a men's room exposing his erection for some other perfectly logical reason.

Curiosity killed the cat, Jake told himself.

He swallowed hard and returned to the men's room, gingerly creaked the swinging door open. Nobody at the urinals. Both stall doors were unlocked.

Jake stepped tentatively over to the stalls, tapped a door open and—there the guy was, still completely naked, erection in hand, standing at the back of the stall, shivering, yet smiling. The guy shook his erection at Jake, then raised an eyebrow in question.

What should Jake do? The man was beautiful—tightly muscled, hairless chest, thick huge erection. Right out of the roll of *Playgirl* microfilm. Someone Jake's age, maybe living in a dorm near Jake, maybe even in Jake's own dorm.

Right here now. The guy hadn't latched the stall door closed. Clearly he was inviting Jake to join him. This guy wanted him. A handsome naked erect man wanted him, and there was nothing to stop Jake except his own hesitations. His moral hesitations. His conscience. His certainty of right and wrong. Would God see?

What do you think? Jake heard God say.

Jake stepped into the stall, ogled the naked man up and down, looked straight into the man's now-grinning eyes.

Jake took a step forward, spat a huge gob smack into the young man's face. "Fucking faggot!" Jake yelled. "Goddamn fucking faggot with no self-control, having sex in a public bathroom! You're disgusting. Disgusting!"

Jake stormed out of the stall and men's room, returned to his carrel, stuffed books into backpack, pulled on his coat, ran upstairs to the first floor and, after opening his backpack for the guard, marched outside into the afternoon cold.

An icy wind had kicked up.

Jake zipped his coat closed, pulled on his hood, and instead of walking back to his dorm to study, he walked down Washington Street. He walked and walked. He walked and walked. Walked and walked and walked, circled the entire campus over and over for hours while thinking of Pecker, the caged pigeon he'd driven insane.

In Jake's Thursday English class, as Jhumpa and the dozen other students sat around the seminar table, Jake presented his composition on animal imagery in Faulkner's novel *The Hamlet*. Of course he included a discussion of the love that one of the characters, Ike, felt for a cow.

"What kind of pervert are you?" asked Ricky, the student with the stringy blond hair. "You into bestiality now?"

"It's in the novel," said Jake, blushing deeply. "Right there on the page."

"Leave it to you to focus on something perverted."

"The question is," asked Jhumpa, "why do we think Faulkner included this incident? What does he intend to show by it?"

"That rural hicks are pervs," said Ricky, snickering.

"Might it be possible that Faulkner's depicting an admittedly unusual romantic scenario to illustrate the nature of ordinary human love and desire? This brings us to a discussion of the literary technique of exaggeration in order to illuminate the ordinary. By embodying empathy and disgust in a single, exaggerated character—like Hugo's hunchback of Notre Dame—an author forces us to consider the boundaries and potentials of both human tenderness and monstrosity. Such characters are known as 'grotesque.'"

"'Grotesque' is the right word for them, all right," said Ricky. Everyone in class chuckled, everyone except Jake, whose stomach clenched so tight that he doubled over and nearly banged his forehead on the seminar table.

"Jake?" asked Jhumpa. "Are you okay?"

He nodded, excused himself to the men's room where his stomach heaved, but he didn't vomit.

After Russian class on Friday morning, Jake felt nervous as he walked to the small pharmacy on Nassau Street, the town's main shopping avenue opposite campus, but he knew he had to. Dad's instruction, "Never hurt the girl," echoed in his head.

Jake had the whole evening planned: he'd meet Marla at her dorm and walk her to Stevenson Hall where they'd eat *Shabbes* dinner with everyone, where Jake would sit among moral Jewish young men and women, where everyone would give sidelong glances of approval and grinning nods to the newest Jewish couple on campus. They'd make him feel good about dating a woman, and being normal. Why had he been isolating himself all this time when what he really needed was to garner everyone else's encouragement and support?

Then he'd lead Marla to the far side of campus where their dorms were, but instead of turning toward her dorm, he'd give a slight tug of her hand, which he'd be holding, and would invite her to his room. "Ted's never there anymore," he'd say, "so we'll be alone. If that's okay with you." He'd give her a long meaning-ful stare and she'd blush and nod. Then they'd go to his room and…no, he wouldn't serve any alcohol. No alcohol whatsoever because that made him lose control and protective inhibitions.

Instead, after taking her coat and draping it over Ted's desk chair, he'd—

He now reached the pharmacy entrance. Predictably, his stomach clenched and he began to hyperventilate. He felt alternately hot and cold. He broke out into a sweat.

Stop it, he scolded himself. Just stop it. You're being stupid. Just do it.

Taking a couple of deep breaths and massaging his stomach, Jake shoved open the pharmacy glass door, heard the jingle of a bell. "Hello there," called a tall man with hair nearly as white as his pharmacist tunic. "If you need help finding anything, just come up to the counter here and let me know."

"Thank you." Jake turned down a narrow aisle of Hallmark cards and poked around, lifting this card and that as though he were considering a purchase. Then he walked along an aisle of pain killers, another of cold and allergy pills, another of digestion medicines. He picked up a large bottle of Pepto-Bismol—might as well since he was here.

A series of quick glances revealed what Jake needed—in a display stand up by the counter cash register. Breathing deeply through his nose, he carried the Pepto to the counter, set it beside the register.

"A tummy ache, eh?" asked the pharmacist. His white eyelashes seemed a bit too long, and his smile was awfully wrinkly. He looked like somebody's grandfather.

"Yes," replied Jake, "my stomach. I get nervous sometimes and it clenches." Why did Jake admit that? Why was he disclosing anything at all to this stranger?

"I feel sorry for you college kids under so much stress. Just do your best, and everything will be fine. And remember to have fun once in a while."

"Thank you, sir," said Jake, genuinely appreciative. "Oh, and since I'm here," he added with forced casualness, "I might as well buy this, too, just in case." He boldly grabbed a red Trojan box from the display stand by the register. "You never know," he added, trying for one-of-the-guys jocularity.

"Good boy," said the pharmacist as he rang up the purchase and slipped the items into a white paper bag. "Being so responsible and prepared, taking care of yourself and your lady friend both. Good boy."

If only the pharmacist knew how opposite of good I really am, thought Jake. But he sure is a nice guy. Any time I need aspirin or anything, I'm coming back here.

/ /

Shutting the door of his room, he wondered where he should place the condoms. "Come on in, Marla," he pictured himself saying. "Take a seat next to the box of condoms. No pressure." He laughed. He needed a spot that would be convenient when the moment came, yet not crudely presumptuous.

He stuck the red box in his top dresser drawer beneath his innocently white socks. No, no good: to get the condoms, he'd have to climb down from his bunk and riffle among the socks; in the process, he might lose his erection, the most embarrassing of all possible outcomes.

Unless he couldn't even get an erection with Marla in the first place.

He just had to be able to get an erection with Marla.

He slipped the red box between mattress and box spring. He climbed up and lay down to test the bed. No, too lumpy, and on the off chance that Ted came to the room one day—lying on the bottom bunk, he'd see the box of condoms staring him in the face.

Removing the strip of 10 attached condoms, Jake crumpled the cardboard package into the white paper bag, which he then shoved beneath crunched-up papers in the metal waste basket beneath his desk. He slipped the strip of condoms under his pillow.

No, no good—if Marla saw him pull out a strip of condoms, she'd think he was a sex maniac. Again he laughed.

He detached one condom from the strip, slipped it beneath his pillow. Okay. This was a convenient solution that yelled "responsible" but not "maniacal." The rest of them went under the socks in the drawer. If he turned out to need more than one, he and Marla would already have done it once, so if his erection ebbed on his way to the sock drawer, the humiliation would be bearable since he would already have proven that *he could do it*.

By the way, exactly how did you put on a condom? Sacrificing one of the remaining nine, he tried ripping open the packet. It wouldn't tear. He held a corner of the wrapper between front teeth and yanked. The wrapper tore; so did the condom. Feh, bitter.

Since the condom was already out in the open—a shame to waste it, right?—and since being torn didn't matter if he were using it solo, and since Jake needed the practice anyway...he slipped off his pants, took the *Playgirl* microfilm roll out from under the pile of briefs in his dresser's second drawer, lay down in bed, unfurled the microfilm to the middle where his favorite guys were—muscular with muttonchop sideburns—figured out how to unroll the rubbery little condom onto himself and....

"**H**ere we are," Jake said, giving Marla a peck on the cheek. He helped her off with her gray wool overcoat, laid it carefully across Ted's bed, tossed his Mighty Mac beside it.

"They look good together," Marla said.

Talk about hinting, thought Jake. "That's Ted's bed. He hardly ever stops by anymore."

"I know. He told me he's practically living with his girlfriend. Very romantic."

"Here, you can sit in his desk chair." Marla did so, and Jake pulled his own wooden desk chair over opposite.

Jake knew what he had to do. He'd thought about it, envisioned it, planned it, practiced it in pantomime no fewer than a dozen times, so he went for it: he leaned forward, caressed Marla's cheek with his thumb, waited for her to lean forward, then brought his lips to hers. An instant later, he felt a sudden moistness…her tongue. It felt spongier than that of the Dinky station guy.

Her hair smelled like peaches. He preferred the scent of Ted's herbal shampoo, but he reminded himself that peaches weren't so bad.

Marla swished her tongue around his. How long was Jake supposed to continue the kissing? He imagined Ted leaning in to kiss him. Jake breathed harder and reached around Marla, who reached her hand behind Jake's head and diddled with the back of his neck. It tickled.

Jake leaned further forward, kept kissing and kissing Ted — Marla — until she finally sat up straight and sighed. "That's so nice," she murmured, smiling softly.

They embraced. They kissed and kissed and kissed, all the while Jake thinking how amazing that he and Ted were finally making love.

"Would you, umm, would you maybe…be more comfortable… umm, lying down?"

She nodded. "On Ted's bed?"

"Oh no." No, that would be too much. "On my upper bunk. I usually climb up the metal frame at the end, but I'll slide a chair over for you. Just take off your shoes."

As she climbed up, Jake found her genuinely graceful. She lay on her side, her back to the wall. Jake hesitated, then climbed up into bed beside her, and again they embraced and kissed.

I can do this I can do this I can do this, he thought with his eyes closed, feeling Ted's hands roam around his back, caress his butt.

But this wasn't Ted. Don't be nuts. This was Marla. A woman. That was the whole point. You're having sex with a woman. That's the whole point. A woman.

He opened his eyes, reached for the flouncy bow of her beige blouse, asking, "Is this okay?"

"Very okay."

He unbuttoned the blouse, tugged the shirt tails out of her skirt, slipped blouse off shoulders. Not only wasn't there resistance from her — she actually helped him. Her bra was ivory-colored and lacy.

Jake removed his best blue shirt and bleached white undershirt.

He wasn't kissing Ted, he reminded himself, he was kissing Marla.

She unzipped her long skirt, he slipped it off her. She undid her bra and slipped it off, too, then giggled as Jake's jaw literally dropped. "I've never…"

"Is this your first time?" she asked.

Looking away, he nodded.

With one finger, she nudged his chin so that their eyes met. "I'm more flattered than I can tell you," she said. "You're so sweet and gentle." She took his left hand, cupped it around her right breast.

He gasped. She kissed him deeply.

He caressed her soft breasts, so unlike a man's firm muscular chest. Don't be an idiot, he told himself while kissing her, while stroking her breasts and listening to her soft sighs.

She guided his hand to her waist, and he reached his fingers into the elastic band of her pantyhose. As he slowly slipped them off, he became totally entangled in their taffy-like, endlessly stretching legs. She giggled and he blushed. A bit of finger-magic and bunching, then he hurled the humiliating bundle of nylon to the floor.

Jake slid off his navy-blue slacks and white briefs in one fell swoop, lay back down beside her and threw himself into his task, doing all the things he'd planned: he kissed her breasts, licked her nipples, all while reaching between her legs and sliding a finger into her warm moistness. Wow, so incredibly slick and tight. Should he reach under the pillow for the condom now? Should he wait longer?

He kept moving and twirling his finger until Marla cheeped.

He pulled his finger out, and Marla drew him up so she could cover his face with light kisses. Jake supposed he'd done it right.

She caressed his erection. Remarkably, he had an erection. Was it those earlier thoughts of Ted? No, no of course not. Jake was sporting an erection because he was making love with a woman. See? he told himself. You can do this. You can have sex with a woman. And your body can respond.

But even as he told himself all this, he realized that for the first time, his erection felt somehow disconnected from the rest of him, that it was responding to Marla's touch the way his foot did when Dr. Peril hammered just below the knee and Jake's foot kicked forward. Jake felt no inner desire whatsoever, no compulsion to place erection where finger had just been, none of the urge to orgasm he experienced every time he fantasized about men.

Certainly nothing like the intensity of feeling Jake had experienced with the stranger at the Dinky station.

Jake simply didn't feel the least little urge to enter Marla's body.

When she whispered shyly that she was uncertain whether they should go further, this being their first time, he replied, "No need to rush."

They spent the night on his narrow bed, he on his back, she curled up beside him, her arm across his chest. He listened to her steady breathing, felt the damp scent of her peach-fragrant hair mixed with…he didn't even know how to define the scent… thicken in his throat such that he needed to turn his head aside to gasp periodically for fresh air. He wanted to disengage from her, but didn't wish to risk her misinterpretation of any movement as an indication of wanting the very opposite of what he wanted.

What he didn't want. He didn't want it. No, he didn't. He just didn't want it.

Jake felt awful. Here she'd given herself to him in the most intimate of ways—well, almost—yet he knew he wouldn't see her again. He'd used her selfishly, thereby totally contravening Dad's instructions never to hurt a girl. At a minimum, Jake owed her an explanation, but how could he explain when he could barely acknowledge the truth to himself? Besides, surely she'd be disgusted and horrified at his truth, might blab all over campus, and everyone would point and stare and call him terrible names.

"Morning," she murmured, stretching awake.

"Good morning," he said, untangling from her and jumping quickly out of bed to the floor. "Here, let me help you down so you can dress."

As she was buttoning her blouse, as he was buttoning his shirt, he could feel her watching him. Did she notice the consternation on his face? Could Marla foresee that in ensuing weeks, he wouldn't answer his room's ringing telephone ever?

"You're probably not all that much of a breakfast person," she said, her tone somewhere between statement and question.

"No, not really." He hadn't even thought about going to breakfast together. That would be too much.

"My roommates will probably be waiting to go to Stevenson for brunch, so I'd better get on my way…unless you'd like to come with?"

"Thanks, but I've got tons of studying to do."

Her eyes took on a sadness, and Jake sensed she knew something wasn't right. "I had a nice time," she said, leaning in and pecking him on the cheek. "I hope I didn't…force anything."

"Oh no, not at all. No no. Not at all."

"Okay, then. You'll call me?"

"For sure."

"Great. 'Bye."

After she left, Jake undressed, took out the microfilm reel, and climbed back into bed to finish what he hadn't finished last night.

Afterwards, he heard, *I can't believe this.*

That was, of course, God.

You cast aside a beautiful and intelligent woman so that you can degrade yourself with microfilm images of men?

'I know,' thought Jake. 'I'm pathetic. Hopeless.'

As long as you don't abandon Me, there's still hope.

'I'm not so sure anymore. I think I'm pathetic and hopeless.'

Your behavior is extremely distressing, but I wouldn't go so far as to call you "hopeless."

'But maybe I would.'

/ /

Jake's own words echoed for days. On his way to Russian class: "pathetic." On his way to psych: "hopeless." When he left Russian class more than a week after that night with Marla, exited East Pyne Hall and spotted her all bundled up in coat and muffler and leaning against an oak tree with her nose in her Arabic textbook as if not actually waiting for him in the hopes he'd notice her: "pathetic." On his way to Wawa to buy peanut butter and jelly and bread so he could eat in his room and avoid Marla just in case she tried "accidentally to bump into him" by showing up for the first time at Commons: "pathetic and hopeless."

M aybe the microfilm was part of the problem, he finally wondered. All those men tempting him day after day. Besides,
how long could he hold onto the reel before "borrowing" turned
into "stealing"?

He rolled up the men in their white box, gave it a kiss, slipped
it into the pocket of his Mighty Mac coat, walked directly to the
library's microfilm room and the "P" shelf. After removing the
microfilm box from his pocket and lifting it toward the shelf's
Playgirl spot, he heard from down the aisle, "May I help you?"

His head snapped to the kindly smiling, same-age-as-Mom
librarian with black hair pinned against her head.

"May I help you?"

"Uh, no thanks."

She stepped away and Jake hesitated: the librarian must have
memorized every title and every shelf spot—she was the *librarian*,
after all—and had seen exactly where he was standing and the
shelf toward which his hand with the box had been aiming so she
had to know precisely which microfilm box he was placing there,
one she'd probably noticed missing, and after Jake left she'd go
back to the shelf to check if he'd done what she suspected and
then, with her suspicions confirmed that he was the crook who'd

just returned the obscene magazine, she'd describe him to the guard at the door who'd seen him a million times, and to a police sketch artist, and Jake would be caught in a matter of days and jailed. Or expelled. Or at the very least exposed on the front page of *The Daily Princetonian* in their Pervert of the Year issue, and a mob of drunken jocks would break down his door to trash his room and beat him black-and-blue. *The Cherryvale News* back home would pick up the story, "Local Boy Makes Bad," picketers would throng their little Cherryvale street, Dad would get fired, and Mom would never be able to show her face at ShopRite again.

Jake moved to the far end of the aisle, stepped away from the stacks, set the white cardboard microfilm box onto a windowsill, held his palm up to the side of his face and splayed his fingers as if hiding from view, then scurried past the librarian, out of the microfilm room, past the guard (who didn't stop him because Jake didn't have a backpack), out of the library, and as far away as possible down Washington Street, away from his dorm, away from anywhere he could be recognized.

He stayed away from his dorm for hours. He stayed away from Firestone Library for a full day. Then two. Then three. No arrest. Hesitantly he returned to Firestone, but stayed out of the microfilm room, not that he had any reason to return there, anyway.

O n a Friday evening exactly two weeks after that overnight with Marla, Ted walked into their room. Jake, studying at his desk, looked up in surprise. "Hi, stranger!"

"Hey, Jake. Mind if I spend the night here?"

"It's your room, too!" Jake was beyond thrilled. "Have a fight with Nancy?"

"Nah, she's way easy to get along with." Ted slung his navy blue pea coat over his chair. "I've kind of been hoping Nancy and I'd bump into you at a movie or play or Commons, but we never see you anymore. Do you get out once in a while?"

Jake shrugged. "So much studying to do."

"You've got to take breaks, Jake."

"I know. So…are you free because Nancy needed time with her girlfriends?"

"Actually…I just thought it would be good for you and me to hang out. If you're not too busy."

"Really?"

"I miss our great conversations."

"Wow, me too."

Ted pulled his desk chair over near Jake's, sat. "So, how's everything going?"

"Okay. My American lit class is interesting, but the other students don't always like my interpretations of texts."

"Very subjective."

"Yeah. And psych isn't as big a pain this semester because I don't have any labs."

"Cool. And umm…how're…you know, other things? I hear you were dating one of my Arabic classmates."

Jake stiffened, stood, walked to the window, looked out. The moon was half-hidden by clouds. "Marla and I dated a couple times. No big deal."

"She says you're really nice."

"She does?" Jake turned to face Ted.

"She says she really likes you. A lot."

"Nice of her, but…I don't know."

"She thinks maybe you're not calling because she slept with you."

"I can't believe she told you about that."

"She knows we're roommates and friends. She wanted my advice. She's afraid you think she's some kind of slut."

"I know you mean well, Ted, but—"

"It's none of my business."

"Right."

"When I was afraid Nancy might be pregnant, you gave me advice about talking to her."

"Nancy's okay, right? You haven't said anything, so I figured she wasn't."

"No, thank goodness. But you really helped me, encouraging me to talk to her. You helped our relationship. I want to return the favor."

"Nice of you, but Marla and I don't have a relationship. It was just a few dates, that's all."

"Is she right about you thinking she's a slut?"

"That's nuts—we both slept together, so if she's a slut, so am I."

"No chemistry?" asked Ted.

"Exactly," said Jake. "No chemistry." Not like the chemistry I feel for you, Jake thought, but didn't say. "I don't have anything bad to say about Marla at all. It's just...no chemistry, like you said."

"Maybe you should just tell her that?"

"I couldn't hurt her feelings that way."

"Is it better to leave her wondering?"

"I know I'm being a jerk, Ted, but I just can't."

"Okay. Not really my business."

"Thanks for trying to help."

"Sure. You want to go to the Student Center for ice cream or something?"

How long had it been since he and Ted spent time together, just the two of them? Months.

At a table for two in a corner of the brightly lit Student Center, they talked about their classes and professors. Various friends of Ted's who used to stop by whenever seeing the two of them together, now gave quick hello's—"Haven't seen you guys here in ages," or "You two see a good movie tonight?"—and Jake was happy. How good it felt just to be with him, to receive all his attention, to watch his lower lip pout out when expressing worry about the quality of the *Song of Roland* paper he'd just turned in, to note the way his cheeks flushed with excitement when wrestling with ethical issues as they were doing this evening when Ted speculated that maybe Dostoevsky's brooding character, Raskolnikov, had been right about some people being more worthy than others and entitled literally to get away with murder.

Ted gave that half-grin Jake loved—when Ted's right cheek lifted higher than his left—as Jake argued: "Dostoevsky's point was that Raskolnikov couldn't live with himself after he murdered the little old lady. It wasn't just that the law was after him, it was that his own conscience hunted him down. Sure, he succeeded in committing murder, but he couldn't get away with it. He drove himself into a kind of fever."

"Want another ice cream cup?" Ted asked.

"No, I've had enough."

"I'll be back." As Ted went to get another dessert Jake watched him, so tall and lean and graceful, taking long strides more like slow loping than walking.

Returning to the table, Ted peeled the paper off his purple ice pop, and his face took on a serious cast, "Jeez, I miss these conversations." Sucking on the ice pop, he stared directly across the table into Jake's eyes. "I mean it," he said, his eyes squinting guilt. "I feel like we got really close, you and I, and then I bailed when I met Nancy."

"That's the normal way," said Jake, meaning it. His chest filled with more love than he'd ever known, love for this brilliant handsome man who was declaring how much he missed me, thought Jake. Either I can try to take advantage of his guilt, manipulating him to spend more time with me, or I can be noble and kind, encouraging him to live a full life, the life I'll never be able to lead because I'm not normal. He's my friend. I love him. I want him to be happy. "It's a good thing to fall for a woman. You have fallen in love, haven't you?"

"I kind of guess so. Nancy's all I can think about. When I'm studying, when I'm in class. Whenever I see her, I feel this little electric shock in my heart."

"That's beautiful," Jake said, thinking how very much he understood those feelings.

As Ted talked endlessly about Nancy, about how funny she was, how cute her way of flipping her waist-length hair over her shoulder, how she loved to trace Ted's nose with her tongue — "Okay," said Jake, "maybe you'd better not tell me anymore!" — how good she made Ted feel about himself as a person, as a man. "I hope you find someone special one of these days," said Ted.

I have found someone special, thought Jake. His name is Ted.

"I'm just thinking," said Jake as they stood and pulled on their coats, "the way you talk about Nancy…maybe you should spend tonight with her, after all. I mean, I'm really glad we got to hang out and catch up, but…well, I don't flip my hair like she does."

Ted chuckled. "And I wouldn't like the feel of your tongue along my nose."

Jake forced a laugh. "So, maybe she'd like you to spend the night as usual?"

"I know she would. She told me I could come back after you and I hung out if I wanted." Ted stopped walking, put his hand on Jake's shoulder. "You're a good friend."

"Always, I hope."

"See you soon?"

"For sure."

Ted waved in his usual way, lifting his palm up straight, holding his departure gaze just a bit longer than other people did. Then he turned and headed toward Nancy's dorm.

Walking alone toward Lockhart—their room—Jake's eyes burned and his stomach tumbled. He knew he'd done the right thing, encouraging Ted to be with Nancy.

Walking through Blair Arch with its gray, four-turreted medievalish tower looming above, Jake glanced at the mass of student fliers taped on the wall. A small one, 8x12, leapt out at him, an orange flier with bold black letters—Princeton's colors, orange and black—"Gay Alliance of Princeton."

Don't slow down, he thought to himself while nearly in shock, someone might see and realize what you're looking at.

Through Blair Arch to the landing atop a long staircase that led down to the quad with Jake's dorm. He stopped, pivoted, walked in the opposite direction, the direction he'd just come from, so that he could pass the wall of fliers again and take another glance at that flier. Not slowing his stride, he walked past and caught a quick glimpse of it. The flier was advertising a dance for next Saturday night.

A gay dance? On campus? Was that possible?—not that he'd go, of course he'd never attend such a thing, but he wanted to know where and when it was being held. Just to know. Just for the heck of it. Just to know. He *needed* to know.

So he pivoted yet again, but before walking back through Blair Arch, he spotted a group of hulking jocks with beer bottles approaching the Arch from the far end. If they saw him looking at the flier, who knew what they'd do to him? He'd better pivot yet again and head back in the direction of the Student Center or anywhere, just to get away.

He wasn't three steps on his path when he heard echoing from behind in the stone Arch, "What the fuck?!"

"You gotta be shittin' me!"

"Fucking faggots on campus? On *our* campus?"

They must have spotted the flier. Jake sped along the path as if they were after him. He was fearful, yet echoed their sentiments—a gay dance on *our* campus? A dance for men who liked men and women who liked women? Right here? Would they actually dance—men and men, women and women—with their arms around each other? In front of everybody? Right here on campus? Not in a library men's room or the Dinky station ladies' room, but at a dance like normal people go to. With music. Maybe even refreshments. A normal place to meet.

Right at the moment, thought Jake, when I'm feeling so alone, I see this flier saying there might be a legitimate way to meet somebody. Is that possible? Could there really be a legitimate way? Could God be giving me a sign? Could God actually approve?

Approve? Jake heard God say. Jake stopped in front of West College, the administration building, looked up at the sky, dark with gray clouds. *You actually think I would condone such a gathering?*

'I just thought,' muttered Jake, 'that maybe I could meet one or two people. Just to talk, that's all…. I don't know.'

No, you don't know. You think it's wise to meet with others who might tempt you into violation of the Torah?

'I don't mean that I'd do anything. Just talk. Maybe ask questions. Maybe feel a little less alone. If there are enough people on campus to have a dance, then that means I'm not the only one with feelings like this.'

If others misbehave, that gives you license to misbehave as well?

'I'm so lonely. And I'm trying to be a good person. I encouraged Ted to be with his girlfriend, didn't You see that?'

True, you're not trying to corrupt the innocent. That's something. But do you really think you should spend time with others who'd reinforce your distressing inclination?

Jake looked down at his shoes. 'I'm sorry.'

If you're sorry then stop once and for all. Stop thinking about such things. Genug, enough.

Dazed from the scolding, Jake continued walking until he realized he'd walked all the way back to the Student Center. He turned around and headed back toward his dorm, noticing some commotion across Cannon Green by Whig and Clio Halls, those white classical Greek temple-like buildings. Probably another protest against South African Apartheid or for women's rights or something, but that was odd for a Saturday night. Jake shrugged — none of his business; he had enough on his mind.

Maybe God was right.

Maybe? What was Jake thinking — of course God was right. God was always right! It was God who determined what was right and wrong, and He'd stated clearly in the Torah that what Jake had done, what he wanted to do again and again, was totally absolutely unquestionably wrong. An abomination. He had to stop thinking about it, to force himself to forget about it. He just had to.

Passing West College once more, Jake bundled his coat against the late February wind picked up. Then he angled toward Blair Arch, and as he walked through it, he slowed again so as to look longingly at the flier, just to find out where and exactly when the dance would happen, not that he'd attend this gay dance or any other one, not ever. Cinderella condemned to stay home from the ball and clean out a filthy hearth.

Sauntering slowly, he searched for the flier, for those bold black letters on an orange field, for the suggestion that at least some people would have a chance at happiness, wicked though they might be. Not that he'd even consider attending the dance. He just wanted to see the flier so he could whisper a final farewell to an unthinkable future he couldn't possibly have.

But the flier was gone.

In its place, taped exactly where the flier had been, flapped a single sheet of white paper with bold red letters stating: DIE FAGGOTS DIE!

Jake practically ran through Blair Arch, down the concrete stairs and across the grassy quad to his dorm.

You see, my son? God said, as Jake shut his room's door behind himself. *You see what I'm trying to protect you from?*

Without so much as turning on his room's lights, Jake undressed, put on his pajamas and crawled into bed. He fell into a fitful sleep.

The next morning, in his robe after showering, as he was leaving his dorm's second-floor men's room, Jake spotted the morning issue of *The Daily Princetonian* left on one of the sinks. He picked it up and froze reading the front-page story:

> Last night outside Whig Hall, gay activist sophomore Doug Braun was attacked and beaten. Witnesses saw Braun fleeing half a dozen pursuers who shouted, "Die, faggot, die!" before catching him as he tried to enter locked Whig Hall. The alleged attackers hurled him down Whig's white marble steps, then proceeded to punch and kick him as others gathered, calling upon the gang to stop. Campus police arrived quickly and took the alleged attackers—all members of Princeton's soccer team and roommates in Blair Tower—into custody.
>
> "They were totally drunk," stated one eyewitness. "They were slurring curses and reeked of alcohol."
>
> Horrified onlookers assisted campus custodial staff in gathering from Cannon Green dozens of

bloodied fliers that Braun had apparently been carrying, notices of an upcoming dance sponsored by the Gay Alliance of Princeton. Braun is the organization's most vocal representative, frequently giving interviews to this newspaper.

Dr. Ackerman of McCosh Infirmary said that, after an initial examination, he transferred Braun to Princeton Hospital on Witherspoon Street because Braun's injuries were too extensive for treatment at McCosh. "In addition to several broken bones, the patient appeared to be suffering from internal bleeding, and risked losing an eye. We at McCosh Infirmary are not equipped to perform surgery." He couldn't venture a prognosis.

The Gay Alliance of Princeton is calling for the alleged attackers to be expelled. "We'll hold our dance next Saturday night as scheduled," said an anonymous representative of the group. "And we demand that the University provide extra security."

The office of the Dean of Student Affairs released a statement promising "a full investigation" and "appropriate disciplinary action pending our findings."

His hands trembling, Jake set the newspaper down. That was the commotion he'd noticed from across Cannon Green: a gay man being beaten.

Broken bones. Internal bleeding. Might lose an eye. Beaten for distributing fliers about a gay dance. Broken bones. Internal bleeding. Might lose an eye.

Jake took the newspaper to his room and stared again at the front page, at the photograph of Doug Braun with his wavy hair

and horn-rimmed glasses. A handsome guy. The newspaper must
have reprinted a photo from some interview with him. He wished
he'd read it. Poor guy.

Jake's trembling turned to shaking: Jake had been right not to
let those jocks see him read that flier in Blair Arch. If they had,
maybe they'd have attacked him, too.

Jake couldn't live his entire life in fear of attack. He just
couldn't. He couldn't. He had to change. Absolutely. He had to
make himself normal.

Maybe he'd already taken a first step by ceasing to indulge his
perverse desires with those microfilm pictures. How could he
have allowed himself to do that? All he'd done night after night
was reinforce his perversion by masturbating to those images.

Jake's thoughts stopped cold. He felt the blood drain from his face.

He retraced his thoughts: "All he'd done night after night
was reinforce his perversion".... Reinforce. Yes, that's exactly
what he'd been doing. By masturbating to pictures of men, by
experiencing orgasms over and over while looking at men, Jake
was reinforcing his perverse inclination. Rewarding himself with
orgasms the way he'd rewarded Pecker, his pigeon, with food
pellets last fall. Jake shouldn't be rewarding himself for fantasizing
about naked men. Instead, he should be fantasizing to thoughts
of naked women. That was the way to give himself positive reinforcement for normal thoughts.

He'd seen Marla naked, right? So, then and there, Jake
climbed into bed, opened his robe, tugged himself while picturing Marla naked, imagining the peachy fragrance of her hair,
remembering the feel of her soft skin, her soft breasts, hearing
her sighs as he slid his finger into her slickness.... Nothing. Not
even a semi-erection no matter how hard he tugged and pulled.
At least in her actual presence, he'd been able to get hard.

This wasn't working, he told himself, because of all the years of faulty positive reinforcement masturbating to thoughts of men. Jake had to undo all that the same way he'd taught Pecker to unlearn pecking at the green tab by getting electric shocks each time he did.

So…to unlearn his attraction to men, Jake had to employ negative reinforcement. Maybe God had sent him to that psych class so he could learn how to heal himself.

'Thank you, God,' Jake thought, gazing up at his white ceiling. 'Thank You for guiding me to my own healing, for saving me from a shadow existence on society's margins.'

You're a good boy, he heard God reply. *Just remember that this approach will require a great deal of discipline.*

'If anyone's disciplined,' thought Jake, 'it's me. I can do it. I know I can.'

I hope so.

'Yes, Sir. Thank you, Sir.'

God hadn't abandoned him, after all. God was giving him a chance. So…what kind of negative reinforcement might work?

Jake was so excited that he rushed to Wawa for a celebratory package of Entenmann's chocolate-covered donuts, his favorite. He ate half the box before he even got back to his dorm room, and when he did, he realized he hadn't even so much as glanced in the direction of the Dinky station on the way to or from Wawa. He'd been so filled with hope that he hadn't thought about sex with men for an entire half hour. The treatment was working even before it started.

So…what kind of negative reinforcement?

He climbed into bed—the scene of the vast majority of his fantasy crimes—bent his arms and laid his wrists beside his head on the pillow and imagined himself strapped onto a gurney as doctors attached electrodes to his scalp. "This will be excruciating, young man."

"I don't care, Doctor," Jake replied out loud. "God wants me to do it."

A nurse shoves a hunk of plastic into his mouth, "So that you don't swallow your tongue and choke."

Then the doctor flips a Frankenstein switch, blue lightning-like bolts travel along wires to the electrodes on Jake's scalp. He feels the searing pain of electricity course through his head, down his spinal column, throughout all of him. Muscles clench and spasm. Arms convulse, legs. He breaks out in a cold sweat. His mouth opens wide as he lets loose an imaginary stream of piercing agony screams and writhes, his wrists still bound to the pillow. Heavy breathing turns to panting as he smells his own singed hair.

The doctor flips the switch off. "That should do it."

The nurse removes the electrodes and uses a tongue depressor to swathe gobs of salve over the burn marks on Jake's scalp. Then she removes the plastic mouthpiece. Jake's jaw muscles ache.

He sure didn't feel like masturbating after that.

He slept well for the first time in months.

While Mrs. Polenko explained the Russian declension of numerals, and Jake nodded his head as if paying attention, his thoughts actually were shaping the next step of his negative reinforcement plan: every time he caught himself having a sexual thought about a man, he would picture a knife plunging into his genitals. "That should do it," he mumbled aloud.

"*Chto, Dzhek? Chto vy skazali?*" What, Jake? What did you say?

"*Nichego, Gospozha Polenko. Izvinitse, pozhaluista.*" Nothing, Mrs. Polenko. Please forgive me.

After class, as Jake walked into Firestone Library, he noticed a husky man whose thick chest just begged caressing.

A long pointy dagger with a jewel-encrusted hilt tore through Jake's trousers as he walked down the stairs, pierced his scrotum. Jake had to grip the banister so as not to lose his balance.

Arranging his books at his usual C-floor carrel, Jake looked up at a thin blond young professor-type in tweed jacket stopped at the stacks in search of a book. As the man pulled a book from the shelf and opened it, Jake noticed the flatness of his stomach, the slight bulge of his crotch that was at Jake's eye level, albeit three feet away. If Jake were to lean forward and lunge, he could—

It was the blond man who lunged, flipped open a switch blade and jabbed straight into Jake's crotch and twisted. "That'll teach you to ogle me, you goddamn queer." Searing pain. Blood spurting everywhere.

Jake crossed his legs, flipped opened his Russian textbook, forced himself to concentrate on numeral declension.

During a break, as Jake approached the small men's room and remembered the naked man he'd seen there with that beautiful huge erection, a razor sliced along the shaft of Jake's penis. Jake nearly doubled over. The pain felt so real that in the men's room, at the urinal, Jake feared what he'd find when unzipping. He looked down: shriveled to a nub, but otherwise okay.

On his way to Commons for lunch, he kept his eyes focused on the sidewalks so as not to notice passing men. All he saw were shoes sidestepping snow-melt puddles: beige Timberland boots, black leather boots, scuffed brown moccasins, blue suede shoes—what?...blue suede shoes? Jake snapped his head up at the man who was just passing—round handsome face with thick brown hair in a bowl cut, husky in jeans and a heavy, camel-colored cable-knit sweater. The same blue suede shoes Jake recalled on the guy he'd spied having oral sex in the C-floor men's room during January's reading period. He'd remembered those shoes so often, he could never forget them. Blue suede with black laces. And black socks.

Jake stared after Blue Shoes, thinking how hot it would be to run up behind him, reach around and hug his thick body, grasp the small belly in his hands while pressing himself against that fleshy backside. Jake felt the stirrings of an erection and—

A Sword of Damocles swooped down from the sky and sliced Jake's erection off. Blood splattered onto the sidewalk as Jake fell to the ground in agony, clutching his crotch, curled into a fetal position. Passing women in pointy shoes and boots kicked his dismembered penis as if it were a dog turd, stomped on it, squished the spongy mass to bloody pulp. "It's not like you're ever gonna use it for God's intended procreation purpose, right?" said one woman in black leather thigh-high spiked heels, a leather corset, patent leather gloves that ran up to her armpits. She cracked a whip at Jake's bloody crotch. "Take that for wasting the Lord's gift. Take that!"

Breathing hard and clutching his stomach, Jake continued to Commons where he filled his tray with a plate of mushy canned peas and tasteless boiled potatoes, a bowl of salad, and glass of milk, walked the length of the dark wainscoted hall to a far table. He kept his head down while he ate until two tall men, one white and one black, sat side by side at the table's far end. After setting down their trays of pork chops and cake, they removed their coats—both wore tight-fitting turtlenecks that revealed muscular chests and biceps, pointed nipples so tempting that Jake couldn't help himself: he walked over to the men, knelt between them, reached up now under one man's green turtleneck, now under the other's blue one, roamed his hands along the firm square pecs, flicked those pointed nips with his tongue, tasting a mix of soap and mild perspiration, taking in the sounds of each man's moans as they unzipped and one grabbed the back of his head, saying, "Here's your lunch."

From somewhere beneath the table, a series of darts shot into Jake's crotch to pierce his scrotum, a paring knife sliced his sack open, leaving his testes to dangle by thin cords; a scissors swooped in and—snip snip. Jake crawled after his bloody testicles rolling the length of Commons as everyone pointed and laughed.

Jake shoved his tray aside, breathed hard. He looked over at the two muscular men and felt…no desire whatsoever. He didn't care if he never saw them again.

How long must he endure the imaginary agonies he was putting himself through? At least one more week, to get himself through mid-terms.

/ /

Saturday evening, Jake wandered all over campus despite the icy drizzle, telling himself he was just trying to exhaust himself by walking, so that he wouldn't have any energy to think about sex and wouldn't need to punish himself. At the same time, he paused at every bulletin board, every wall of fliers, hoping to spot one that would mention where the gay dance was being held that very evening. Not that he'd attend, he assured himself, but so that he could stand outside the venue and spot who was going into the dance—that way, he'd know which young men on campus to avoid.

He found not a single flier.

/ /

Fernando, his psych class TA who handed out the midterm, left the top two buttons of his shirt open to reveal a tuft of black hair. What sort of hair pattern covered his chest? Did the hair encircle the nipples, did he have a sexy treasure trail down the middle of his belly?

'Stop!' blared in Jake's ears as he felt scrotal rip, tear, jab.

Cut tear impale.

/ /

In partial response to his English class midterm's question seeking analysis of Tennessee Williams' *Cat on a Hot Tin Roof*, Jake wrote, "The main character in *Cat on a Hot Tin Roof*, Brick, suffers from guilt at having abandoned his best guy friend with whom he was in love. Maybe if he'd approached his friend, declared his love, the friend would have reciprocated the feelings. In that case, the two of them might have…" What? Might have…what?

Jake pictured those two male characters—one resembling himself, the other looking like Ted— embracing and gazing into one another's eyes, declaring their love, vowing to keep it secret.

A cleaver rose up from the floor under the seminar table where they were taking the exam and castrated Jake then and there. He nearly passed out.

After ripping up that response and writing some bullshit about Brick's wife being too difficult a woman to live with, Jake ran to Firestone and the small C-floor men's room where he dashed into a stall and puked. If the treatment were working, then why did he keep having these lusty fantasies all the time? Sure, each treatment interrupted a given fantasy or even arousal, but the next passing man prompted a new horny thought and started the cycle all over again, sometimes mere minutes later. The negative reinforcement experiment was a failure. A total failure.

Having resisted masturbating for so long, Jake's desire seemed more overwhelming than ever.

He dropped his pants and sat on the toilet. That's when he saw a hand-written note on the tissue roll saying, "For bj be here 12:30."

"Why is evil temptation everywhere I turn?" he moaned aloud. "I'm trying as hard as I can, but what more can I do?"

Jake tore off the tissue square with the note, pulled a pen from his backpack and scrawled onto the roll's top fresh tissue square, "Die Faggot Die."

Then he grabbed the tip of his erect penis—erect at the thought of that 12:30 bj he was missing?—grabbed the tip between the nails of right thumb and forefinger and pincered until he bled. For real this time. Not another useless fantasy, but true genuine mutilation. Over and over he pincered as tight as he could, digging fingernails deep into flesh until fingertips were bloody.

He had to grit his teeth and clamp his lips to keep from screaming. Then he let out a long-held breath.

Panting.

What had he just done?

What was he accomplishing by actually tearing into his flesh?

Did he truly want to cut his own penis off so that his problems would then be over and done with?

As if that would solve anything. Even without a penis, he'd still long for men, desire them, fall in love with Ted…with men. The problem wasn't in his penis, but in his brain.

He tore off the toilet tissue square he'd written on and dabbed the head of his bleeding penis.

Yes, his brain. Something was wrong with Jake's very brain. That must be why, according to one of those books he'd read, homosexuals were forced to have lobotomies.

He pictured himself with shaved head and a massive skull scar like he'd seen in *The Planet of the Apes* after the ape doctors did brain surgery on a human astronaut. Was that the only way to fix himself, to cut out part of his brain and drift through the world zombie-like with dead eyes, an expressionless face, a non-existent libido?

He'd rather be dead.

Had he been wrong in regarding the negative reinforcement therapy as God's plan? Had God turned His back on Jake?

Come to think of it, Jake hadn't heard from God in over a week.

'God?' he thought to himself.

Yes, I'm here. I've been watching.

'It's just not working. I've been trying, but it's not working.'

I had such hopes for your plan. But now…I'm deeply disappointed. I don't know what more I can say. You've got to fix this.

'But how, God? How?'

Silence within Jake's head.

'God?'

Silence.

Was God fed up with him? If so, could Jake blame Him? Wasn't Jake an abomination like the Torah said? An abomination was a being so revolting that even God cast him out from among His children. Maybe God didn't want him anymore.

/ /

That afternoon in his dorm, Jake put on his blue terry-cloth bathrobe and thought, 'Please, God, don't let anyone else be in the men's room so I can wash my scabby penis in the shower and not risk being naked in front of other guys or seeing them naked and risking getting an erection that they might see and that would probably hurt with all the scabs on my penis tip.' He slapped himself across the face, mumbled, "You've got no right to talk to God, you abomination. He doesn't want you. You're on your own." Jake's stomach clutched and he doubled over, his pulse raced, his breathing sped up. He cinched the blue terry-cloth belt tight and trudged up the stairs.

The next morning, on his way to Russian class in East Pyne Hall, he thought, 'Please God, let the midterm be easy.' Again he slapped and berated himself for daring to address God. Stomach clutch, pulse race, breathing. He kept walking.

'Please, God, help me write a decent paper on Edward Albee's plays.' Slap.

'Please, God, let the C-floor men's room be empty and with no notes on the toilet tissue so I can use the stall quickly for its officially designated purpose with no nasty distractions.' Slap slap slap slap.

'Please, God, let me bump into Ted at dinner and let there be an empty chair near him while his girlfriend is off having dinner with other friends.' How dare you pray to God for such a thing, you disgusting, loathsome slime. Slap!

'Please, God, don't let me get caught in the rain on the way home from Commons I know I should have brought my umbrella but I'm so distracted lately that I forgot it's not my fault I'm trying to be good but I don't know how to fix myself I can't fix myself what the hell am I supposed to do?'

Slap slap.

'I can't take this anymore, God, I can't. I don't know what to do. Please, God.'

Slap slap slap slap slap.

That night, as Jake struggled to fall asleep, he spoke out loud: "This is not a prayer, God. I'm not asking for anything. Instead, I'm making a promise—I'll find a way to be good in Your eyes. I will. I promise."

No slaps.

J ake tossed and turned throughout the night. At first, he was awakened by nightmares of mutilation, of arrest, of public shaming, of being doused with spit from the sky. He watched pitchfork-wielding students chase him from town, all led by that stringy-haired Ricky from lit class. Then he watched them string him up by a rope and hang him from Blair Tower. They bound him to a stake in front of Whig Hall and burned him on a pyre of library books and microfilm boxes. Then ancient Hebrews—leathery-skinned, white-bearded old men in robes—flung him into a desert pit, proceeded to hurl stones that tore his flesh until he bled and crumpled, completely covered by a mound of stones, obliterated from the sight of man and God.

It was only then that the nightmare feeling of terror subsided. Horror melted into strange calm.

Jake continued dreaming—visions of tranquility as he lay peacefully with his arms folded across his chest in a *Dark Shadows* cemetery crypt coffin. Peacefully. Peacefully with no stomach aches, no frustrated longings, no sense of shame, no loneliness. Peacefully in a coffin.

Jake awoke with unusual clarity of thought and an awareness that he realized had been lurking on the periphery of understanding like a bumblebee banging up against a screen in hunt of a hole in the mesh to squeeze through so as to reach target, to sting.

Yes, he thought, initially shocked. Yes, he thought as he calmed. Yes. He knew what he had to do.

For the first time all year, Jake skipped Russian class. Forging a path in new inches of snow, he walked past the Dinky station, past Wawa, past the Graduate College and onto an open field covered in clean whiteness marred only by Jake's own foot prints, as if he were marking private space on some heaven cloud.

'I understand why You've stopped speaking to me, God,' Jake said within himself. 'I don't merit Your attentions anymore. You warned me, but I didn't obey. I've tried, You've seen me try. But I can't. It's so lonely, God. I can live without friendship or another person's love, but not without You. There's only one way I can think of proving that I really want to be a good Jew and obey Your laws.... A bad Jewish boy in life, but a good one—a *yeled tov*—in death.'

Death? Jake heard within. What are you saying—death?

'I'll show You, God. I'll prove my devotion.'

Jake, stop that. I never meant for you even to consider—

'It's the only way, God. The only way. I'll prove that I'm a good Jewish boy.'

Prove to whom? To Me or to yourself? You think I could possibly want you to—?

Jake shook his head, covered his ears. No more. God meant well—of course He did. He always did. But Jake had to do this. It was the only way for Jake to free himself from the struggle. (And find peace.)

He breathed deeply, filled his chest with clean cold. The anxiety in his stomach—gone. He extended his arms and hands and fingertips up to heaven as if grasping all of God's Creation. He spun in joy. "From dust to dust is the way of all things," he mumbled out loud as he spun, growing dizzier and dizzier. "It's the natural way, the normal way. I can be part of nature instead of apart from it. I can return my body to earth the normal way. I can be normal normal normal normal." So dizzy that he fell, laughing.

He lay in the snow, flapped his arms to make a snow angel. The sun shone down, the white field glistened all around him, white stringy clouds sped across the sky.

Was that a sign of God's approval? In his head Jake heard a muffled sound like some sort of moaning. But he shook his head to ignore.

The only thing left to consider was how to execute this path to redemption.

PART 7

As he finished *davening* musaf, the additional Saturday morning prayer service, Jake nodded to himself. He mustn't put off executing the decision he made the day before. If he didn't do it soon, he might chicken out and spend the rest of his life in misery.

This weekend. It had to be this weekend.

But not today, Saturday, because killing himself on *Shabbes* just felt wrong. Tomorrow, then. If he did it in the morning then his corpse would surely begin to smell by afternoon and someone would find him by dinner time, which would give everyone in the dorm all evening to deal with the situation and calm down. It's not like they'd really care.

Just as he shut the *siddur*, the prayer book, he heard a key in the door lock, and turned. In walked Ted. "Hey, you're here. I've stopped by a couple times, but kept missing you. How's it going?"

"Super, thanks," said Jake, genuinely delighted to see him. He hadn't seen Ted for weeks, didn't like the idea of leaving without saying goodbye, although he wouldn't actually utter "goodbye." But here Ted was, showing up all on his own, almost as if he knew this was the right weekend to drop in.

Ted slipped off his pea coat and sat on his own bed. "I came by to ask if you'd like to room together next year. I picked up a room draw application, and it's due in a couple weeks."

Room together next year? "Wow, that's really nice." A warmth filled Jake, even though he wanted to tell Ted not to waste his time. "I guess I haven't been paying attention to the calendar. Didn't realize it's room draw time."

"It's not like I'd be hanging around the room a whole lot, assuming I'm still with Nancy, so you'd kind of have a single mostly. It's nearly impossible for a sophomore to get a single."

"You're trying to sell me on rooming together by saying you won't be around?"

"I guess I am. Kind of dumb."

"Kind of nice. Thanks for asking. I'd be happy to room with you, even if you are around." I'd be happy to room with you forever, Jake thought.

"Cool. The next step is for us to check out available rooms and rank preferences. I've got the list. Want to poke around some of them tomorrow after dinner? I could stop by here and we could go look."

Tomorrow after dinner—Sunday evening. Jake's body would be cold by then. If others found Jake before Ted showed up, they could break the news to Ted; or if Ted were to come by the room and be the first to find Jake…it would work out either way. Jake couldn't have planned it better.

"Tomorrow after dinner sounds good."

"Cool." Ted stepped over to their closet. "I need to grab some clothes for tonight. Nancy's parents are in town for her birthday and they're taking us to dinner. Lahiere's on Witherspoon Street."

"Fancy."

"Yeah, and then…" Ted continued talking as he riffled through his half the closet, but Jake stopped listening, just stared at Ted's shoulder muscles rippling under his thin beige sweater with each shove of this hangered shirt and that, his biceps flexing when he lifted a pair of slacks. Such a handsome profile.

Roommates again? Maybe Ted would lose interest in Nancy. Jake pictured himself and Ted lifting his bunk bed frame off from above Ted's, setting the two beds side-by-side. They'd lie in one another's arms every night, Ted cuddling Jake close, telling him how much he—

"So if you're here, I'll see you then?" said Ted.

"What?"

"Tomorrow."

"Of course I'll be here," said Jake, wondering at Ted's question. Hadn't they already agreed to meet at the room after dinner tomorrow?

"Cool," said Ted. "So…any plans for tonight?"

"I figure I'll go to a movie on campus. *Cabaret*."

"Oh yeah, we missed it when they were showing it last fall. Okay, gotta run. Don't forget now."

"Uh, okay." What was Jake not supposed to forget? About checking out rooms tomorrow night? "Wish Nancy a happy birthday for me."

"Will do." Ted lingered that extra goodbye second as he always did, with his characteristic wave, then he was out the door.

So incredibly adorable, thought Jake. And yes, tomorrow would be perfect. All Jake needed was the courage.

/ /

Jake went to the 8:00 PM showing of *Cabaret*, wondering whether he chose that particular film as opposed to Kubrick's *Clockwork Orange* to be the last movie he'd ever see because he knew it was partly about Jewish suffering during the Nazi rise

245

to power—a final honoring of his people? A final moment of connection?

As the movie unfolded, as Jake realized the Michael York character to be a closeted homosexual who just couldn't make the relationship with Liza Minelli's character work, Jake regarded the film as confirmation that he was right about his own future. If he were to live, it would never work.

Afterward, Jake returned to his dorm and went to bed early so as to be fresh the next day. He recognized the irony in wanting to be at his most alert when killing himself.

As he finished *davening* Sunday morning, Jake added a prayer of gratitude for all God had done for him, and expressed hope that God would understand what he was about to do in a couple hours' time "all in the name of Your glory."

As he had once before, Jake heard a sort of moaning in his head, but he chose to ignore it.

Jake sat at his desk, retrieved two envelopes from his drawer as well as a yellow legal pad. He wanted to declare his love to Ted, but that would only horrify Ted and make him loathe Jake's memory. So he just wrote, "Sorry to mess up your room. Thanks for being a super roommate and the best friend ever. Have a happy life."

The letter to his parents and Artie was longer: "I can't explain the pain, it's just too much to bear. I know this will hurt you, and I'm so sorry. Thanks for being a terrific family. I love you all. Artie, maybe one day you'll name a son after me. I'd like to have engraved on my tombstone that phrase from the Passover *haggadah* about 'all his bones proclaim His glory' or something like that. So that I'll be remembered as a good Jewish boy."

Jake sealed the letters in separate envelopes, wrote "Ted" on the one and "Mom, Dad, Artie" on the other. He secreted them into his desk's top drawer.

Then he telephoned his parents, knowing they'd be enjoying their usual Sunday bagels, lox and cream cheese right about then. He told them mid-terms hadn't been all that difficult.

"Attaboy!" said Dad.

Throughout the conversation, Jake took great care to keep his voice cheerful but not overly so. This would be the last conversation they had, he and his parents. They'd be better off without him, but he didn't want them later to think he'd given clues that they'd somehow missed. He didn't want them to blame themselves for anything. It wasn't their fault he was perverted.

After saying a casual goodbye and "Love you lots," he hung up, dressed, and headed out into the wintry morning. He felt anxious trudging through sidewalk slush along Nassau Street. Violence — hanging, wrist slitting, stabbing, shooting — was terrifyingly unthinkable. But Jake had heard that some movie stars — Marilyn Monroe? Judy Garland? — had died from sleeping pill overdose.

As the bells atop the shop door jingled, the tall fatherly pharmacist smiled at Jake from behind the counter.

Just the way he'd done when coming to buy condoms, Jake hovered a bit in the greeting card aisle, pretended to peruse birthday and congratulations cards. Then he glanced around until finding the sleep-aid shelf. He recognized Sominex from TV commercials, heard the jingle in his head: "Take Sominex tonight and sleep…safe and restful sleep, sleep, sleep." Reading the ingredients, he saw that the active ingredient was an antihistamine; he recalled the time a year ago when the combination of muscle relaxant and antihistamine had made him nearly catatonic. If such a small dose of medicines could render him speechless and practically immobile, an entire bottle of pills would probably knock him out for good.

Concentrating on appearing casual, he took the bottle to the cash register. The white-haired pharmacist smiled kindly, rang up the purchase, offered a sympathetic look. Could he read Jake's thoughts? "Midterms are over, but you still can't sleep?" asked the old pharmacist. "They work you kids too hard. Too much stress."

Jake smiled wanly as part of him wished this tall scarecrow with too-long eyelashes and wrinkly smile would walk around the counter, pull Jake to him, press Jake's head against his strong shoulder, then kiss his forehead and say that Jake looked like a good boy, and that everything would be all right.

After Jake paid, the pharmacist slipped the bottle into a small white paper bag and handed it to Jake with a quiet smile, but no further conversation.

/ /

Back at the dorm, Jake went up to the men's room, washed hands and face, filled a plastic cup with water, carried the cup downstairs to his room. Inside, he stepped over to his desk, withdrew the envelopes with notes he'd written to his family and Ted, placed them on Ted's pillow. Whoever found Jake would see the notes for sure.

Wanting to make this ceremonious somehow, to show God this wasn't a rash, impulsive decision, but one that had been weighed carefully, Jake put on a *yarmulke* and set his *siddur* up on his bunk.

He removed the Sominex bottle from the white paper bag—its crinkles sounded like whimpers…asking him to hurry or asking him to stop?

His hands were shaking.

He popped the cap off the bottle. He tossed a handful of oval blue pills into his mouth, took a big swig of water.

Tears started to run down his cheeks, tears of relief, tears of fear.

He swallowed. His stomach heaved and he spat up a few undissolved pills…as if his body were trying to thwart rather than cooperate. More water. He re-swallowed those half- dissolved pills, then swallowed still more. A bitter taste on the back of his tongue. More water. He repeated the process until the bottle was empty. He left the empty Sominex bottle on Ted's dresser.

Then he climbed up to his bunk, opened the *siddur* and recited the *Shema*, the prayer asserting the singularity of God, the central tenet of Judaism, the most important prayer, the one that, according to Dad, every good Jew should recite just before dying: "Hear O Israel, the Lord our God, the Lord is one." These would be Jake's final words. If not a good Jew in life, then at least....

He lay back and waited to die. His thoughts swirled: was he doing the right thing? A pointless question because now it was too late. How long would it take? How long before he drifted off to sleep, never to wake again?

Was he doing the right thing? Too late to change your mind, Jake. You're adhering to the Torah, so of course it's the right thing. The Torah condemns abominations, although...it doesn't condone suicide. Does the Torah actually say anything about suicide? Jake hadn't thought to look. He wasn't making a mistake, was he?

Tingling in his fingertips. The pills were working. A good thing, right? Of course a good thing.

Tingling in his toes. Yes, the pills were working. Eyes starting to get heavy.

Tingling up his calves. Good. Really working. 'God, am I doing right?'

Jake heard a soft weeping in his head, but couldn't make sense of it.

Tingling up his thighs. Tingling at the base of his spine. His spine? Oh no, his spine! What if he didn't die, but ended up paralyzed? Tingling creeping up his spine. Oh God, up his spine. Up and up, one vertebrae at a time toward his neck. "Oh God," Jake mumbled, "please don't let me be paralyzed. Dear God, hear this, my final prayer even though I have no right to pray to You.

Please don't let me be paralyzed. Show me mercy. Take me and do whatever You wish with my soul, but please don't let me be paralyzed. Please please please."

The tingling stopped. Everything felt so heavy. Arms heavy. Legs heavy. Whole body heavy.

Yet Jake remained awake. How could he be...still awake...all those pills...still awake. Spine—paralyzed? Maybe. Maybe he wouldn't...fall asleep. To stop self from...paralyzed. Part of him wanted...no...no.... Oh God, did part of him want to...live? "Help," he mumbled in a volume he himself could barely hear.

He thought to vomit, but couldn't move.... Help help, inside his head.... Vomit and live.... Help...can't move.... Too late.... Arms heavy, legs.... Too late.... Spine...neck.

Heavy.

Vomit.

Can't.

'God?'

Jake heard the key in the lock. Ted walked in.

Summoning all his energy, Jake opened his eyes. "Te...," he murmured.

Jake saw Ted look at him lying there, dart his eyes to the empty Sominex bottle, to the envelopes on his pillow. "Jake—what did you do!" Ted grabbed the envelope addressed to him, tore it open, scanned it quickly, dropped it to the floor, leapt to the telephone, dialed. "My roommate's trying to kill himself—what should I do?"

Relieved—yes...relieved....

Jake blacked out.

"Come on now, get up."
What?

Shaking. Someone shaking arm.

"Come on now, we're getting you up."

A man yanking.

Tired. So tired. Heavy. Sleep.

"Come on now. We're proctors. We're getting you up."

Eyes half-open. Bleary. Two men. White man. Black man.

"We got ya."

Slipping down off the top bunk. *Yarmulke* slides off. "My *yarm* —"

"Stand tall now."

On feet. Knees weak. *Yarmulke*?

Man holding each arm.

"Walk."

"Can't." So heavy. No *yarmulke*. Bad Jew.

"Walk!" Firm. Insistent.

Legs barely move.

Half-dragged out the room, out the dorm. University Place? Car. Back seat. Ted beside. Ted holding hand.

Ted holding his hand.

Driving.
Stopping.
Proctors dragging Jake upstairs.
Ted? Where's Ted?
Blackout.

/ /

Toilet. Retching. Vomiting. Someone's hand against forehead.
Vomiting.
Blackout.

/ /

Dave, whom Jake hadn't seen for ages now, his brownish-red
hair teased up like a wild halo around his head, flew in through
the window, stood all wrapped in a black cape, stepped toward
the bed, leaned over, bit Jake's neck and lapped his blood.
Blackout.

/ /

"I'm Dean O'Malley."
Jake opened his eyes. Through the haze, he made out a
woman. Short-haired brunette wig that was on crooked.
"You're in McCosh Infirmary. We want you to get well, Jake.
We all care about you."
Blackout.

/ /

Two Puritans, a man and a woman dressed in characteristic black and white, looking suitably dour, stood side-by-side in front of Jake. Was it Thanksgiving?

The Puritans dissolved.

The worst sight Jake had ever seen: Mom's face twisted in agony. "Jake," she said with a sob. Leaning over his hospital bed rail. "My little Jake. My baby."

Dad held Mom up. His own face struggling. "We're here, son. You're going to be okay."

Blackout.

/ /

"Why'd you do it?!"

Groggy, Jake turned his head on the pillow, looked at a black man in white lab coat. Frizzy white Afro. Staring over horn-rimmed glasses. Sitting on a chair beside the bed. Holding a notepad. Why bark at Jake? Jake was groggy, not deaf. The man wore a stethoscope around his neck—a doctor? Not Dr. Peril.

Jake's heavy eyelids drooped closed again—so sleepy.

"Wake up!" The doctor jostled Jake's right shoulder. "Why'd you do it?!" he demanded again, his voice louder now.

Jake summoned all his energy—could the doctor tell he was shrugging? Jake didn't care.

He felt so groggy. Jake stared at the white wall behind the doctor, up at the white ceiling, over to the open doorway opposite his bed, at the bedside IV with plastic bag and tube descending down…into Jake's left arm.

An IV in Jake's arm.

"A glucose solution to flush your system."

"Pee."

"Here's a urinal." The doctor placed a plastic container in Jake's hand, closed Jake's fingers around the handle. "Got it?"

Jake dragged the container beneath the blanket, shoved it between his legs, up under his hospital gown. He let loose a stream. Ahhh.

Then a warm wetness—his thighs, his buttocks. Odd pee smell.

"Missed," Jake mumbled.

"Nurse!" called the doctor.

A tall thin white woman entered. In white uniform and cap. The doctor stood. "Please clean him up and change the sheets. Then come get me."

The doctor left. The nurse stroked Jake's forehead. "You're having a difficult time," she said, her voice soft as a kiss. "Things will get better. We'll help you."

Jake opened his eyes wider, stared into her deep hazel ones, at her gentle smile. He wanted to reach up and hug her, but no strength. Who was this woman who cared without knowing him? Maybe she'd tried to kill herself once, too?

"I'm a nurse, and I'm also the mother of a teenage boy, so don't you be shy. I'm going to wipe you down with a washcloth, then I'll change your sheets and gown, okay?"

Jake gave a heavy half nod.

So gentle. Jake felt the way he had when eight years old with scarlet fever and Mom gave him alcohol sponge baths to bring his temperature down. Mom. Mom was here before, right? In the infirmary—that's where he was, right? Mom this morning? Yesterday? With Dad. What were they doing here at college?

The nurse rolled him onto his side, undid the bed sheet behind him and tucked in a fresh one, rolled him back toward her onto the fresh half-sheet, tugged up the other half of the soiled one, tucked the end of the fresh one into the bed's other side.

"It's the IV," she explained while disconnecting the tube from his arm, sitting him up, pulling his arms through a fresh white gown, then reconnecting the IV. "Filling you with a solution to flush your system. To get rid of the sleeping pills." She again caressed his forehead. "There you go." She bundled the soiled sheet into a big ball. "Dr. Ackerman's the best doctor at McCosh Infirmary."

"Seems mean." The grogginess was a shade lighter now.

"He only wants to help. Let him."

She parted with a smile, and a moment later, Dr. Ackerman returned. He stood at Jake's bedside, clasped Jake's forearm, stared into his eyes, asked, "You awake now?"

"Yes."

"I had to be firm to keep your attention. You kept falling asleep."

"Okay."

"I need you to tell me, Jake. Why'd you do it?"

Jake looked aside at the wall.

"Are classes too hard?"

"I'm doing okay."

"Yes, you are. Last semester you got an A+, an A, an A- and a B+."

"I'm okay."

"Your father wanted me to ask if you're feeling guilty over that pigeon lab experiment last fall in your psych course."

"Yes. But no. It's not that."

"Then what, Jake?"

"I don't know."

"You don't know why you swallowed a bottle of sleeping pills?"

No response.

"Do you like girls?"

Jake's head snapped forward. What? How did this stranger know to ask that question? Who was this stranger to ask Jake such a personal thing? Jake wouldn't disclose anything private to him or anyone. It was too shameful. What he felt. What he'd done at the Dinky station. Twice.

Even in his lingering grogginess, Jake knew to protect himself. But if he gave a knee-jerk, defensive-sounding reply—"Of course I like girls. What's the matter with you?"—the answer might seem too pat. The doctor might wonder if Jake were lying.

"Sometimes," Jake replied. "I like girls sometimes," Jake replied. That was a non-defensive answer. That should throw the doctor off track.

"Okay," said Dr. Ackerman. He scribbled notes. "At least we're talking. You rest now. And take your time to think about things. We're going to keep you in the infirmary for a week or so."

"But I'll miss classes."

"You just tried to kill yourself, young man, yet you're worried about missing classes? Don't you realize how serious this is?"

Jake didn't know how to respond.

"I'll arrange for your professors to send assignments."

"But don't—"

"Don't what? Don't tell them?"

Jake nodded.

"Don't you worry about that. I've already spoken to your room-mate. He volunteered to bring your books."

"Where's Ted?"

"No more visitors today," continued Dr. Ackerman. "I sent your parents home. They didn't want to leave, but I told them it would be too emotional for you to see them right now. Was I right?"

Jake nodded.

"I thought so. I'm on your side, Jake."

Their eyes met. Jake believed him.

"Your parents will be back later in the week. For today, just rest. If you need anything, call the nurse. Or me. Any time."

These people were being so nice. Strangers. But, thought Jake, if they knew the truth, they wouldn't be so nice. They'd probably let him die.

Dr. Ackerman left.

Jake dozed then woke, dozed then woke throughout the rest of the afternoon and evening and night.

"I told Mrs. Polenko you were in the infirmary with the flu."

"Thanks." Jake couldn't bring his eyes to meet Ted's.

"Here's your Russian text book. Mrs. Polenko circled this week's exercises for you to do. If you want, I can bring them to her after you do them so you can keep up."

"Really great of you, thanks."

"Jake," said Ted, standing beside his bed. "Dr. Ackerman and Dean O'Malley asked my opinion, whether I thought you really wanted to kill yourself. If you did, they won't let you stay at Princeton. That'd be too much of a risk for you…and for them."

"Are they forcing me out like Sheldon?" Jake hadn't considered the possibility of what might happen if he survived the pills. "What did you say?"

"I told them the truth—that you didn't really want to kill yourself."

"You said that? But, I swallowed a whole bottle of pills."

"Saturday afternoon when I stopped by the room. I told you I'd come by the room on Sunday."

"In the evening. After dinner. You said you'd come by in the evening so we could check out rooms for next year."

"Yeah, and while I was getting clothes at the closet, I told you I'd also come back to the room Sunday at 11:00 in the morning to change clothes for brunch with Nancy and her parents. I said it would be good if you could be there then so we could make a specific plan about which rooms to check out later that evening. I told you I'd be at the room twice on Sunday."

"You told me that?"

"I sure did."

"I didn't hear you. The whole time you were talking at the closet, I was daydreaming."

Ted tilted his head in question. "About what?"

"Doesn't matter." Jake searched Ted's eyes. "You really said you'd be coming to the room at 11:00 in the morning?"

Ted nodded. "And you said you'd be in the room then."

"I meant in the evening. I didn't hear you about being at the room in the morning."

"Maybe not consciously, but part of you heard. That's why you took the pills when you did. Part of you knew I'd come find you before it was too late."

If what Ted was saying was true—and why would he lie?—then Jake had known he'd be saved and wouldn't actually die. Was it possible that Jake wanted to make the gesture of trying to end his life—to show God that he, Jake, was willing to respect and obey God at any cost—but at the same time, he still wanted to live?

"You didn't really want to die, Jake. You didn't. You just needed to scream for help." Ted pinched the bridge of his nose. "I heard your scream, Jake. I've been neglecting you for months, and I'm sorry. It wasn't intentional. It's just that I'm so nuts about Nancy, and—"

"Stop. You didn't do anything wrong. You were just living. Normally, that's all. This isn't about you."

"I'm not so sure about that."

"What do you mean?"

"Dr. Ackerman asked if I knew why you did it."

"And?"

"I told him I had no idea."

"Of course not, it's private."

Ted just nodded, reached down and took Jake's hand. "Jake, you're my pal. I'm here if you want to talk."

Each morning for the next three days, Jake spoke on the phone with his parents. Every evening before bed, too.

Mom sobbed through the entirety of each conversation, and Dad repeatedly asked if they could come visit. "I'm not ready," Jake said.

He asked if Artie knew what had happened.

"No," said Dad. "We told him you were very ill with an unusually bad flu that was highly contagious to adolescents, so Artie can't come see you. He sends his love."

Ted visited every day, bringing assignments and books, taking back homework Jake finished. Jake steered conversations away from anything personal. On the fourth day of Jake's infirmary stay, Ted arrived looking unusually tired with bags under his eyes. He slumped into the chair.

"You okay?" asked Jake.

Ted breathed in deeply through his nose. "Jake, listen, there's something I need to tell you."

"Okay." Jake felt suddenly nervous.

"It's about room draw."

Jake looked away. Of course Ted wouldn't want to room with a suicidal maniac like him. Of course. "That's okay," said Jake, meaning it. "I understand. I wouldn't want to room with me, either."

"It's not what you think."

"I don't blame you, Ted. Every time you'd come back to the room, you'd wonder if you'd find me dead in bed. I get it. It's okay. Don't worry about it."

"It's not just that."

"Then, what?"

"Dean O'Malley asked me to call her once a week to let her know how you're doing."

"That's not fair to you."

"I understand why she asked, but it's too much. I mean, what if I said you were fine, but then...you know..."

"But then I killed myself for real. You'd feel responsible."

"Exactly."

"I get it, Ted, really."

"Besides, I don't want to spy on you. You're my friend."

"I understand."

"And so..." Ted stood and turned his back. "It's not just about next year. I've asked to be assigned a different room for the rest of *this* year."

"This year?" Jake felt his stomach cave in.

"I asked Dr. Ackerman if now was the right time to tell you. He said it'd be better while you're here. In case you reacted badly."

"Everybody's afraid I'm going to try to kill myself again, I guess. I really made a mess of things, didn't I?"

"I'm sorry, Jake. Really."

"I know."

"You hate me?"

"You saved my life. You visit me every day. You're the best friend I ever had."

"We're still buddies?" Ted extended his hand.

Jake shook the strong hand, grateful for the touch. "Did they find you a room already?"

"At the Graduate College, away from the main campus."

"And away from me. Okay, I get it."

Jake's parents walked into the room.

"Mom? Dad? What are you doing here? I told you—"

"You told us it was too soon to come visit," said Dad. "Maybe it's too soon for you, and I apologize, but it's not soon enough for your mother and me. We need to see you. We can't wait any more."

Mom, eyes like puffy red slits, rushed over and hugged Jake, covered his face with kisses.

"Ted," said Dad, shaking his hand. "Ted, with all the turmoil Sunday night, we didn't get a chance to thank you, to thank you for…for…."

"You don't need to thank me, Mr. Stein."

"Oh yes, we do," said Mom, standing and clasping Ted to her. "You saved our boy's life. We can never repay you."

"Mom, stop. You're embarrassing him."

Mom pulled back, blew her nose into a tissue.

"I'm gonna go and give you folks some time together," said Ted.

"See you tomorrow?" asked Jake.

"Sure. Tomorrow."

Jake's stomach filled with lead as Dad gently pulled Mom back, seated her in the visitor's chair, then shook Jake's hand and stood beside her. "So, Jake, you're looking well."

"Food's not bad. I told them no meat because it wouldn't be kosher."

Dad shook his head. "You're a good boy, Jake. But you don't need to worry about that. You know the Talmud lets us break rules for medical reasons. Health comes first. Life before everything."

A wail escaped Mom's lips. She covered face with hands.

"Millie, you promised."

"I'm sorry," she whimpered, composing herself.

"No, I'm sorry, Mom," said Jake, twiddling thumbs on his chest. "I'm sorry I hurt you so badly."

"This isn't about me, it's about you. When I think that you could be so distressed that you'd—"

"Millie, stop. The doctor told us not to upset him."

"As if he's not already upset? He tried to kill himself! My son tried to kill himself!" She jumped up and fled the room.

"Forgive your mother, Jake. She's having a tough time." Dad ran out after her.

What have I done? wondered Jake, finally allowing himself to think the questions he'd been blocking: Who was it that had called Jake's parents to tell them? How was Dad able to maintain enough calm to drive the hour or so to campus on Sunday with Mom hysterical at his side? Was there traffic? Did they yell at Dr. Ackerman or Dean O'Malley, blaming them? Did they interrogate Ted? How long had they waited at Jake's side while he was unconscious? Did they want to yank Jake out of school? Did the doctor advocate locking him up in an asylum?

And the biggest question of all: did they suspect Jake's shameful truth?

A few minutes later, his parents returned. "I apologize for being so emotional," whispered Mom as she dabbed a tissue at her nose.

"It's okay," said Jake. "Really, it's okay."

"Just get well, my darling. That's the only thing that matters. Whatever's bothering you—it's not worth…. I couldn't bear life without you." She caressed his cheek as her own face crinkled into misery.

How could Jake have thought his parents would be better off without him? If he didn't want to bring shame on them, he could always run away and live somewhere they'd never have to see him. They'd miss him, but wouldn't be devastated like this.

Again guiding Mom into the chair, Dad asked, "Is there anything you want to talk about, son?"

"No."

"You can tell us anything," said Mom. "We love you."

Jake shook his head.

At that moment, Dean O'Malley walked in, her wig sitting straight this time. "How's our boy?"

Mom stood. "He's looking well, Dean O'Malley," said Dad, reaching out to shake her hand. Mom followed suit.

"Please take my seat," offered Mom.

"No, thank you, I won't be staying. I just heard that you were both here. I've wanted to speak to the three of you together."

"Of course," said Dad.

"Jake," said Dean O'Malley, "I hope you realize that your actions are serious. Very serious."

"Yes, Ma'am," he said softly.

"Dr. Ackerman and others in the administration and I have been consulting."

Oh God, was she about to expel Jake?

"We want to act in your best interest."

"Please let me stay in school," he blurted. "I'll be good. I won't do it again. Honest. It was a mistake, that's all. Please let me stay."

"I'm glad to hear you refer to this as a mistake, Jake. That's truly wonderful. Dr. Ackerman believes in the get-right-back-on-the-horse theory. He thinks you should jump back into university life."

"Yes, please."

"But I'm not so certain. What would be different for you now than a week ago? Whatever troubled you then…why wouldn't it trouble you now? We're so lucky your roommate found you when he did. We don't want to risk being unlucky next time."

"There won't be a next time. I promise. It was a mistake." What exactly was the mistake? wondered Jake. Was it that he took the pills, or that he did so when part of him knew Ted would be returning to their room before the pills could take full effect?

"If your parents agree—their agreement is essential—we're willing to let you stay on a trial basis."

"But what sort of supervision can you offer?" asked Mom. "At home I can look after him every—"

Dad interrupted: "I would assume there'd be conditions to Jake's trial stay, Dean O'Malley?"

"Yes. Jake, in order for you to stay, you'll be required to see a psychiatrist for as long as he deems necessary."

"A psychiatrist?" Jake pictured a psychiatrist ordering him into a straight jacket. Electric shock treatments. Lobotomies. "No. No psychiatrist. I'm not crazy."

Her voice softened. "No one's calling you crazy. But we do believe that you're troubled. Deeply troubled. Obviously so. If you wish to stay on campus, you'll need to meet regularly with a psychiatrist. This is not negotiable. I know a warm friendly therapist in town, Dr. Enríquez. He'll report weekly to Dr. Ackerman—not about the content of your conversations because those will remain confidential. But he will let us know whether or not you're attending your weekly sessions. If the occasion arises when you feel depressed again and you and Dr. Enríquez think you'd benefit from returning to the infirmary for a short period of time, we'll be able to accommodate you."

"You mean," asked Mom, "you're sending Jake back to his dorm room? Unsupervised?" "We're a campus, Mrs. Stein, not a—"

"Not an asylum," mumbled Jake.

"Not a rehab facility," said Dean O'Malley.

"I don't like the idea of Jake living unsupervised," said Mom.

"Millie," interjected Dad, "these are experts on college kids."

"If they're such experts, then why didn't they see this coming!"

"Millie!"

"He didn't try this at home, did he?" Mom demanded. "He tried it here. What's wrong with you people?" She yelled at Dean O'Malley, "Letting a perfectly healthy boy—"

"Millie!" Dad grabbed Mom by the shoulders, whispered something into her ear.

Mom slumped against Dad. "I apologize, Dean, for blaming you," Mom mumbled. "I don't know what I'm saying."

"Yes, you do. You're a loving mother protective of her child. I'm a mother, too. Two little girls. I understand. Believe me."

"Thank you," squeaked Mom.

"Mrs. Stein, there's another option if you'd prefer," continued Dean O'Malley. "Jake could take an indefinite leave of absence from school, return home to you, and petition for return to Princeton at some point in the future. Keep in mind there's no guarantee we'd grant that petition. And I can tell you we would do so only with certification by a psychiatrist of our choosing that Jake is well."

The idea of discussing personal things with a psychiatrist nauseated Jake. But clearly he'd have to talk to a shrink either here or at home. He looked over at Mom, at her sniffles and crinkled red face, her nose peeling from all the tissue rubbing. At Dad pretending so hard he was okay that his face was pale. Did Jake want to live with them and every day see the pain he'd caused? No way. Nor did he want to take the risk of never being allowed to return to college. His whole life would be ruined. "I'll stay here and see your psychiatrist," he said.

"Shouldn't we discuss this?" asked Mom.

"I want to stay," said Jake. "Whatever I have to do."

Dad squeezed Mom's hand. She lowered her eyes.

"I was hoping you'd decide that," said Dean O'Malley. "Clearly you have a sensitive soul. We need young men like you here at Princeton."

"Like me?" Jake surprised himself by voicing the question.

"Exactly like you." Dean O'Malley stepped to his side, squeezed his forearm. "Dr. Ackerman will keep me apprised, but you're welcome to stop by my office. Any time. I'd be happy to see you."

She shook Jake's hand warmly.

"Thank you, Dean," said Dad, standing and shaking her hand. Mom nodded tearfully.

Dean O'Malley left.

"Sounds like a great plan," said Dad with too much enthusiasm.

"You sure you don't want just to come home?" asked Mom.

"He'll be under a doctor's care, Millie. He's making an adult decision. Everyone stumbles. The mature thing is to take a helping hand, get up, wipe yourself off, and try again. I'm proud of you, son, for being willing to face whatever's weighing on you."

"Thanks, Dad."

"We're always here if you need us, your mother and I."

"I know."

"There are a few more things I need to say," continued Dad, his voice flattening.

"Sol, the doctor said not to be confrontational, not yet, it's too soon."

"He's my son and I'll speak to him as I see fit."

Dad didn't have any suspicions about…did he? "I'm tired, Dad."

"This won't take long. You're your own man now, but you're still my son. I will speak my mind."

"Okay." Jake steeled himself for what might come next.

"I asked Ted—a good boy, that Ted, he really cares about you—I asked him if you've been eating at Stevenson and attending services. He says he doesn't think you have."

"I only eat kosher food," protested Jake. "Even when I eat at Commons. Only kosher food. And I *daven* a lot in my room."

"That's good, but that's not what I mean. Actually, I mean the opposite. This isn't easy for me to say, Jake, but I have to: if you no longer wish to be observant, that's your business. You're a man now. I've educated you in Jewish tradition, so now it's up to you. If you want to be less observant than me, well, that's your

270

choice. There's no shame in it. You've got a good Jewish heart. Your Uncle Irv and Aunt Flora are way less observant than I am, but we're best friends, right? I'm less observant than my parents were, right? I married a woman less observant than me because she's such a wonderful person."

"Oh, Sol."

"What I mean, Jake, is...I remember what it's like to be young and in love...maybe you've fallen in love with a non-Jewish woman and think it's an impossible situation. If that's the case, I won't be happy about it, but...."

How Dad surprised him. "Thank you, Dad."

"Whatever it is...I don't care what decisions you need to make in order to live your life, as long as you live it. Or maybe you don't want to go to law school the way I was expecting. Whatever it is, I'll adjust. But even if I can't, even if I can't adjust, Jake, it doesn't matter. This is your life, not mine."

Jake had never heard Dad talk this way. Of course Dad didn't really know the implications of what he was saying, but still.

In his hospital gown, Jake climbed over the bed rail out of bed, embraced Dad, rested his head on Dad's shoulder the way he used to do as a little boy.

When Ted showed up the next day, he shuffled into Jake's infirmary room looking even more exhausted than the day before.

"You don't look well," said Jake, sitting up in bed. "Your skin's sallow, and dark under the eyes."

"I didn't sleep at all last night. I haven't been sleeping well for days."

"My fault, isn't it?"

Ted shrugged.

"Sorry."

"Dean O'Malley told me you'll be staying on campus. I'm glad."

Jake relayed the previous day's conversation, emphasizing how "Mom's fairly hysterical."

"That surprises you? How did you expect her to react?"

"I don't know. But she acts like—"

"Like what?" Ted's voice was rising. "Like she's afraid you might try it again?"

"Hey, calm down."

"Maybe I'm tired of being calm. Maybe we're all tired of tip-toeing around you and pretending everything's okay. It's not okay, Jake. Everything's not okay."

"Whoa, where's this coming from? You've been so cool. But now— Hey, you need some sleep."

"And exactly how am I supposed to sleep after what you did? What'll you do the next time you get depressed—jump off Blair Tower? What if I'm not there to catch you?"

"I've never seen you angry."

"I've been putting my feelings aside for days, but now they're erupting and I can't help it. When you hurt yourself, everyone who cares about you feels like a total fuck-up for not being a good enough friend or parent to realize you were suffering so badly." Ted's face reddened. His fists clenched. "I just saw you on Saturday. We had a conversation on Saturday like normal. We talked about rooming together next year, and I thought everything was fine, then the very next day you tried to off yourself." Ted punched his right fist into his left hand. "How do you think that makes me feel?"

Jake mumbled, "Pretty bad, I guess."

"I feel so damn responsible, I can't bear it."

"Responsible? It's not your fault I—"

"Isn't it? Aren't I part of your problem?"

Jake felt suddenly cold. This was too close for comfort. "I'm really tired, Ted, maybe you'd better go." Jake pulled the covers up to his chin.

"I spent last night figuring it out," Ted said. "Finally the pieces started to fit together."

"I'm sleepy. You need sleep, too. Please go."

"You don't date girls, and when you do, you don't like them."

"Marla's one girl, Ted, just one. Stop it, it's none of your damn business."

"And last night, as Nancy watched me grab a shirt from her closet, something finally clicked, something I always thought was just me and my own dumbass narcissism. The way you always look at me, especially when you think I'm not noticing. From across Commons when I'm at a table with Nancy. Or the way you looked at me Saturday when I was getting clothes from the closet, Jake."

"Stop it. You're making things up."

"Am I? You always look at me the same way Nancy does."

"You're ridiculous." Jake turned onto his side, facing away from Ted.

"You look at me with love in your face."

Jake pulled the pillow out from under his head, covered his face with it.

"Jake," he heard in muffled tones. "Come on."

He felt Ted's hand on his shoulder and tried to shake it off.

Ted squeezed his shoulder, waited a few moments, then pulled the pillow off Jake's face. "So, I'm right," he said.

Jake stared up at him. "I'm so ashamed."

"You shouldn't be. When I first started seeing Nancy, didn't you tell me it was normal for two people to have sex if they both wanted it? Why is that less true for you and any man who wants to be with you?"

"Nice of you to say," mumbled Jake. "But it's not what you actually think deep inside. You really think that your roommate—your former roommate—is a disgusting faggot."

"No, I don't think that. Maybe you do, but I don't. Don't put words in my mouth. You're my friend, and my friend is a great guy who fell in love with the wrong man. That's another reason we can't room together anymore, Jake. It wouldn't be fair to you, and to be honest, I'd always be uncomfortable."

"Of course you would. Why would you want to live with a homo who might creep up and attack you in the middle of the night?"

"Cut the bullshit. For months we slept in bunk beds and you never tried anything. I'm not afraid of you. But I don't want to feel you looking at me the way Nancy does. Or the way I look at her.

I'm always checking out her body, the way she moves, everything. If you and I room together I'll always feel self-conscious. Besides, I think how I'd feel if Nancy and I roomed together but she told me we could never have sex—I'd be frustrated out of my skull. How could that possibly be good for you?"

"It couldn't. It's not. It's awful. But it's not your fault, Ted."

"I know that. I didn't set out to frustrate you. But I don't want to do that in the future."

"You're right."

"And there's something else. It's about you being so religious."

"I'm not really, not by Orthodox standards."

"But you are by your own standards. You know I'm an atheist, but last night I imagined what it must be like to believe that God declares certain things right and others wrong. And what if you think that something inside you is one of those wrong things? That must hurt. A lot."

"You really were up all night, weren't you?"

"You're my friend. I want to understand you."

"I don't need to see Dean O'Malley's psychiatrist. I just need to talk to you."

"You can talk to both of us."

"But how can I talk to a stranger about such personal stuff?"

"That's exactly the point—who gives a damn what a stranger thinks? If the psychiatrist doesn't like what you say, fuck him." Then with a shy, tentative half-smile, Ted added, "I don't mean that literally."

Jake blushed deeply. Was it really possible that Ted was okay talking about all this…even joking about it?

PART 8

The first thing Jake did after Dr. Ackerman signed him out of the infirmary was rush to his dorm room and check: the blanket and sheets were off Ted's lower bunk bed, and the drawers of Ted's wooden dresser and desk were empty, as was his half the closet. It was true, Ted had moved out.

Jake felt emptier than at the end of a long Yom Kippur fast.

At least Ted said he still wanted to be friends. His daily visits to the infirmary proved he was sincere.

Jake looked at his watch, changed clothes, and headed off for his first visit with Dr. Enríquez. Walking down cloudy Nassau Street, Jake noticed that although his stomach felt full of butterflies, it wasn't clenching nearly as badly as it had been before.... Maybe Jake had just needed a good week's rest in the infirmary?

He turned down residential Chestnut Street, walked a couple blocks and found the old three-story white house Dr. Enríquez had described on the phone. As instructed, Jake walked up the side staircase to a second-floor private suite and knocked. The man who opened the door was around Dad's age, pudgy, with thin graying hair and black-rimmed glasses, wore loose beige slacks and white button-down shirt. He welcomed Jake with a smile, extended a hand. The two shook.

Dark wooden bookcases along the office walls, a large desk covered in papers and pads. Leggy philodendrons in pots on a shelf over a radiator by a wide window that looked out at a white-barked birch tree full of buds. Dr. Enríquez pointed to one of two overstuffed green armchairs, each with a coffee table beside it. A box of tissues stood on the table beside Jake's armchair.

All morning Jake had been telling himself he should open up to Dr. Enríquez the way Ted had advised. But the moment the doctor asked him, point-blank, "Do you want to tell me why you overdosed on sleeping pills?" Jake replied reflexively, "No, I don't want to tell you."

Dr. Enríquez nodded, crossed his legs, scratched under his chin, and said casually, "You know you need to talk to me in order to stay at the university."

"I'm not going to talk about that."

"Because…?"

"It's personal."

"Don't you think my job is to help you resolve personal issues?"

"Your job is to keep me in school." Jake didn't intend to be rude, but knew that's how he was sounding.

"The way I give you the chance to stay in school is to help you figure out how to deal with personal issues, don't you think?"

"You're a stranger."

"That's true. So, maybe we need to get to know one another better first. Tell me—how does it feel to be back in your dorm room?"

"Good."

"No discomfort? Difficulty sleeping?"

"Why would there be?"

"Well, that's the bed where…you know."

"Where I swallowed the pills and planned to sleep forever."

"Exactly."

"No. No discomfort. It's just a bed. It's not inside my head."

"Is that where the discomfort is, Jake? Inside your head?"

"Duh."

"That's a private place, inside one's head."

"You better believe it."

Dr. Enríquez nodded again, uncrossed his legs, recrossed them. "How're classes going?"

Jake didn't mind discussing classes, started by talking about Russian and then the other subjects, about grades and how much more comfortable he felt with the workload this semester than last. Non-threatening topics of conversation.

"Do you think maybe you've been working too hard?"

"Did anyone tell you that?"

"No one had to. It's a common problem around here—over-work, insufficient downtime."

"I guess that's true," Jake said. "Especially first semester, I was scared I'd flunk out."

"But now you've proved to yourself that you won't."

"I guess. But I've got to get good grades to get into law school."

"You won't get into law school if you're dead. To be blunt."

Jake gave a nervous chuckle. "I get your point."

"So can you ease up a bit? Maybe cut back study time enough to give yourself a couple hours a day to relax?"

"I could probably do that."

"I'd recommend it. In fact, as your doctor, I'm prescribing it."

Maybe Jake wouldn't mind talking with this man a little more. (Just a little.)

J ake continued attending classes as before, and spent afternoons studying and doing homework; but taking into account Dr. Ackerman's "prescription" to cut back on study time, Jake spent early spring evenings walking and thinking. He walked all over campus, all over town, replaying all the questions Dr. Enríquez posed, reliving the days leading up to the pill-taking, the days in the infirmary, the conversations there. Over and over and over.

/ /

"Jake, please stay after class for brief conversation."

From his seat, Jake nodded at Mrs. Polenko, waited as the other students filed out. She stepped over to him. "Good boy doing all homework while in infirmary."

"I just needed to rest, that's all. But I could still study and do homework. A bad flu."

"Bad flu you say. Your roommate said same thing. I understand. I understand why you lie. But to me you don't need to lie."

Jake's face burned. "Lie? I'm not lying. I was—"

"Stop." Mrs. Polenko sat in the chair beside Jake's, took both his hands in hers. "Dr. Ackerman was afraid you work too hard, so he explained to me everything. I told him I can help with classwork. But I think you don't need such help because you are very good student on your own. But if you do need my help, you will tell me, okay?"

Jake nodded.

"Good. Now I will tell you something. Something you will not tell other students, please, okay?"

"Okay."

"In Russia, in Second World War, millions died. Millions, you understand? Nazis shot and murdered. Bombs. Freezing. Famine. My baby died because I had no food and nothing…here." Mrs. Polenko pounded her breast. "No milk."

"Mrs. Polenko, I'm so sorry. I had no idea."

"My baby would be older now than you. Many times I wanted to kill myself, Jake, many times."

Jake didn't know what to say. Why was Mrs. Polenko telling him this?

"Every my baby's birthday, still, I wish to die. But if I do, then who will teach you correct Russian grammar?" She smiled. "All you students—you are my babies. Little babies I teach to speak. You understand?"

He nodded.

"You are good student, and nice boy. Jake, everyone has problems. I never thought I would live in different country, in United States. I never thought I would teach at big university, live in safety again. But I do. If you kill yourself—you have no chance. If you live—you have chance. We cannot know our future. So Jake, from me please take advice: give yourself chance." She squeezed his hand. "You understand?"

How kind this woman was being. "Yes, Ma'am. I understand."

"Good boy."

Jake leaned down and kissed the back of Mrs. Polenko's hand as if it were the most natural thing in the world to do. She patted the top of his head. Then she stood, turned, went to the blackboard and, with her back to Jake, picked up the eraser and said, her voice cracking with emotion, "You go now, Jake."

"Yes, Ma'am. Thank you."

During the following week's session with Dr. Enríquez, Jake replied that he would be okay discussing Mom and Dad's reactions to his…"suicide attempt. There, I said it. Suicide attempt."

"That's a good step, Jake. A very good step."

"Just words. No big deal. The big deal is what I did to them, Mom and Dad."

"Tell me."

"I nearly murdered their child."

Dr. Enríquez nodded.

"I devastated them. Especially Mom."

"They love you. They're crushed to think they might have lost you, and that you've been so depressed that you'd attempt suicide."

Jake shared Ted's theory that Jake had wanted to be found and hadn't really wanted to die.

"Perhaps," said Dr. Enríquez. "Perhaps you did this as a call for help. If so, that was a scream through an enormous megaphone."

"I guess."

"Even if you wanted to be saved, you took the risk that you might not be. What if Ted had changed his plans and didn't show up at your room in time?"

"Then you and I wouldn't be having this conversation now."

"Exactly. Don't dismiss your suicide attempt as some mere bid for attention. Are you saying that you haven't genuinely been in deep pain? That there's no possibility you sincerely wished to end your life?"

"No. I'm not saying that. The pain's been real. I did want to end my life because I deserved to die."

"Why did you deserve to die? Had you done something so terrible that you needed to punish yourself with a death sentence?"

Jake grew silent. He'd disclosed more than he'd intended. But Dr. Enríquez's question was a good one. Death sentence. Did Jake deserve a death sentence for what he'd done at the Dinky station? For what he might do in the future? For violating God's rules? A death sentence? Really?

"Jake?"

"I'm all confused."

"That's normal. Let's get back to your pain. Can you tell me about that? About what it felt like?"

Jake explained the stomach clenchings every time he left his dorm room or a class or the library. The rapid breathing.

"Sounds like panic attacks to me," said Dr. Enríquez. "The body's way of responding to stress overload, fear. Not just fear, but terror. Does that make any sense?"

Terror. Jake was terrified of being what he and Ted had talked about. How could Jake deny what he was feeling toward Ted, toward men in general? Jake was terrified of those feelings and their implications.

"Are you still experiencing them, those panic attacks?"

"A lot less." On the way here, Jake hadn't doubled over at all. "Why is that?"

"Good question. Have you been sharing thoughts and feelings with anyone, maybe releasing a little pressure?"

Ted. Mrs. Polenko. Dad. And although Jake hadn't said much to Dr. Ackerman, he seemed to care. And that tall nurse who spoke to Jake. Dean O'Malley giving him a chance. And Dr. Enríquez. "It's like all of a sudden I don't have to hide being depressed. I can let it be just obvious."

"Hiding can be incredibly burdensome and stressful. When we hide something like depression, we sometimes exaggerate the potential consequences of being discovered. Depression itself makes everything seem more dire than it objectively might be. Depression distorts our perceptions of reality. Does this make any sense?"

"Yes." Jake suspected that Dr. Enríquez understood more than he was saying. "Yes, it makes sense. Everything you say makes sense."

"Let's get back to your parents. How does it feel to talk with them now?"

"Mom's a basket case. Dad's putting on a good front. I feel guilty."

"Understandable. They're probably terrified you'll try it again."

"Probably."

"Are you thinking about trying it again?"

Jake sighed. "But it's not like I have any specific plans. I just think of it as a way out, that's all. Like there's an escape hatch."

"Escape."

"Yes."

"Escape from...?"

"Myself."

"From what about yourself?"

"From being—" Jake caught himself. He was just about to say it, those words. Those words he'd said to Ted. But if he said them to Dr. Enríquez, to a professional, then it would be even more real. Official somehow. Jake stared into Dr. Enríquez's eyes, remained silent.

"Nothing you say ever leaves this room unless you want it to. Your truth is safe here, whatever it is."

Jake shook his head.

"Okay, Jake. We've covered a lot of ground today. A lot of emotional ground."

J ake chose to begin the next weekly session with Dr. Enríquez by stating, "My parents just don't understand me."

"Have you given them much chance to understand? Have you asked them to understand...whatever it is you're referring to?"

Jake looked down at the brown, indoor-outdoor carpet, at a loose flap beside Dr. Enríquez's chair that needed more tacking down. "No. No, I haven't given them a chance."

"Parents raise us with a set of standards and expectations and hopes, so we think those are the only things they understand. But sometimes—not always, but sometimes—they can change and surprise us."

"Dad surprised me in the infirmary when he said he'd be okay with me living a different kind of Jewish life than he does. Well, not that he'd be okay with it, but that he'd manage."

"Is that an issue for you, Jake? Living a different kind of Jewish life than your father?"

Jake nodded as his eyes drifted above Dr. Enríquez's head and out the window, at the birch tree budding light green leaves, at the robin standing on a branch tilting its one-eyed side of the head now up, now down.

In the weeks since his suicide attempt, Jake periodically heard mumblings in his head that he suspected were God's efforts to engage in conversation. But Jake didn't feel ready. Hadn't God tried to stop Jake from trying to prove his devotion by ending his life? Would God be pleased that Jake had failed? Or would He secretly wish that Jake had succeeded?

"Is there someone Jewish you can talk to, Jake? Other than your parents, I mean. A friend?"

"My best Jewish friend is Deb. But she's in Philly and I can't just call her up and tell her I tried to kill myself. She'd freak out. She'd want to miss classes to be with me. That wouldn't be fair to her. I could probably see her at Passover." Yes, he needed to talk to Deb, to see the absence of disgust on her face when he acknowledged aspects of himself that she'd already seemed to understand and accept when they talked about Steve. "And my Uncle Irv and Aunt Flora. They're not really my uncle and aunt, but are my parents' best friends. They're Jewish, but way less religious than Dad. Their son—" Jake stopped himself. He was going to say that their son was like Jake, or at least Jake thought so. Had Dave told his parents about how he and Jake played in bed? About Dave's own attractions to men? Maybe they'd already been through all this with him. Maybe Jake could talk to them. Uncle Irv was way cooler than Dad.

"You were saying something about their son?"

"Just that we were good friends once. He's at Berkeley now. I could probably talk to them about Jewish stuff."

"That's good, Jake. When can you speak with them?"

"It'd be weird for me just to call. Besides, like I said about Deb, it's not stuff I want to talk about over the phone. I'll see them at Passover. Maybe I could find private time with them, I don't know."

"A good possibility. Any rabbi at home you could talk to?"

Jake recalled the Yom Kippur sermon against gay Jews. "No, no rabbi at home I can talk to."

"How about the Hillel rabbi on campus?"

"I don't know him."

"That's sort of what he's here for. To be someone Jewish students can talk to about things."

"Maybe."

"Or a Jewish friend here? There's a whole Jewish dining hall, isn't there?"

"Stevenson, yes. I'm a member, and I've been a few times."

"Why just a few?"

Jake shrugged. "The only person I really know there is Marla, but I couldn't talk to her."

"Because…?"

"We went out for about a month, that's all."

"Recently?"

"It didn't work out."

"Because…."

"Just didn't."

"Because…."

"It just didn't, okay?"

"Jake, what's the worst that could happen if you were to share honest thoughts with me? What's the very worst?"

The very worst would be for Dr. Enríquez to say that yes, Jake was an abomination to be destroyed, which, Jake had to admit, didn't seem all that likely for him to say.

"Jake, listen. I don't want to push you—you're really doing great in sharing thoughts. But have you noticed that each time you mention someone Jewish to talk with, you find reasons you can't talk to them now, or at all? It's as if part of you won't permit personal conversations with anyone who's Jewish. Why do you think that is?"

"Good question," replied Jake, thinking that he didn't want anyone Jewish to condemn him the way he'd been condemning himself. The way he'd convinced himself that God condemned him. But God hadn't wanted Jake to kill himself, had He? He'd told Jake that. Had Jake gone too far in the name of Torah? "I need to think about this."

Jake was sleeping better than before. The churning in his stomach continued to decrease, as though some sort of fever had broken. Yes, he thought, crossing this street and that, strolling the extensive grounds at the Graduate College (where he hoped to bump into Ted, but didn't), walking through a woodsy path at Princeton's Institute for Advanced Study—yes, it was as if a fever had caught hold of him, had distorted his thinking before, a fever he couldn't shake. Although he could still acknowledge the reasoning that had led him to the pills, he no longer felt the same sense of doom. Maybe if he'd talked to Dr. Enríquez beforehand, or even Ted, the fever never would have taken such hold. Or Jake would have been able to cope with it better.

Should he tell Dr. Enríquez about his secret feelings? Sometimes their conversations already felt like they were talking about the same thing without actually voicing it. Like Ted said—if Dr. Enríquez didn't like the fact that Jake was…was…gay—there, Jake articulated the word to himself, the word, the very word—if Dr. Enríquez didn't like the fact that Jake was…gay…then fuck him. But not literally, hah hah.

"Jake, hi."

What?

"I haven't seen you in a long time."

It was Marla. Without even realizing, Jake had made his way down Nassau Street as the sun was beginning to set. In jeans and a yellow windbreaker, Marla had stepped out of Woolworth's just before a clerk locked the door behind her.

"Shampoo," she said, lifting a small plastic bag.

"Peach-scented?"

"You remember."

He gave an awkward nod.

"How are you, Jake?" she asked, her voice full of caring. Full of meaning.

How much did she know? "Uh, I'm okay," he said. "You?"

"I'm fine. I know you were in the infirmary, Jake. Ted told me in class."

"Oh."

"And I know it wasn't the flu, even though Ted told me that's what I should say if anyone asked."

"You mean…?

"Don't be embarrassed," she said. "I feel just awful for you, that's all. How depressed you must have been."

"Yeah, well, Ted shouldn't have said anything," Jake said. "He knows you and I aren't—"

"He knows I like you, and he thought I'd want to know. He was right. I wanted to visit you, but then I thought I shouldn't because you don't like me."

"Don't like you? I like you fine."

"You never called after that night." Marla swallowed. "I've been meaning to apologize to you."

"Apologize? What for?"

"For being so forward. You must think I'm a terrible person. I don't sleep around, Jake, really. It's just that with you, I—"

"Stop. Don't. It's me, not you. You didn't do anything wrong."

"Didn't I? I kind of had a feeling, but didn't pay attention to it."

"What feeling?"

"I'm not some woman of experience, but I did have a boyfriend my senior year of high school. He never pushed sex on me, and I always thought it was because he was a gentleman. We decided that graduation night would be our first time. He even rented a motel room. But as soon as we sat on the bed, he got all fidgety, he hemmed and hawed and finally blurted out that he couldn't because he was gay."

"How did you react to him?"

"At first I slapped him."

"You were angry."

"You bet I was. He'd used me. But then I realized he could have used me much worse that night and not told me until morning. He didn't do that. He stopped in time. So I thanked him."

"Did you stay friends?"

"Not at first. I was really hurt. I loved him. And felt like a total fool. It took all summer for me to be willing to talk to him again, but eventually we became friends. I mean, we were friends already, so we just resumed our friendship, that's all."

"And the reason you're telling me this is…"

"Just in case it's relevant." She stared into his eyes.

Jake looked down at his purple Keds sneakers. "I feel like a big jerk."

"You're not a big jerk, just a small one."

He looked up to see her smiling. "Am I right?"

Damn, was everybody figuring him out? "Is it that obvious?"

"I don't think to most people, no, but I seem to have a talent for attracting gay men." Marla turned, knocked on Woolworth's darkened plate glass window and called out in a loud voice, "Anybody in there want to turn gay? Come spend a night with me!" She spun back around to Jake and giggled.

He hesitated for a moment, then burst out laughing. In relief. And maybe a little in joy. "You don't think I'm disgusting?"

"*I* like guys, so why shouldn't you? Some guys are darned attractive." Without warning, Marla slapped him hard across the face.

Jake recoiled, massaged the sting on his cheek. "What the hell did you do that for?"

To get it out of my system. I reserve the right to slap you once more, but at least now we can be friends." She linked her arm through his and led him further along Nassau Street that had grown dark now. The street lights gave everything a hazy glow.

"You honestly don't think it's wrong, Marla? For me to be this way? From a Jewish perspective, I mean. It's forbidden in the Torah."

"A lot of things are forbidden in the Torah. Like eating shellfish. But you don't see half the Jews in the country hanging themselves because they like shrimp cocktail, do you?"

He winced.

"I'm sorry," Marla said, "for being so flip about suicide."

"I've got to get used to remarks like that, I guess."

"I'm no Torah scholar," she continued, "but what about Jews who work on *Shabbes* or who disrespect their parents or covet a neighbor's husband or wife? Those are violations of the Ten Commandments, the most important rules. Not even the ultra-Orthodox go around killing *Shabbes* violators or disrespectful children or people who moon over someone else's spouse. The prohibition against…homosexuality…doesn't rise to the same level of importance as the Ten Commandments. So why freak out over violating that lesser rule?"

"I never thought of it that way."

"I don't know anybody who follows all the Torah's rules. There are so many ways of being Jewish, Jake."

"That's what my Dad says. And of course you're both right. But when talking about…my situation…the Torah uses the word 'abomination.' It doesn't get any stronger than that."

She stopped, faced him. "Jake, is that the reason you did it? Because of the Torah?"

He looked squarely into her eyes. "I want to be a good Jew, Marla."

"My dear friend." She stroked one finger along his cheek. "We're supposed to live by the Torah, not die by it."

"I talked to a Jewish friend," Jake told Dr. Enríquez the following week. "Like you suggested."

"Which friend was that?"

"Marla, the woman I dated."

"Really? And how'd that conversation go?"

"Super well. She's so nice."

"Are you two thinking of dating again?"

Jake studied the doctor's face. Could Jake detect any irony? Any surprise? No.

"No. You've figured out the reason she and I won't date anymore, haven't you?"

"I only know what you tell me, Jake."

"Ted figured me out. Marla did too. She says it's not obvious to everyone, but now I don't know."

"Whatever it is you think may be obvious—would it bother you for people to understand you better?"

"I sure thought so a few weeks ago. But now I'm not sure. It's like my friends feel closer than before."

"That often happens when we share privacies."

"You know about me, don't you?"

"As a therapist, it's part of my job to formulate possibilities about my patients. In order for me to guide conversations in ways that will be most helpful. Have I formulated possibilities about what's been troubling you? Yes. Yes, I have."

"You know that I'm...a homosexual."

Without flinching or showing any facial reaction at all, Dr. Enríquez replied, "That's one of the possibilities I've had in mind, yes."

"You're awfully calm about it."

"Shouldn't I be?"

"I've read books about psychiatrists declaring homosexuals insane and locking them up in institutions and using electric-shock therapy or giving lobotomies. Are you going to do that to me?"

Dr. Enríquez leaned forward, reached out a hand as if to pat Jake's knee, pulled back. He sighed. "You've been afraid of that, haven't you?"

Jake nodded.

"Then you're extra courageous in discussing this with me so honestly."

"Like we said last time, hiding is hard."

"I love my profession, Jake, but we've sometimes done awful things in the name of treatment. A few years ago, we psychiatrists finally moved out of the Middle Ages and came to recognize that there's nothing clinically wrong with being homosexual. 'Gay' is a less medical-sounding word, don't you think? The problem is not with a gay orientation, but with the way the rest of society, including psychiatrists, have stigmatized it. I don't believe your depression grew from being gay, but from being made to think there's something wrong with being gay, with being made to feel ashamed. Do you see the distinction I'm drawing?"

"Are you saying I'm not insane?"

"Well," said Dr. Enríquez with a grin, "I can't say that with certainty." Dr. Enríquez chuckled a moment before his face took on the most serious cast Jake had seen. "But I can say with certainty, that gayness is neither a reflection of moral laxness nor a symptom of mental illness."

Jake burst into tears.

How pretty Prospect Garden seemed to Jake in late April, the blue and pink crocuses in bloom, the lavender hyacinth, yellow and orange tulips, red roses. Jake walked slowly along the gravel paths, enjoying the colors and light fragrances. He was contemplating the essay he planned to write for lit class about Lillian Hellman's play *The Children's Hour*, a tale of two women teachers falsely accused of having a lesbian relationship at a girl's boarding school. Just let Ricky whine in class about me seeing homosexuality where it doesn't exist, he thought. Just let her!

Tomorrow, Dad would come to take Jake home for the Passover *seders*. Jake was thinking about maybe taking Uncle Irv and Aunt Flora aside to discuss everything, to ask their advice on how best to explain to Mom and Dad. If the opportunity arose. And he'd call Deb and ask to get together. If he told her he needed her, she'd make the time for sure.

Sounds like a good plan, Jake heard echo softly in his head.

'God? Is that you?'

Who else? The voice was familiar, but gentler than Jake remembered.

'It's been so long since You've spoken to me.'

I've been trying. It's been quite a while since you were calm enough to listen to Me. I tried to stop you from…you know.

'I know. I'm not sure what to say to You. All of a sudden, everything's topsy-turvy. I guess I…I….'

Tell me.

'I guess I'm worried about what You'll think of me now.'

Now that you tried to kill yourself? Or now that you're on the verge of accepting your feelings as legitimate?

'Both, I guess.'

I won't lie—your behavior shocked Me. Sex with a stranger in a toilet. And everything else. But nothing distressed Me like your suicide attempt, Jake. That's such a perversion: attempting to end the life I gave you, and to do so as an alleged act of devotion. Awful. Just awful. You broke my heart. To think that My child's distress could be so profound as to lead him to….

'I'm sorry, God.'

As am I. You won't do that again, will you, Jake?

'No, Sir.'

Promise Me.

'I do.'

I must admit that the shock of your attempt prompted Me to contemplate things in ways I haven't before.

'You? I made You start contemplating?'

Parents assume they know what's best for their children. Generally they do until the child reaches maturity. But at some point, the parent should listen to the child. Perhaps I need to do more listening.

'I'm not sure what You're saying.'

Humanity's matured since I first granted the Torah millennia ago. Perhaps it's time to take humanity's mature needs into greater account, to hear what many of My children—including you—have been trying to tell Me.

'What? Are You talking about changing the Torah?'

Not at all. The Torah's flexible enough for its meaning to take on different nuance over time. After all, scholars have been interpreting My words from the beginning, and those interpretations vary from place to place and time to time. Why not be open to varying interpretations concerning the Torah's guidance about love?

'Really? Are you serious?'

I'm always serious. You're a good boy—you try so hard to do the right thing. Don't you deserve love? I've been asking Myself that—doesn't this good boy deserve love like everyone else? If the love you need is that of a man…although that's not what I initially considered proper…well…perhaps I should listen to what you say you need. I'll need time to try getting used to this idea, but perhaps I can. I'm not promising anything, mind you, except that I'll try.

'Wow. That's amazing.'

And keep in mind, Jake, that I'm talking about love—I expect your behavior to reflect good judgment and appropriate self-control. The same as I expect from everyone else.

'The same as You expect from everyone else.'

Exactly.

'I can live with that.' Jake shut his eyes, breathed in deeply through his nose. 'This means that You don't hate me, God?'

Hate you? Never, My boy. I love you.

How brightly the sun was shining now, directly overhead. A few fluffy clouds dotted the blue sky.

'I love You, too, God.'

I never doubted.

'I don't really know what the next step is for me. I'll need Your help.'

No.

'No? You won't help me?'

There are times when a man must make his own decisions. You're a man now, Jake. It's time I let you decide for yourself how to live. How to live, *Jake. How to* live.

'That's scary.'

Yes, being a man is scary, indeed. Give yourself time. There's no rush. I'm going to step aside now. But I'll always be here. Make Me proud of the life I granted you. Be good to yourself.

'Yes, Sir.'

Jake listened for more, heard only stillness.

An orange and black viceroy butterfly flitted up off a red rose bush, flew over a low boxwood hedge, brushed against Jake's shoulder as it winged high toward the sun until it disappeared somewhere in the blue.

As he watched, Jake saw a cloud swirl slowly across the sky, almost as if dancing.

"'Bye, God," he murmured aloud, suspecting that from now on, he would hear God less in his mind, but more in his heart.

"**E**njoy the bread while you can," teased Ted as he tossed four empty hamburger rolls onto Jake's tray. "Starting tomorrow night, it's all matzoh for you."

Jake smiled, stepped past the hamburger station to the salad bar, filled his dinner plate with greens and tuna salad. Ted had made a point of inviting Jake to dinner at Commons tonight—just the two of them—before Jake headed home tomorrow for the Passover *seders*.

"Let's sit in the back." Ted led the way toward a long table where a single man sat.

Jake followed, and as they approached, he recognized that man from his picture in *The Daily Princetonian*—but now with an eye patch: Doug Braun, the student who'd been attacked and beaten for posting fliers about the gay dance. Bruises still marred his face. Poor guy.

"Mind if we join you?" Ted asked Doug.

"Ted," whispered Jake, "what are you doing? Do you know who this is?"

"Sure, sit down."

Ted set his tray beside Doug's, leaving the space across the table from Doug for Jake. Doug extended his hand; Jake put his tray down and shook the hand. "I'm Jake."

"I know," said Doug.

"You know?" asked Jake, sliding out the wooden chair and sitting. "How could you know?"

"Don't all you gay guys automatically know each other?" Ted grinned. "What's it called—'gaydar' or something?"

Doug gave a chuckle, then asked while pointing at the four rolls on Jake's tray, "You opening a bakery?"

"Ted," said Jake, ignoring Doug's remark. "Is something going on?"

"Take it easy," said Doug. "Your buddy here looked me up. He thought maybe you and I'd enjoy meeting."

Ted tucked into his hamburger with a look of exaggerated innocence on his face.

"This is a set-up?" Jake shoved his chair back. "Some kind of blind date?"

"I'm not fully blind," said Doug. "The doctors say there's a good chance my eye will heal, although they can't be sure."

"Oh gosh," blurted Jake, "that's not what I meant."

"Besides, I don't date just anyone," said Doug. "If you want a date with me, you're gonna have to charm me first with your intellect and wit."

Jake didn't know how to respond.

Doug reached a hand across the table, gently took hold of Jake's wrist, spoke with deep seriousness. "Your friend's worried about you. He told me you've been having a tough time."

"Exactly what did he tell you?" Jake then turned to Ted, "What did you tell him? Did you tell him about…?"

"It's okay, I've been there," said Doug, retrieving his hand. "Well, maybe not exactly, but I went through years wondering if my life was worth living."

"I can't believe you told him, Ted. That's private."

"Of course it is, and I apologize," said Ted, his eyes bearing an earnestness Jake had never seen. "But I didn't know how else to help you. I never met any gay guys before you. So I contacted Doug to see if maybe he could give me advice. After we chatted a couple times, I thought you'd like him. I felt him out first—"

Doug grinned. "He felt me *out*. Not *up*. Just to be clear."

"—I'll always be your friend, Jake, but you need a gay friend. Someone who can understand you in ways I can't."

"You're lucky to have a straight friend like this," said Doug. "He's not a dime a dozen."

Jake thought for a moment, sighed. "I guess you're right. I guess I am lucky."

"Aw, shucks," said Ted. "You gay guys sure know how to make a straight man feel good."

"Don't get any ideas," said Doug. "I don't do straight men."

The three shared a laugh.

Ted clapped a hand on Doug's shoulder, "Any more news about those assholes?"

"The guys who attacked me?" asked Doug. "The university held a hearing yesterday. I don't know what'll happen to them."

"They should be expelled," said Ted. "And go to jail."

Doug shrugged. "If it were up to me, I'd force them to attend meetings of the Gay Alliance for a few months. So they could see we're just normal people. That's the way to prevent future violence."

"Wow," said Jake, "you're incredibly generous."

"You should come to our meetings, too," said Doug. "To prevent future violence against yourself."

Jake's eyes welled up.

"Sorry," said Doug, "I know that's really personal."

Jake swallowed hard. "But maybe it's the advice I need," he whispered.

Ted stood. "Excuse me, guys, but Nancy just walked in." He hailed a wave toward the opposite end of the dining hall. "She'll get on my case if I don't join her." He lifted his tray. "You okay with that, Jake? Hanging out alone with Doug?"

Jake looked at Doug, who winked, then back at Ted. Jake nodded. "Yeah, I'm okay with that."

As Ted walked away, Doug elaborated on his stay in the hospital, on the difficulty his ribs were having in healing. Jake tried to concentrate on Doug's words, but kept thinking up question after question he wanted to ask: what was daily life like for a homo—for a gay person who didn't hide? What happened at a gay dance—did everyone have to dance, or could you just stand around? How did one man approach another and ask another for a dance? Were there slow dances? If so, how did you decide which man led? And outside of school dances, how did Doug meet men to date? Did he actually go out on dates like normal people? Did he have friends—gay friends? Straight friends? Did gay people have to dress a certain way (not that Doug's powder-blue polo shirt and jeans were any different than anyone else's)? Would law schools accept Jake if they found out about him? Would Jake ever find a job?

And besides all these questions, Jake kept thinking how amazing it was to be sitting here in the open, discussing personal topics with a man who could truly understand, deep down inside, what Jake had been feeling these last weeks, months, even years. A man whom Jake could talk to honestly without fear of rejection.

Yes, here Jake was, sitting and chatting with a potential new friend. A gay friend. In public. And nobody seemed even to notice.

Two gay men sitting in Commons enjoying dinner and conversation. Just like everyone else.

ACKNOWLEDGMENTS

Many thanks to the Norman Mailer Center and Writers Colony for a fellowship providing time and space to pour much of this material onto the page. Thanks, as well, to the editors of *The Florida Review, Speechless-The Magazine, Kosher Meat, Found Tribe,* and *Mentsh: On Being Jewish and Queer,* each of whom published parts of this novel in different form as personal essay.

My heartfelt appreciation to Steve Berman and Ron Suresha of Lethe Press for encouraging this project, and for Steve's suggestions that helped strengthen the manuscript.

Deep love and appreciation to my family for sticking by me through the tough times, most especially to my husband, Leo Cabranes-Grant—you protect my heart and buoy my soul.

ABOUT THE AUTHOR

Daniel M. Jaffe holds degrees from Princeton University (A.B.), Harvard Law School (J.D.), and Vermont College (M.F.A.). Jaffe's writing combines Jewish cultural, religious and family life with queer sensibilities. He resides in California with his husband.

CPSIA information can be obtained
at www.ICGtesting.com
Printed in the USA
BVHW032144240919
559341BV00001B/4/P

9 781590 216712